PRAISE FOR MARK OF THE LEAST

"A wildly original and magical twist on the Robin Hood narrative, Kendra Merritt's *By Wingéd Chair* is packed to the spokes with complex characters, wry humor, and flawless world building."

-Darby Karchut, best-selling author of DEL TORO MOON and FINN FINNEGAN

"With a wonderfully crafted blend of swords and sorcery and characters based on Robin Hood, Merritt tops this story off with the lead character readers need nowadays; a strong, independent, powerful female mage who also happens to be in a wheelchair. Readers will be constantly turning pages to see what happens next to this fun group of characters through the twists and turns they won't see coming."

-The Booklife Prize

"Kendra Merritt's prose is fresh, with one-line descriptions that crack like a whip, and she doesn't miss an opportunity to surprise the reader. From the first line to the last, I was enchanted with *By Winged Chair*."

-Todd Fahnestock, best-selling author of FAIRMIST and THE WISHING WORLD

ALSO BY KM MERRITT

<u>Mishap's Heroes Series</u>

Magic and Misrule

Death and Devotion

Trust and Treason

Illusions and Infamy

Sparks and Scales

Wastelands and War

<u>Mark of the Least Series</u>

By Wingéd Chair

Skin Deep

Catching Cinders

Shroud for a Bride

A Matter of Blood

Unmasked

After the Darkness

The King in the Tower Collection

<u>Daybreak Colony Duology</u>

Surviving Daybreak

Daybreak Sentinel

<u>Eldros Legacy</u>

The Pain Bearer

The Truth Stealer

The Death Bringer

MISHAP'S HEROES

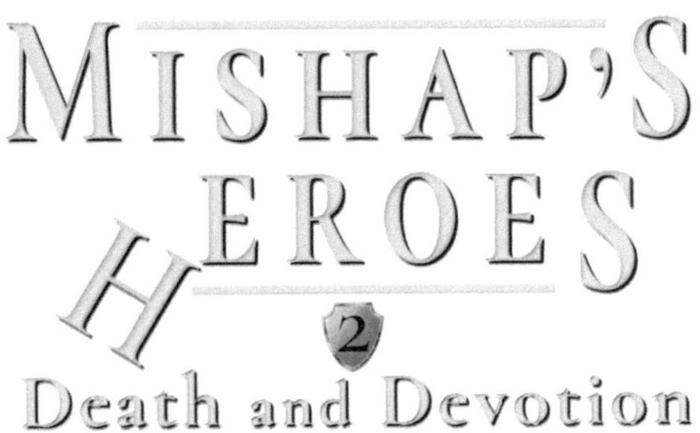

Death and Devotion

KM MERRITT

BLUE FYRE PRESS

For all my DMs. Thanks for not killing me. Yet

ONE

A THICK FISHY pall hung over Brisbene harbor like a wet blanket that had lain in a corner too long. But after a week cooped up on a transport ship, Vola was willing to breathe anything if it meant standing on dry land again. She stood at the railing, and her chest swelled. Then her lungs seized, and she bent over coughing.

A delicate hand tapped her back as if that would help anything. "Oh, dear," a lyrical voice said. "Take a deep breath. Oh wait, don't. That might be the problem."

Vola hacked once more, then straightened. She cast a rueful glance at the woman beside her. Lillie stood only a little taller than Vola's elbow with plump curves in all the right places, even after a week at sea with nothing but dried rations to eat. The sky was overcast and gray, but of course, a single shaft of light broke through the clouds to glint off her red-gold hair. Vola was pretty sure there was a law of the universe somewhere that said blonde hair and sunlight always went together, no matter the weather.

Vola tossed her own black braid over her shoulder and squinted up at the sky. But no sun shafts sought her out.

"It's noisy," another voice said, this one gravelly with mystery and disuse. Talon hadn't said much during the voyage. They'd conveyed everything they'd needed to with grunts and gestures. Of course, it was all things like, "get out of the way," and "don't wake me up before noon."

A decent breeze made the sails snap overhead, but Talon's hood remained firmly in place, concealing their face. The dark edges of their cloak ruffled against the rough planks beneath their boots.

"Why is it so noisy?" they said.

Vola glared out at the city stretched before them. Buildings with real slate and tile roofs marched all the way to the water's edge where docks jutted into the harbor. Houses, warehouses, shops, and taverns crowded each other, spreading from one end of the world to the other as far as Vola could see. A low buzz crept across the water, and Vola could just make out the rumble of carts, the hum of conversation and shouting.

The spires of temples and cathedrals dedicated to the Virtues poked out of the masses here and there, and off to the right, up a cliff, lurked a wide squat fortress of black stone.

"I suppose I'd better go fetch Miss Sorrel," Lillie said. "If we're going to dock soon—"

"Is that fresh air I smell?" another voice said. This one didn't even reach Vola's elbow. More like her hip.

A pale halfling with dark circles under her eyes and curly hair matted with sweat scampered to the railing and climbed up to take a huge sniff. Then she sagged against the wood, arms dangling over the side.

"Are you going to vomit again?" Lillie said.

"Ugh, don't say that word," Vola said.

"Which word? Vomit?"

"Can't you just say barf like the rest of us? Barf at least doesn't make me want to barf."

"And vomit makes you want to vomit?"

"Please stop talking now," Sorrel said, voice thin. "I'm not going to barf. Wait," Sorrel said toward the sea rolling beneath them. "Y—no." She gulped. "Not this time."

She sucked air in noisily through her nose and let it out through her teeth.

The swell of the waves pushed them closer to shore. The noise got louder.

Talon drew back farther into their hood, which Vola hadn't thought possible. As if trying to escape without moving their feet. A huge black wolf padded up to their side, and the ranger buried their hand in his thick ruff.

"I didn't expect it to be so big," Vola finally admitted.

"What? A city?" Lillie said. "Brisbene is actually the smallest port in Southglen." Though she didn't sound too happy about it.

Vola shifted from foot to foot. "I haven't been in many cities."

"How are we supposed to find Lord Arthorel's slaver in that mess?" Talon said.

Vola rolled her lip between her tusks. It looked like a big maze, but it had to be better than that. Otherwise, people wouldn't flock to live in cities. Would they? Maybe humans were really herd animals and they just hadn't noticed yet.

"The same way we tracked down Lord Arthorel," she said. She opened her mouth to continue, but Lillie beat her to it.

"By accidentally getting him to hire us and then letting him kidnap one of our friends so we could swear vengeance on him and get lost in his castle of illusions before letting him escape again and running him to ground in the harbor?"

Vola shut her mouth with a snap as Lillie tilted her head in thought.

"That's pretty much what happened, isn't it?" Sorrel said with her head draped over the railing.

"I really don't think that will work a second time, do you?" Lillie said, finally.

"I meant methodically," Vola said with a low growl in her voice. "That's all I was getting at. One step at a time. We know Lord Arthorel was selling the people he captured to someone in Brisbene, and we know where the captain was supposed to drop them off. We can go from there."

They stared out at the bustling mass of humanity and non-human species as the ship slid up to the dock and the sailors threw lines to those waiting ashore.

"You make that sound so easy," Talon said.

Vola blew out her breath. It wasn't that bad, she thought to herself. They at least knew where to start, and that was a whole lot better than last time. Vola's palms itched for her sword. She'd always thought of that impatience as the orc side of her. But like Henri had told her, while a paladin *had* to answer a call for help, a real paladin *wanted* to answer a call for help. So she took it as a good sign.

The captain of the ship sidled up next to them, eying Talon and the wolf warily. Vola grinned, baring her tusks. It was a good day when she wasn't the scariest thing around.

"We'll be parting ways here, sir," she said.

"Good." His hand crept up to clutch his wild gray hair. "Oh, wait. I mean, so soon? You didn't want to ride with us to Gerricksbane?"

He glanced at Sorrel as she groaned.

"No, our quarry is here," Vola said. "We just have to find him."

"Oh, darn," the captain said, snapping his fingers.

"Pretty sure that's sarcasm," Talon said. The wolf stood.

The captain raised his hands. "Your monster will be waiting for you on the dock in thirty minutes. I've got a tide to catch, and if you need a ride back to Water's Edge, please, please find some other ship."

He spun on his heel and stalked across the deck to yell at

some deckhands.

"That wasn't very nice," Lillie said. The party turned toward the hatch.

"Well, we did get his employer arrested and free his cargo," Vola said.

Talon crossed their arms. "And I'm pretty sure holding his crimes over his head to get a discounted ride is called blackmail. I don't think he likes us very much."

Lillie jerked back as if affronted, making her long, bright hair sway. "He was going to be transporting slaves. People bought as property. We saved him from not being arrested himself. The least he could do is give us a ride."

"Not sure he sees it that way," Vola said. "Come on. Let's get off this tub."

"Wait," Sorrel said behind them.

They glanced back at her.

Her knuckles went white against the railing, and then she heaved her guts into the sea. Vola and Lillie winced.

Sorrel wiped the back of her mouth. "Last one," she said and followed.

It didn't take them long to collect their things. None of them had much. Just a change of clothes each and their weapons.

In less than twenty minutes, Talon stood on the dock, bow and quiver secured to their back. Lillie had already cracked open a book to pass the time, and Sorrel leaned on her quarterstaff as if it was the only thing holding her up.

Vola slung a round shield—scarred and gouged by battle— over her shoulder and carried her sword and sword belt in her other hand. She'd stopped wearing it on the ship when she kept getting stuck in the narrow corridors, but she fastened her blade and shield to her back as soon as she got out into the open air.

As Vola drew even with her friends, a scrabbling and a squeal drew their gazes down to the other end of the dock. A second gangplank spanned the gap between the ship and the pier where the sailors unloaded their meager cargo. Three sailors had hold of the end of a ragged lead rope, and they pulled and heaved, their feet slipping along the gangplank.

At the other end of the rope strained a…creature. Like a cross between a donkey and an angry crocodile. It raised its filmy crest in anger and bared its yellow teeth at the sailors as they dragged it to shore. One more sailor brought up the rear, putting his shoulder to the creature's tail.

The creature's claws flexed and left gouges down the gangplank as the sailors yelled and prodded and pulled.

Vola grimaced.

"I really wish we'd found someone to buy it back at Water's Edge," Sorrel said.

"Maybe here…" Vola glanced back at the city. Surely someone here in this vast gathering of humanity would have use for an ornery swamp monster that ate just about everything and everyone.

Lillie glanced at the altercation down the dock, and her brow screwed up in thought. Then she twisted her fingers and whispered a spell, and a very surprised looking turtle popped into existence on the dock at their feet.

"Here you go, Millford," Lillie called. "A nice tasty turtle. Come on, boy."

The swamp beast's eyes narrowed. Its scaly nostrils flared as it snorted. Then it squealed and barreled past the sailors, knocking two of them into the water.

It slid and skidded to a halt beside them and chomped on the turtle.

Then it looked up in consternation and tried again.

"It's only an illusion," Lillie said as the swamp beast's teeth closed on air over and over again. "I didn't have a turtle handy."

"Can we just go?" Sorrel asked, leaning heavy on her staff.

"Before I barf again. I don't have anything left to barf up and that's even worse than if you have a whole meal. It makes your throat burn and your stomach hurt and—"

"Yes, fine," Vola said. "We're leaving. It's not like the dock is moving, though. This is almost as good as dry land."

"I'd rather put as much distance between myself and the ocean as possible, thank you—Ahh!"

Vola spun to see the swamp beast hoist Sorrel into the air by the back of her tunic. It chewed maliciously, its eyes narrowed as if daring them to do something.

Vola rolled her eyes as Lillie and Talon lunged forward.

"Millford, put her down this instant. I thought we were past this. You can't eat party members."

Talon took a more direct approach and bashed the creature on its nose. It dropped Sorrel with a squeal and backed up a step.

Sorrel darted forward and tugged her tunic straight, breathing heavily. "Watch it." She wagged her finger at the creature. "Or we'll see if anyone in this town likes fried fish."

Lillie's brow furrowed. "Is that even a good threat? I'm pretty sure it's part reptile, not fish."

Sorrel threw her arms in the air. "And part horse, so we'll find a glue factory, okay?"

Vola glanced around to find the captain and make sure they were square, but the sailors had all disappeared except for the one fishing himself out of the water, and when she looked toward the ship, all she saw was six pairs of wary eyes watching them from over the railing. They ducked when they realized she was looking at them.

Vola shrugged.

"Let's go." She took hold of the swamp beast's lead rope and gave it a glare. "If you bite me, I'll muzzle you. Lillie, you've got the address, right?"

No time like the present to get their investigation started.

They all had a personal stake in this one. Lord Arthorel had tried to kidnap a bunch of orphans and unlucky townsfolk to ship off to this slaver, and then he'd done his best to kill Vola and the others when they'd tried to stop him. Vola's nature wouldn't let her leave without tracking down this slaver, but she'd discovered in the last few weeks paladins weren't the only ones with a sense of honor and a heart for rescuing people.

Lillie nodded and stepped away with a pronounced limp. A shaft of guilt zinged down Vola's spine. She'd hoped the wizard's wound would have healed more in the week of rest they'd had on the ship. But from the deep lines at the edges of Lillie's frown, the long slice still pained her.

Vola opened her mouth to insist Lillie ride the swamp beast, but the thing was likely to take a chunk out of the wizard if she tried. And if Lillie insisted she didn't need help, Vola didn't dare suggest otherwise.

Lillie led them off the docks, onto a cobbled street lined with open market stalls. Vendors shouted from either side of the lane, hawking spices, fruit, and cloth. A fish as big as Sorrel flew past them and landed with a wet thunk on a bed of ice.

Vola's head came up, and she sniffed. Somewhere, someone was barbecuing wargle, just like her Aunt Urag made, and Vola's mouth watered.

Unfortunately, Lillie headed in the opposite direction, taking them along the wharf where the water slapped the stained stone.

"Where was the captain supposed to deliver the slaves?" Vola said. "Surely not in the middle of the city?"

"He told me it was a warehouse," Lillie said, checking the weathered signs on the buildings lining their route. "Here." She stopped in front of one that had been red once before the salt air had had its way. The big sliding doors where cargo could be loaded in and out were shut and padlocked, but the little door for humanoid traffic stood open to the breeze.

"Was it really that easy?" Sorrel's face was still a pale green and she breathed through her mouth, but her eyes surveyed the open door.

Vola frowned. The halfling was right. This was too straight-forward.

She left the swamp beast tied outside and led the way through the door. A desk stood across the space just a few feet in, occupied by a pair of feet propped on the surface. Whoever owned the feet remained hidden behind a broad newspaper.

Through a door to their left, Vola could see the rest of the warehouse proper. Rows and rows of cages and crates lined the space, each labeled with a number. Some held animals, pacing behind their bars. Some held boxes and bundles of indeterminate origin and contents. There weren't any people out there. At least none that she could see.

"What is this place?" she whispered.

"Looks like some sort of storage depot," Talon said. "A drop-off for goods and cargo."

Vola stepped up to the desk and tapped her finger against the surface. "Excuse me."

Her only answer was a grunt.

"Do you run this place?"

The newspaper never lowered, but finally, a voice drifted past the headlines. "I sit here," it said. "I make sure nothing goes in or out that's not authorized. And I take payment for new contracts."

"So, you're in charge. You would be able to tell us who's been here."

The voice snorted. "Each box is rented separately, and there're over a hundred. I'm not that observant."

"But surely you have records," Lillie said, stepping up beside Vola. Usually, her looks and lyrical voice could charm whoever she was talking to, but that wouldn't work if the voice never bothered looking up.

The newspaper rattled in annoyance. "Every box is rented to an anonymous account number. This is the kind of place where people don't want their names written down."

"What about box number 57?" Lillie asked.

"Also anonymous."

"So, you don't care that illegal dealings are happening out of your depot?" Lillie asked, drawing herself up.

"Nope."

"Well, at least that's straightforward," Talon said.

Vola rubbed her forehead. "I take it waving my sword around won't do any good?"

"Lady, I have no loyalty to any of these people. I also have no details on any of them. Threats won't get you anything, 'cause I've got nothing to give."

"We could go to the authorities."

"Go ahead. My bribes are paid up."

"What about records of anything else that's been stored in box 57?" Talon said.

Vola pursed her lips. That wasn't a bad idea. Track him down from the other side.

The paper rustled. "We don't document what comes in and out longer than a week. Just enough to make sure nobody's taking things out that they didn't put in. All records are burned after that. It's that sort of business."

Vola tapped the rough edge of the desk. "What if we bought the box?"

Lillie raised an eyebrow.

"Then we could check it out ourselves," Vola whispered.

"Box 57 is already paid up for the month. Won't be renting it out again any time soon."

Sorrel blew out her breath in a sigh.

"Means he's probably still expecting a shipment," Talon said.

"Probably the one we just set free," Vola mumbled. To the

invisible clerk, she said, "Could we offer you something in exchange for, say, sending word if anything else gets stored in box 57?"

"Probably not," the voice said.

"What self-respecting criminal won't take a bribe?" Sorrel cried.

"Oh, I'd take the bribe. I just wouldn't bother with the whole telling you anything part."

Vola threw up her hands. "Fine." She herded the rest of them out the door.

Lillie paused at the threshold to say, "Thank you."

"What are you thanking him for?" Talon said. "He literally gave us nothing."

"No, but he was very honest about giving us nothing."

TWO

VOLA STOPPED JUST outside the warehouse, breathing hard. Words were always so frustrating. It was so much more satisfying to hit a problem over the head and have it fall at her feet.

"This…this is going to take longer than I imagined."

The problem was Vola had a great imagination. It was wonderful at imagining things like riding into town on a valiant steed, waving her sword, and magically rounding up all the bad guys in one go. Grateful crowds would throw flowers and favors at her.

It was also good at imagining those same crowds throwing rotten vegetables and stabbing her with sticks when she failed to deliver the bad guys as she'd promised.

Vola winced.

"I did think that was too easy," Sorrel said faintly.

Vola planted her hands on her hips and stared around at the city. "I think our best bet is to stake this place out. See if anyone comes to use box 57."

"That means we're going to be here a lot longer than we thought," Talon said.

Vola sighed. "Yeah. We're going to need to hunker down. We need a base of operations."

"What kind of base are you imagining?" Sorrel asked. "One that doesn't go up and down, I hope?" She eyed the water lapping the edge of the wharf.

"We could set up camp outside town," Talon said. It was hard without being able to see their face, but Vola detected a hopeful note in their voice.

Vola shook her head. "We need an inn. Somewhere in the city. Close to our investigation."

"Great," Sorrel said. "Anyone know how to find a good one? I don't know about the rest of you, but I grew up in a monastery in the mountains. We didn't really have any cities."

Vola had grown up in a tiny village east of Water's Edge. And Talon had been raised by wolves. Literally.

They all looked at Lillie.

"Oh. Oh, I really don't like the crowds in cities," she said, eyes widening. "And the smell. I prefer something quieter."

"Yeah, but you would know how to find your way around, right?"

"I..." Lillie looked around at their faces and her shoulders sagged. "I guess I do."

"Great." Vola slapped her on the shoulder, making the half-elf stagger. She made a mental note to pat gentler next time. "You're our guide, then."

Lillie reluctantly led them deeper into the city. The further they moved from the bustle of the harbor and the dank smell of fish and rot, the better Sorrel looked. Her color heightened to its normal healthy brown, and she finally lifted her head to gaze about her with shining eyes.

"Do you suppose they like living all squished together?" Sorrel said, gesturing up at the houses that crowded each other for space on the street, like old women trying to get a good view of a scandal. The upper stories were built out over the street so neighbors could shake hands across balconies or steal each other's laundry.

"Maybe they start off liking it," Talon said. "Then slowly go mad." Their hood jerked at a couple arguing from the gutter.

"Or deaf," Vola said.

The big black wolf, Gruff, stalked along the street in Lillie's wake, leaving a wide path as people noticed him and leaped back. For once, those looks of terror weren't directed at Vola. She kept glancing around for the torches and pitchforks but only found baskets of goods and the occasional shovel. In fact, the worst looks were directed at the swamp beast, trudging at the end of its lead.

"I don't understand," Vola said. "No one's running from me."

Talon snorted. "No one's even noticing you."

"It's weird."

Sorrel raised an eyebrow. "Would you rather be run out of town by a mob?"

"No, but…it's throwing me off. Like running to kick a ball, only to have it pulled out of the way at the last second."

"You must not be the strangest thing they've seen today."

Lillie didn't carry a map, but she did move unerringly through the streets like she knew where she was going. She kept her elbows tucked and her chin down to avoid eye contact but made straight for a cross street. Vola didn't ask if she'd been here before. There were things Lillie didn't like talking about and where she'd been before they met in Water's Edge was one of them.

They turned the corner and something told Vola they'd stepped into a different world. The crowds were better dressed and better smelling for a start. And the signs outside the shops had actual writing on them rather than just crude pictures. The din from the harbor retreated to a nice background hum.

"Oh, wow," Sorrel said, staring at her feet. "Even the cobbles line up all nice."

Lillie stopped in front of a cheery facade, painted a bright yellow, and she gestured toward a pair of red doors. Lacy curtains fluttered in the windows.

"We can get some rooms and some food here," she said. "That's what we're looking for, right?"

"May's Bed and Breakfast," Sorrel read off the sign. "But what if it's lunchtime?"

"That's not really the point," Lillie said.

Vola squinted at the sign, trying to make the letters stand still, then she reached into the wallet that hung from her belt.

"Um, Lillie. I don't know if this is exactly what we're looking for," Vola said.

Lillie blinked. "But it looks just like Becky's Tea and Tap Room in Water's Edge."

That was true. Becky had decorated her tavern using clippings from women's magazines. And this could have been the original source for those clippings.

"It's just they have the prices posted outside here." Probably to prevent the riff-raff like them from treading on the carpets. "And I don't think it's in our price range."

"Oh." Lillie's face fell. "I'm sorry. I didn't know we had a price range."

To be fair. Vola hadn't either. The coins in her purse would have stretched a lot further anywhere else, or at least that's what this sign seemed to tell her.

"What is our price range?" Sorrel asked.

"Er." Vola pulled the coins out, and the others gathered around to stare down at the tiny pile in her calloused palm. "About three gold, looks like."

"What happened to the money Becky gave us?" Sorrel asked.

"It paid for our voyage here," Vola said. "She was very

generous after we saved the townsfolk. But it's not like we were actually paid for that job."

"That's what happens when you arrest your employer," Talon said.

"Hey, he turned out to be the bad guy," Sorrel said. "What else could we do?"

Vola sighed and tucked the coins back in her coin purse. "Nothing for it. Do you think we can find someplace a little less… er…nice?" she asked Lillie.

Lillie tucked her hair behind her ears, revealing their lightly pointed tips. "I'm not as familiar with those areas of the city, but it shouldn't be too hard."

She turned and trudged back down the street, and the rest of them followed.

Vola didn't think the streets could get any narrower. She was wrong. The section of the city that Lillie led them to this time had trash floating down the gutters and the houses arched over them, blocking out the light completely so it seemed like they walked through a mean, damp tunnel of splintered doors and peeling paint. Women in ragged dresses squinted at them from their narrow stoops, and men gave them suspicious looks as they hauled up their sagging patched trousers.

"Just keep an eye out for a sign," Lillie whispered. "Usually a flagon or joint of meat. Something like that."

"How about a happy face?" Sorrel said. "A big smile. I could use one of those right about now."

"In a place like this," Vola said. "I think that's called baring your teeth."

Instinct made Vola glance over her shoulder.

"Don't look now, but we've got some new friends," she said.

Talon and Sorrel both glanced back at the small mob forming behind them. The group of hulking men and thin-faced women lingered far too close, watching them with covetous eyes.

Vola was tempted to just let the swamp beast go and see what happened. But there was probably a law against cruel and unusual punishment in the city. And the mess afterward wouldn't be worth the trouble. Vola's knuckles tightened on the lead rope.

"There," Talon growled and Vola glanced up. The hooded figure pointed to a sign less than a block away which depicted both a flagon and a joint of red meat. Some cursive lettering was scrawled underneath, which Vola didn't even try to interpret.

"Jackpot," Sorrel said.

And that was when Vola felt the back of her neck prickle.

"Hey. Greenie," a voice said from behind her.

Vola's lips peeled back in a snarl, and her chin lowered. She spun, dropping the swamp beast's lead and drawing her sword in the same motion.

The mob behind her had spread out across the skinny street. Half the neighborhood turned out to try their hand at overwhelming a group of adventurers. The man in front, dressed in sagging overalls with a puckered scar over the remains of his left eye, gave her a lopsided grin and leaned against a half-rotted signpost. He lifted a finger, and a flame flickered at the end of it, casting little shadows across his craggy face. He used the ethereal flame to light his cigarette.

"What did you call me?" she said.

He blew out a puff of smoke. "You and your friends are walking our street," he said, not answering her question. "But you didn't pay our tax. That's rude, that is."

Vola could feel Sorrel and Talon forming up behind her and wished she had some little telepathy that would tell one of them to protect Lillie. The wizard could hold her own but did that better from the middle of a group where she wouldn't be hit as easily.

"You didn't have a sign," Vola said, evenly. "Everyone knows tax collection points must be posted clearly."

The man took his cigarette out of his mouth and spat on the ground.

"Must have slipped my mind. We'll just take our tax and be on our way."

Vola's grip tightened on her hilt. "We don't have anything worth taking."

"I think you're bluffing." The robbers all grinned, and Vola counted one full set of teeth between them.

"Maybe," she said with a shrug. "How many limbs are you willing to lose to find out?"

"Now Miss Vola," Lillie said, pushing to the front and placing a hand on her arm. "Is that any way to treat a citizen of this fine city? Really, gentlemen. All you had to do was follow the proper procedures and all this could have been avoided. But of course, I'm willing to overlook it this once."

The man's eyes narrowed. "You talk like a nob. What's a nob doing down here?"

Lillie flushed to the roots of her perfect hair. "I don't know what you're talking about."

"Really?" Sorrel said. "You think everyone talks like that?"

Vola kicked her.

The lead robber's grin returned, and he snapped his fingers, conjuring his little flame again. He tossed it from hand to hand, making it weave through his fingers as he smirked at them. "Where're you from?"

"Nowhere important," Lillie replied.

"I'll bet I could make you tell me," he said.

Lillie snorted. "I'll bet you could, too. With a more impressive spell. One like this," she conjured her own fire, but this one filled her hand. "Or this one." She sent the flame streaking to scorch the cobbles at his feet. "Or this one." She stomped her foot and a wave of air shot out around her, making the ground buckle and the would-be tax-collectors stagger.

Lillie waited while they picked themselves up. She stood, arms crossed and hip cocked as if at ease, but from where she waited, Vola could see the wizard's knuckles were white and a thin layer of sweat gleamed on her brow.

Vola was just glad Lillie was concentrating on one thing. She'd seen the wizard nearly set fire to a tavern trying to walk and spell cast at the same time.

Lillie spread her hands and spoke again. "Please, gentlemen. My friend was right. We're cash poor at the moment. But we will happily pay your tax." She tapped her lip as if thinking and surveyed their group.

Talon cleared their throat and jerked their head at the swamp monster.

Lillie only hesitated a moment. "What about a trade?" she said. "We picked up this rare specimen in the swamps south of Water's Edge, and he's a faithful companion to whoever he calls master. His name is Millford."

Vola fought not to snort. Lillie was the only one who'd ever called the thing Millford.

Lillie took the swamp beast's lead rope and limped over to place it in the scarred man's hand. She beamed at him, and Vola saw him stagger again.

"There, see? No harm done. We'll forget the incident if you do the same." Lillie didn't wait for a response. She turned on her heel and made her way as quickly as she could to the tavern they'd been aiming for.

Sorrel and Talon followed with Gruff crowding close on their heels, and Vola brought up the rear, walking backward to keep an eye on the mob.

As she slid into the dingy tavern and warm, moist air closed around her, Lillie slammed the door shut.

They waited, each holding their breath.

There was some muttering beyond the door and then a short

sharp scream. The sounds of running feet and a quick squeal made Vola blow out her breath.

"It's gone," Talon said. "The swamp beast is gone."

"Did you see their faces?" Sorrel said, slapping her knees.

"I actually feel a little bad about swindling them like that," Lillie said and bit her lip.

"They were going to rob us," Vola said. "I think it serves them right that they managed to rob us of something we haven't been able to give away."

Lillie finally chuckled. "You're right, of course. I kind of hope it eats them."

"If only we could be so lucky," Vola said. She straightened away from the door and finally took a chance to look around.

The interior of the place matched the street outside. It was dark and dank, smelled of spilled beer and sweat, and the man behind the bar wore a dirty apron and wiped a mug with a gray cloth. The clientele seemed little better. Scattered around the tables sat small groups of armored men and women carrying a variety of weapons. They didn't look that friendly but Vola got the impression they glared at everyone who came through the door.

"Hey, animals have to stay outside," the barkeep yelled across the room.

Talon growled and Vola's hand shot out to keep them from lunging. Gruff stood at their side, hackles up.

"Let's not make trouble," Vola said in the ranger's ear.

Talon didn't respond. At least not with words. They growled again low in their throat, and this time, Gruff joined them.

"We need a place to stay while we hunt down the slaver. And I don't think we get to be picky. He'll be able to defend himself out there just fine."

She and Talon both glanced down. Gruff thumped his tail and lifted his lip so one gleaming fang showed.

"That's not what I'm worried about," Talon finally said and

stalked to the door. They pushed it open and Gruff darted outside.

A couple fainter screams drifted through the patched walls as Talon returned to Vola's side.

A long piercing howl rose, rattling a nearby window.

Sorrel covered her ears. "What is that?"

"What I was worried about," Talon said. "He doesn't like it if he can't see me."

Vola winced. "He didn't make that noise when we were in Arthorel's manor."

Talon shrugged and headed for the bar. "He could hang out in the woods there. Cities make him nervous. But at least this way I know where he is." They flicked their fingers at the bartender. "Happy now?"

Vola tried to ignore the sound of an unhappy wolf and strode up to the bar. She took a stool three seats down from a barbarian dressed in a fur loincloth who curled around his beer like a dragon around its gold.

The bartender studied them out of the corner of his eye.

"Fighter, paladin, or troublemaker?" he asked, jerking his head at her shield.

She blinked. "Paladin."

He relaxed a hair. "Don't see a lot of orc paladins around," he said. "Even here."

Vola opened her mouth, but before she could respond, Sorrel piped up.

"Half-orc," she said with a glare for the bartender.

He raised his hands palm out. "Sure, sure," he said. "We see some now and then, serving the Obstacles." He craned his neck to see if her shield had any insignia. "You're not carrying an emblem."

Her teeth clenched. But she put her hand to the neckline of her chainmail and pulled out her emblem. A little fish knife hung from the silver chain.

The bartender snorted. "Cleavah? Really? Isn't she a little—"

"Don't finish that sentence." Vola leaned forward so her sword hilt clanked against the counter. "She chose me, and I am well capable of defending her."

His eyes flicked to the signs of battle scarring her shield and cleared his throat. Vola fought to control her breathing. Would she have to defend her goddess against every ignorant unbeliever for the rest of her life?

"Why is your inn called the Snuggly Bunny?" Lillie said, joining Vola at the bar.

"What?"

"The sign out front. It says the Snuggly Bunny."

The bartender's jaw went slack. Then he snapped it closed. "Can't read," he said. "Just picked the words that looked the prettiest."

"Oh," Lillie said with a bright false smile. "And uh, do you have any rooms available?"

He chewed the inside of his lip before answering. "Yup. Clean, too. That'll be a gold each."

Vola blanched. "Um. What if we shared one room?"

The bartender spit behind the bar. "That'll be a gold each."

Vola thunked her head against her fist. "Of course it will."

The bartender grumbled then put his mug and cloth down. "If you need extra coin, there's a job board over there."

Vola sat up and followed his pointing finger. In the back hallway, a dim lantern illuminated a mangled cork board. A couple of scraps of paper hung from thumb tacks.

"A job board?" Sorrel said. "People just post jobs they need done?"

"Yeah. See a job you want to do, grab the posting, and go do it." The bartender shrugged. "Brisbene ends up being a hub for most adventurers. This saves time and cuts down on in-fighting."

"In-fighting?" Vola said, but Sorrel had already scampered toward the board. Lillie followed and the two of them stared at the scraps of paper fluttering on the corkboard.

Vola pushed back her stool. "Anything?"

"Well. Yes," Lillie said. "Something."

Sorrel stood on tiptoe and stretched for the nearest paper. "If he's right and a bunch of adventurers have already been through, then they picked the options clean. We've got flower picking."

"What? Let me see that." Vola snatched the scrap from Sorrel and squinted at the scribbled writing, willing the letters to hold still. "Gather seventeen bushels of Broken Grace blooms. Cash on delivery. You've got to be kidding me."

"Didn't we do this already?" Talon said. "The last time we were sent for flowers, they tried to eat us."

"Well, at least it would be easier the second time around," Lillie said.

Talon snorted. "What if I want to spill some blood?"

"That would be this one," Sorrel said and jumped to grab the second scrap. "There're rats in someone's basement. Why bother paying someone else to get rid of your rats?"

Vola screwed up her nose. Neither option was great. They could be gardeners or exterminators. Would either of those make Henri proud? She'd only just left him back in Water's Edge and here she was scrounging for jobs again.

"It's not like we have a lot of other choices," Lillie said. "I doubt we could find cheaper lodging."

"And earning some local goodwill might be a good idea," Sorrel said. "Who knows how long it'll take to find this slaver?"

Vola took the two meager postings back to the bar. "'Scuse me. Is this all there is right now?"

"What's posted is what's available," the bartender said, digging a glass out from under the bar and setting it under a tap.

"Pretty picked over," she said.

"Yeah. New postings trickle in all the time, but the adventurers around here snatch everything up in the morning. Nature of the business, I'm afraid. Here you go, sweetheart," he said, placing the full glass in front of Lillie. "On the house."

"Oh." Lillie went bright pink and stammered. "I didn't… What's that for?"

He just winked before he bent to another task.

"I mean…thank you?" She leaned over to ask in Sorrel's ear. "Would you like this?"

"Of course," Sorrel said. "What is it?"

Lillie sniffed the drink and grimaced. "Beer."

"Yeah, but what kind?"

Lillie's brow furrowed. "There are different kinds?"

Sorrel rolled her eyes and took the drink. She took a sip and held it in her mouth while gazing at the ceiling. "Decent pale ale," she said. Then took another sip. "With hints of citrus and banana."

"If you say so," Lillie said.

Vola sighed. "Drinking comes after the victory, Sorrel. We have to pick one of these. Or we won't have beds to sleep in tonight."

"I vote rats," Sorrel said. "That, at least has the possibility of fighting."

"I also want to hit something," Talon said.

Vola and Lillie exchanged a glance.

"I mean, flowers could be nice," Lillie said. "But probably boring."

Vola grinned, showing off her tusks. "Rats it is. We just have to wait till Sorrel's done drinking."

"Done." Sorrel smacked the glass back down on the table and smacked her lips. "Let's go kill something."

THREE

"THOSE ARE NOT RATS!" Vola said. She made sure Lillie and Sorrel had made it out of the cellar before slamming the door behind her. Something heavy hit it from the other side with a thud and Vola put her shoulder to the wood.

"I mean they were kind of ratty," Lillie said, puffing. Talon stood behind her on the stairs, bow drawn to cover their retreat. "They had beady eyes. And pointy teeth."

"And tails," Sorrel said. "I remember the tails."

Several more bodies hit the other side of the door, and Vola's feet slid against the flagstones.

Sorrel threw herself at the door. Her weight wouldn't do anything to help, but Vola appreciated the gesture.

"I take it back," Sorrel said. "I would definitely pay someone else to do this right now."

Another thump knocked Sorrel back a couple of paces. Vola resettled her feet and gritted her teeth. The cellar floor was worn smooth and didn't offer a lot of traction but at least the ceiling curved above the stairs far enough Vola didn't have to duck.

"What have they been eating?" Lillie said.

"Things," Sorrel said. "Lots and lots of things, by the look of it."

"Okay, I have an idea," Vola said.

"Does it involve running away very, very fast?" Lillie said.

"No!" Vola said. "Look, we were unprepared before. We ran in there thinking 'rats.' But we know better now."

"So, now we'll run in there thinking 'really big rats?'" Lillie said.

"With really big teeth?" Sorrel said.

"And really big tails?" Talon pointed out from their vantage point.

Vola glared over her arm as she held the door shut against the onslaught. Claws scrabbled the wood from the other side, sending a violent shiver down Vola's spine.

"If we do this right, we won't have to run in at all. Sorrel, I want you to hit this door, hard enough to send anything against it on the other side flying. Then Lillie, you're going to lob your biggest spell in there. You still have a good one?"

"Or two," Lillie said with a confident nod. She straightened up and raised her hands.

"I see." Sorrel slung her quarterstaff back onto her back and planted her feet.

"Talon…" Vola started but when she glanced back, Talon had already knocked three arrows to their string at once. Gruff lay behind them on the steps, panting. Not much for him to do in such a narrow space.

"All right," Vola said. "Three, two, one."

Sorrel took a deep breath, closed her eyes, and wound up her fist then she shot forward to punch the door. Vola's hands stung from the force that went through the wood, but without hesitating, she flung the door open.

Large shadows tumbled away from the force of Sorrel's blow,

and Vola leaned back as Talon's bow twanged and a ball of light and heat rushed past.

Then she slammed the door shut again, just in time to guard them against the resounding boom.

Heat puffed out from the gaps around the door, bringing with it the stench of burnt fur.

"That ought to do it." Vola sagged against the wall. Nothing tried to push through the door this time.

Sorrel peeked through the crack. "One, two, three, four, five, six, seven, eight. I think that's all of them. Singed to a crisp. Does Gruff eat rat?"

Gruff blew out a violent snort and lay on his side, uninterested.

Sorrel closed the door again and plopped on the ground right at the bottom of the steps. Lillie brushed her hands off on her pants, then grimaced at the grime they'd left.

Above them, the house stood silent. They'd told the man and his family to vacate while they took care of the "pest" problem. Vola was glad now. She was going to have a hard enough time explaining how everything in the cellar ended up torched.

Vola surveyed her party. "Anyone get hit while we were in there?" She paid particular attention to Lillie. She wasn't about to make the same mistake twice and the last one had cost Lillie greatly.

The wizard shook her head.

Sorrel raised her head. "I got bit. Ew, do you think they had rabies?"

"Probably," Vola said. "But we can take care of that."

She laid her hands on either side of the bloody bite on Sorrel's forearm and whispered the words "Lady bless."

An intense white light flashed between her hands and the bite smoothed out, replaced by clean, brown skin. A matching mark appeared on Vola's arm, accompanied by a dull ache. But the teeth marks faded even as they watched.

Sorrel rubbed the blood off on her pants. "I'm glad your goddess is so obliging. Makes for a really handy recovery."

Vola sat back against the wall and let her head thump the wood. "So, this is going to be a lot harder than we thought it was going to be," she said, voicing what she knew they all had to be thinking.

"Yeah, even the easy quests almost kill us," Sorrel said, examining her arm. "With our luck, the flower one will have some awful thing that tries to murder us. Just like the swamp blossoms."

"To be fair," Talon said. "These rats were nothing compared to the swamp."

"What else are we going to do?" Lillie said. "We need money to stay in town and we need to be in town in order to track down the slaver."

They fell silent. No one suggested quitting. Vola had been the only one to see all the prisoners packed in the bottom of Lord Arthorel's slave ship, but they'd all been part of the rescue. They all knew what would have happened to those people if they hadn't gotten to the harbor in time.

"We have other resources we could try," Talon said.

"Like what?"

Their deep hood nodded to Vola and Sorrel. "Don't you two belong to some sort of order?"

"That's true," Lillie said. "There are usually local chapters dedicated to the Virtues and Obstacles. We could go to them for help."

Sorrel shifted on the stone floor, looking at her feet.

"Maxim is revered everywhere," Lillie said. "Isn't he? All we have to do is find one of his temples."

Sorrel rubbed the back of her neck. "I guess."

"What's wrong?"

"Nothing," she said quickly. "I just don't really want to go begging to my order."

"But you're supposed to be finding Maxim's Warhammer," Lillie said. "Surely that warrants some help."

"I'm supposed to be able to do this on my own. We have that receipt Astrid got from the man she sold it to." Sorrel dug the limp paper out of her pocket. "Myron Vidal. Too bad she didn't get an address, too."

"Tracking him down won't get us any more money for food and lodging," Talon said.

"Yeah, and Maxim isn't the sort of god who likes to interfere in mortal affairs," Sorrel said. "Not like Vola's goddess."

Vola shifted and banged her shoulder into a sconce on the wall. She fumbled to steady the candle before it set fire to her braid. She opened her mouth but couldn't think of anything to say. Sorrel had neatly turned the conversation away from her and her order.

"That's true," Lillie said. "Cleavah has helped us in the past. Maybe she will help us again."

Vola winced. "Probably not this time."

"Why?"

"You don't just send a prayer up to your goddess saying, hey I need some money. She's not a health and wealth Virtue. If you follow her, she promises a lifetime of hard work."

"All right, but why don't we find a devotee of Cleavah and see if she has any jobs that need to be done."

It seemed so reasonable when Lillie said it like that. And Sorrel was right. Cleavah was much more likely to stick her nose in than Maxim. Still, it didn't feel great to admit to her goddess that she was broke. Even if Cleavah knew it already. The goddess was great at hanging over her shoulder.

"Fine." She sighed. "It's fine. I'll go find out if the local temple has anything that could help us. I'll meet you guys back at the inn. We can plan our next move either to stake out the drop-off point for the slaver or going after this Myron Vidal."

Sorrel stood. "Isn't it nice to have leads for once?"

"Don't forget to collect our payment from the man upstairs."

"Leave it to us," Sorrel said, dusting off her pants.

"Just don't tell him about the damage."

FOUR

ALL SHE HAD to do was step onto the street and close her eyes. A warmth beat in Vola's chest, easily ignored until she concentrated on it. Like a homing pigeon, she turned until the feeling seemed stronger and started walking.

The city was full of temples, cathedrals, abbeys, and tabernacles. Some sprawled across several blocks. Some were tiny, tucked into corners or basements. With over a hundred gods to choose from, all split into the Greater and Lesser Virtues and Obstacles, there was always at least one fanatic or priest within walking distance. You couldn't throw a rotten tomato without hitting one.

Cleavah's nearest devotee practiced her faith in a hovel off Broad's Way. Splintered boards covered the windows and soot stains climbed up the bricks as if someone hadn't quite succeeded in burning it down. "Get a real god" was scrawled across the wall in bright, pink paint.

Vola eyed the grimy facade, then glanced up and down the street. A couple of prim housewives sauntered down the cobbles, baskets over their arms. They giggled to themselves when they saw Vola head for the door. She glared at them and made sure to bare her tusks. They gasped and hurried away.

Vola sighed and slid through the door. How did you convince the world to respect a goddess when she resided in places like this?

With the windows boarded up, she'd expected the space to be dark and foul, but a couple of sweet-smelling candles lit the interior with a clear light. Vola straightened in surprise. The light revealed clean-swept flagstones and cheerful rugs leading up to the altar. Fruit and flowers lay arranged nicely in a bowl plus one very long fish knife, the light glinting off the edge.

"Ah, Vola. At last, here you are," a voice said from the door in the back corner, smooth and clear and deep like a mountain pond. "I've been waiting, though I know you come from afar."

Vola spun, searching for the owner of the voice. A woman in a black bodice and a full dark blue skirt cocked her head in the candlelight and gave Vola a smile.

Vola's brow furrowed. "Er, were you expecting me?" She knew for a fact she'd never been to Brisbene. And she seriously doubted she'd have met this woman at the paladin academy. She would have remembered the smooth gold skin and the masses of dark brown hair cascading around her shoulders.

"The lady of sharp implements watches all those who serve. And the bonds between her chosen we must conserve."

Oh, great. A true believer. One who spoke in verse. Vola rubbed her temples. She probably had a scrying orb in the back and a pack of licensed prayer knives, but Vola wondered if she'd ever even talked to Cleavah. Or whether the goddess had talked back.

"Right, so you've been keeping tabs on me?"

"Tabs is a strong word when the line between sisterhood is blurred. We two must collaborate; only then can we..." The woman's forehead wrinkled and she finally rolled her eyes. "Oh, screw it. Where am I going to find a word that rhymes with collaborate?"

"Elaborate?" Vola suggested.

"Oo, I'll write that down for next time. But no, I'm done for now."

Vola chanced a grin. "Thank Cleavah, I thought you were going to go on forever."

The devotee shook her head. "So many who come here expect all the bells and whistles. But it's too easy to talk yourself into a corner. Now. You've come looking for a job."

Vola blinked. "How did you…"

The devotee winked.

Right, Cleavah must have told her. The devotee was the real deal then.

"Um, yeah. Preferably we'd like something that pays."

The devotee gave a gusty sigh. "I understand. There's a time for the spiritual but we must also leave room for the practical."

"So, you're familiar with the concept."

"Yes. Taxes caught me off guard last year." The woman tapped the side of her nose. "But I won't let the damn things catch me blind again. I'll ambush them myself."

Vola's brow furrowed. "How do you ambush taxes?"

The devotee stooped to retrieve the fish knife lying beside Cleavah's altar. She tested the edge with her thumb and didn't answer.

Vola shook off a sudden shiver. "So, you wouldn't have any jobs lying around for a paladin of Cleavah, would you? Anyone she needs smited? Or smote?" Vola hid a wince.

The woman's lip twitched. "As it happens, the lady of sharp implements is in need of a champion."

Vola straightened. That sounded promising.

The devotee stepped away from the altar with a distinct hitch in her gait. She swung her leg as if it either pained her or it would collapse if she put too much weight on it.

Vola was strongly reminded of Lillie, and suddenly she was swamped with a wash of guilt so strong it staggered her.

The devotee paused and glanced back at her and for a second Vola wondered if she'd made some sort of noise.

"Are you all right?" the woman asked.

"Fine," Vola said, voice rough. She cleared her throat. "Fine," This time sounded like she meant it. They were weeks away from that drab manor populated by illusions, and she and Lillie had resolved it. There was nothing between them now except trust.

"Would you like a hand?" Vola said and stepped forward to offer her arm.

The devotee tilted her head. "No. I would not." She hesitated while Vola pulled her arm back and rubbed it with her other hand. "But thank you for offering."

Vola bit her lip between her tusks while the woman ducked through the door where she'd first appeared and came back, a delicate flower between her fingers.

"This is what Cleavah needs of you, Vola," she said.

"Um, a flower?"

The woman took Vola's hands and placed the blossom in her large calloused palms. The blue petals faded to white in the middle and seemed to shimmer a little in the flickering candlelight.

"This is called Broken Grace. Cleavah requires fifty blossoms by next week. Delivered here. And there will be payment for those worldly needs."

Flower gathering. Vola sighed.

"Did you by any chance put a notice on the job board at The Snuggly Bunny?"

The woman's face brightened. "I did. Was it helpful? Is that what brought you to me?"

"More like divine coincidence." Vola closed her fingers around the petals and tucked the flower in her pouch. At least these wouldn't try to eat them. "I think I should get back to my party. They might burn the bar down without me."

"Will you retrieve the blossoms?" the devotee asked as Vola made for the door.

Vola rubbed the back of her neck. It wasn't like she had much of a choice. Seemed like there wasn't anything in this town that was actually worth getting bloody for. But her party needed to eat.

"Yeah, sure." Eventually. At some point. Flower picking wasn't particularly urgent, after all.

Vola trudged down the street toward their inn as twilight descended. There was probably a spectacular sunset somewhere, but the buildings blocked out the sky until all she could see was a kind of purple-gray above.

Outside the inn, Vola cocked her head. The sign swung above, the script crossed out with a thick red line. Scrawled across it in blocky letters big enough for her to read was "The Sharp Ax."

Vola shrugged.

Gruff sat on the doorstep, his head thrown back in a mournful howl. Well, at least she knew she was in the right place.

"Talon's fine, you silly creature," she told him. "You're just going to worry them if you make all that racket."

He slitted one golden eye at her and continued howling.

Vola rolled her eyes and stepped through into the common room. A wash of voices and shouting rolled over her, making her falter. Bodies crowded the tables, ranging from heavily armored fighters to spell casters wrapped in so much silk they were probably arrow proof. In the corner, a ranger shouted his order over the general hum of conversation, and by the big fireplace, a bard stood with one foot on his stool while he strummed out a parody of the national anthem.

This place filled up as the sun went down, apparently.

Vola frowned and scanned the crowd, looking for a menacing hood, a fall of strawberry blonde hair, and a small hand raised for a beer.

There they were, clustered at the end of the bar. Lillie and Talon had secured seats but Sorrel sat right on the bar between them.

Vola started through the crowd. She expected them to part around her, like every other bar she'd ever been in, but the other adventurers seemed oblivious to the half-orc trying to shoulder them aside. A barbarian, wearing what could generously be called a kilt, stepped on her toes and didn't even flinch when she growled at him.

Her tusks didn't get her any sort of respect. It was almost refreshing, even if it was also extremely annoying.

She finally made it to the bar just by putting her shoulder down and plowing through the bodies. An elf in a stained robe and tarnished circlet found himself bumped fifteen feet away from the stool he'd claimed. He swore at her just as she joined her party.

"Step off, little man," Sorrel said, brandishing a mug at the elf. "She's with us."

"He's taller than you," Lillie said as the elf faded back into the crowd with a grumble.

Sorrel wiggled her butt on the bar and swung her feet. "Not right now, he isn't."

"Any luck?" Lillie asked Vola.

"Not unless you want to go flower picking after all." She braced her hands against the bar and thumped her forehead down on the smooth wood.

"Oh. Well, perhaps we shouldn't be so picky. We were paid for the rat job but only enough to cover tonight."

"And only after Talon glared at him," Sorrel added.

Talon didn't react. They perched on the edge of their stool, hood twitching every time someone nearby guffawed or drunkenly leaned too close.

If Talon and Gruff were used to the wilderness, it was no wonder they were both jumpy. Maybe they should retreat to their room. Their very expensive room.

Vola took Sorrel's mug and glared into it. "Can we afford this?"

Sorrel snatched it back. "It's Lillie's."

Vola glanced at Lillie, who flushed. "The bartender just keeps giving them to me."

"He does?" Vola said with a raised eyebrow.

"Perhaps it's a local custom?"

Or perhaps Lillie was too lovely for her own good. The funny thing was she had no idea. She'd told Vola once that fat and clumsy wasn't attractive.

Vola sent a look down the bar, trying to decide who was the most likely culprit. A couple of men down the way noticed her looking and straightened. One with an instrument case slung over his back twiddled his fingers and wiggled his eyebrows.

Vola drummed her fingers against the bar and glared. The man gulped and slid off his stool to disappear into the crowd.

"Hmm," Vola said.

"What can I get you?" The bartender stepped into her line of sight, scrubbing a mug.

"Tea," Vola said, turning back to her party.

"Come on, Vola," Sorrel said, taking a swig, leaving a smear of foam across her upper lip. "Just one drink."

"We haven't even come close to victory yet," Vola said. "I don't want to anger my goddess, do you?"

"She's the one who likes fish knives, isn't she?" Sorrel said. "No, I don't want to mess with her."

"Then we must find the slaver," Lillie said.

"How are we going to do that if we can't afford to stick around long enough?" Sorrel said.

"Heads up," Talon said under their breath, and the rest of them stiffened.

A boy wove through the crowd, clearly not belonging among the adventurers but comfortable enough to make his way to the back of the common room, a crisp piece of paper in his hand.

He stood on a chair and reached to pin the paper to the job board, right in the center. A little breeze made the edges rustle.

The boy turned to jump down and found every eye in the place on him and the lone job posted in the center of a big empty board.

His lips tipped in a jaunty grin, and he gave them all a cheeky salute. He left the bar amid a hushed silence.

"Get it, get it!" Vola hissed under her breath.

Everyone moved at once.

The floor shook under the sudden stampede of boots. Glasses and mugs danced across the bar and crashed to the floor. Vola found herself wedged between a massive fighter on one side, who smelled of sweat and steel, and a sorcerer on the other, who had apparently bathed in incense that morning.

Vola sneezed with enough force to shoot her back a foot into the chest of the kilted barbarian. He growled and made a lunge for her. She ducked out of the way and ran into the bard with the lute.

She'd never make it to the job board. There was already a pile of adventurers writhing under it shouting things like, "I've got it! I've got it! Wait where'd it go?" and "No biting, Anton! That's cheating!" and "Shit, she's slippery."

Swords shinged from their scabbards, and Vola decided to cut their losses.

The bartender stood behind the bar, polishing a glass as he heaved a great sigh.

Vola caught sight of Lillie's bright hair disappearing under a tangle of bodies, and she waded forward to grasp one of the wizard's arms and pull her free.

"Thank you," Lillie said a little breathlessly.

"Stay close." Vola squinted through the fray.

The flash of a dagger drew her gaze to the edge of the massive fight where Talon's hood was just visible. The ranger ducked forward, but Vola got an arm around their middle and pulled them out.

"Hey, I was in the middle of something."

"Well, I'm not waiting until you get to the end of it. Where's Sorrel?"

"I lost track of her immediately," Lillie said, hiding behind Vola's broad back. "She's so small and fast."

Vola planted her feet. It was a little better here where she could see the occasional floorboard between adventurers. Closer to the job board, the ground was buried at least three bodies deep.

She cupped her hands around her mouth. "Sorrel!"

"Coming!" came the reply.

Lillie gasped and pointed. From the pile of bodies, a hairy arm emerged, the piece of paper clutched triumphantly in its fist.

Sorrel's curly head appeared as she clambered up the pile and plucked the piece of paper from the hand. She spun and slid deftly down the bodies to land on her feet.

She scampered over to them.

"Ta-da!" She brandished the job posting.

Vola gaped. Then grinned. "Great job. Now let's get out of here."

"They've got it! There, by the door."

The other adventurers spun, and suddenly they were the focus of every eye in the building.

Vola's gaze darted between her party and the enemy, taking stock.

"Lillie, I want you to set fire to this place if they come even a step closer." She spoke loud enough to make their position clear.

The bartender sighed again.

"Sorrel, protect that job with your life. Talon—"

Behind them, the door burst open and Gruff plowed through.

"Talon, I believe you were in the middle of something."

The hood dipped, and Vola could imagine the smirk underneath.

The front line of adventurers took in the bared teeth of the wolf and the fire between Lillie's hands and stepped back a pace.

"Geez, it's just a job," the barbarian in the kilt said. "Calm down. No one has to die for it."

"Yeah, get a grip," a bard said.

"Animals outside!" the bartender bellowed, finger pointing.

"That's what you're upset about?" Sorrel called.

"Just go." Vola herded them out the door as the adventurers behind them subsided with grumbles. She slammed the door shut, and they huddled together on the front step of the bar.

"Well done, Miss Sorrel," Lillie said. "What does it say?"

Sorrel unfolded the piece of paper and held it out. The words danced and swam for Vola, but Lillie obligingly read it aloud.

"I require a band of heroes to find a missing adventurer. Cash on delivery. Come to the Rutger Sea Corporation warehouse by the docks for more information."

Sorrel let out a whoop. "A missing person. That's great!"

The rest of them stared at her.

A frown line formed between Lillie's delicate eyebrows. "I think you've confused great with terrible."

Sorrel's face fell just a bit. "Well, I mean obviously not great for the adventurer. I just mean we're good at kidnappings now. They're kind of our thing."

"I'm not sure if you can say it's our thing if it's literally the only thing we've done," Vola said as Lillie took charge of the paper and folded it neatly to store in her bag.

"Which means it's literally what we do," Sorrel said. "We rescued all those people in Water's Edge, didn't we? And Henri."

Vola hesitated, images flashing through her head. Carnivorous flowers nearly eating them, illusory assassins getting the drop on them. Almost drowning in a sinking tent.

"Yeah, I remember it going really well," she said.

Talon turned to stalk down the darkened street, Gruff following. A few shady figures lounging outside the bar took one look at the hooded figure and thought better of whatever ambush they were planning.

"Where are you going?" Vola called.

"To find the warehouse," they answered. "Unless you want to sit there wasting time all night?"

FIVE

OUT BY THE SWAMP, everyone had gone to bed around sundown, leaving the little town dark and quiet. In the city though, it seemed like the party was just getting started.

Light spilled from unshuttered windows and open doorways, painting the cobblestones with gold. Music wound through the air as Vola and the others passed through the lower parts of the city. Minstrels busked from popular corners and the tinny strains of a distant piano wafted to them from an open doorway. The luscious scent of meat pies made Vola's stomach rumble, and she realized they hadn't eaten yet.

She sighed. This whole adventuring thing wasn't nearly as romantic as the academy had made it out to be.

The world grew quiet as they drew closer and closer to the docks. There were fewer public houses and more warehouses and the only light came from the lamps down by the wharf where the night fishermen launched their boats.

The cobbles under their feet grew slick as they passed onto a street lined with weather-beaten buildings gone gray from salt spray. Vola was hard pressed to tell which smelled worse, the fish or the mildewed cobbles.

"Is this it?" she asked.

Talon led them unerringly to the third building down and pointed.

"How do you know?" Vola said.

"I'm a tracker. I find things," the voice grated out.

Lillie conjured a little ball of light and sent it soaring upwards to illuminate the clapboard sign over the door. "Rutger Sea Corporation," she said.

"Neat trick," Sorrel told Talon. "Could you find dinner? Like if you lost it or something."

"What does that have to do with anything?" Lillie asked.

"I'm hungry. What about our missing person, could you find them?"

Talon shifted from foot to foot. "Only if they've left a trail. It's easier with things that stand still."

Vola glared at the weathered facade, trying to decide if the clench in her gut was the smell or a nasty premonition. "I don't like this."

"Well, it is pretty ugly," Sorrel said.

Lillie pouted. "It's just seen better days. There's no call to be mean."

"How can you be mean to a building?"

"I meant," Vola said, halting the conversation before it could fall off the track completely. "That I have a bad feeling about this. Why would an employer want to meet in a warehouse down by the docks? Where no one can see?"

"Perhaps they're shy?" Lillie said.

Vola straightened and loosened her sword in its sheath. "Talon," she said with a hand gesture. "You want to find a good vantage point to cover us?"

The hood nodded. "There are windows along the roofline. I'll bet I can get in from there. Gruff can flank from inside."

"Good. Lillie, Sorrel, stay alert. Let's be ready for anything."

Talon disappeared into the dark around the corner while Vola stepped right up to the big front door and slid it aside just far enough that they could slip inside.

Vola nearly gagged as the smell of dried fish washed over them. Holding her breath wasn't going to be an option if the whole place smelled like this, but holy Cleavah, that was bad. The stench seemed to reach down the back of her throat, coating her tongue and tonsils.

She cleared her throat, then gestured them forward.

Crates were stacked on their right, almost brushing the support beams near the roof. And on the left stood drying racks covered in millions of noisome little fish.

Vola had never been a fan of fish, and now she was rapidly hurtling toward detesting it.

Four lamps hung from pillars in the middle of the warehouse, creating a pool of warm, yellow light. One man stood in the middle, wringing his hands.

Vola stepped into the circle.

He jumped and raised a hand to protect his face. "Ahh!"

Sorrel and Lillie stepped up beside her as Vola surveyed the man. He wore a pair of fisherman's overalls with a white linen shirt underneath. Completely ordinary for this part of the city. But something about him made Vola's skin tingle.

She waited for a second to give him a chance to get used to her appearance.

He peeked around his arm, then dropped it and cleared his throat. "Uh, terribly sorry about that," he said. "I'm afraid you quite startled me."

"I'm sure I did," Vola said with a sigh.

"You know, if you put some more lights in here, that wouldn't happen," Sorrel said. She surveyed the warehouse, tapping her teeth. "This place could use some brightening up."

"It's not like you can put up curtains," Lillie said dubiously.

Vola cleared her throat. "Are you the one we talk to about finding the missing person?"

The man brightened. He wore his dark hair swept to the side and his face was clean-shaven. "Yes. Are you…are you qualified?"

"Well, we were the ones who snatched your job posting," Sorrel said. "So, yeah—"

Vola kicked the halfling to shut her up. "We're experienced in bringing back missing people," she said. "It's kind of our thing." She avoided looking at Sorrel. "Who's missing?"

"My…My g-girlfriend." He gulped and Vola's eyes narrowed.

"Uh huh," she said. "And what's her name?"

"Rilla?" His eyes darted around them.

"You don't seem terribly sure of that."

"What?" he said. "Yes, she's called Rilla. She's dark, with curly black hair, and the last time I saw her she wore a green and gold jacket. Please, I'm very worried about her. I'm afraid some calamity must have befallen her."

Lillie tilted her head. "How do you know she's missing?"

The man looked baffled. "Because she's not here."

"I mean, she's her own woman. You don't control her. Maybe she just left."

He shook his head so that his perfectly combed hair flopped in his eyes. "She would never just run away. She has responsibilities here."

Sorrel stepped up to the man. Her head only came up to his waist, but she reached out and poked his belly button. "You're not the bad guy, are you?"

Vola started and almost reached over to grab Sorrel and drag her back, but the halfling was advancing, driving the man against the nearest pillar.

"You are, aren't you? You kidnapped her yourself. Admit it."

"What? No, no of course not. Why would I kidnap my...I mean why would you even ask that?"

Vola rubbed her forehead. She knew why Sorrel was asking. They'd been burned by their employer before. And Vola herself wanted to know why they were meeting in a warehouse after hours, but scaring off their only contract didn't seem like a good idea either.

Sorrel let him go and turned away with a shrug. "You never know."

"I didn't do anything to Rilla." The man raised his gaze to Vola, pegging her as the least hostile. A nice change for once. "She's an adventurer. She was on a quest investigating some strange thefts, but she stopped coming home at night. I think something has happened to her. Please. You have to help find her. I even know where she was going to investigate next."

Vola met Sorrel's gaze. The halfling shrugged again, not exactly helpful. Lillie stood, biting her lip, but eventually, she nodded. Vola raised her eyes to the darkness around them, but she couldn't spot Talon wherever the ranger had hidden themselves.

Out of the black, Gruff padded toward them as if in answer. He stopped beside Vola and licked her hand. The man squeaked.

"All right, then. We'll find Rilla," Vola said.

He blinked between Vola and Gruff before he clapped his hands together. "Oh, wonderful. She was heading to the Broken's Hospital in the Verdant district. You can start there."

That was actually a pretty good lead. The Broken was one of the Greater Virtues and had clinics and shrines everywhere. But if he had an exact location that was even better.

"I will pay you three hundred gold when you find her. That is a fair price, is it not?"

Vola fought to control her expression. More than fair. They

would have only been paid a hundred to find the entire town of Water's Edge. That is if they hadn't ended up arresting their employer.

But all she said was, "It is," and she reached out to shake his hand.

He hesitated a brief second, and she took special care not to crush his hand in hers.

"We'll be in touch," Vola said.

"Speaking of," Lillie said, holding out her hand. "How can we contact you when we find her?"

"Rilla will know how to get a hold of me. I don't…I don't give out my personal address. It's the principle of the thing."

"I understand," she said with a brilliant smile.

The man—who obviously didn't give out his name for similar reasons—flushed to the roots of his hair.

They left ahead of him, meeting Talon on the street just outside the warehouse.

"Did that seem odd to anyone else?" Vola said. Mist fell on the docks near the waterfront, making the leather joints in her armor squeak.

"Odd how?" Sorrel said. "Big empty warehouse. Employer who wouldn't give his name. Mysterious quest. Seems like a normal day for an adventurer."

Vola glanced at Lillie, convinced the wizard would have picked up on everything Vola caught if not more.

Lillie bit her lip.

"He wasn't exactly who he said he was, was he?" Vola said.

"Do you think he was lying?" Talon said.

"Not so much lying as leaving something out. Something important."

Sorrel's brow furrowed.

"He wore fishing gear, but it was brand new," Vola said. "Pristine with no stains, and I think he was the least smelly thing in there. And when he shook, his hands were soft. No callouses."

"He did talk a lot like Lillie," Sorrel said.

Lillie nodded. "I think he works for someone much loftier than he was letting on."

"Anyone you might know?" Vola asked, examining her nails.

Lillie glanced at her sharply. She opened her mouth as if to deny it but then must have thought better. "I didn't recognize him. And I don't know anyone named Rilla. If that's even her name."

"Do you think we should still take the job?" Talon said. "If he's not being honest about it?"

Sorrel, Lillie, and Talon all looked at Vola.

Vola scratched her chin, then rolled her shoulders. "Yes. We'll find the girl. She may actually be in trouble. Either at home or wherever she disappeared to. So, we'll find her. But that doesn't mean we have to turn her over to him until we know what's going on."

SIX

THE NEXT MORNING, Vola and the others left The Snuggly Bunny aka The Sharp Ax bright and early only to stop short on the doorstep.

"Ugh, tell me I'm hallucinating," Vola said, covering her eyes.

"If you're hallucinating, then I am, too." Lillie passed a sad look over the menacing figure of the swamp beast, who stood in the middle of the street crunching something between its teeth while it glared malevolently at anyone who dared pass.

A woman with two children in tow spun on her heel and hurried the other way.

"I thought we got rid of it," Sorrel said. "Or at least I really, really hoped we'd gotten rid of it. What do you suppose happened to those thugs who took it?"

"It probably ate them," Talon growled.

The swamp monster swung its head around to eye them, making the broken rope hanging from its neck sway wildly, before it turned to snap at a burly man in dirty overalls. The man yelped and shot back up the street.

"Well, we can't leave it here to terrify innocent citizens," Lillie said, though she made no move to go collect the beast.

"Why not?" Sorrel asked, brow furrowed.

Vola sighed. She had to agree with Lillie. Much as she hated to admit it, the beast was here because of them and it would be their fault if it razed the whole city.

She stepped forward, but the beast saw her coming and dodged. She lunged, rolled, and snatched at the broken lead rope, finally getting it wrapped around one arm.

The beast narrowed its eyes. Vola knew that look well and managed to twist out of the way before the nasty yellow teeth closed on her flesh. She bashed the thing in the nose. "Behave."

"It's a full gold to stable your horse overnight," a voice said.

They all glanced back at the door to see the bartender leaning against the door frame. He didn't even look at them as he lit his cheap cigarette and took a drag.

"What if it's not a horse?" Vola said.

"Then it's two gold a night." The bartender blew a stream of smoke into the humid morning air.

"Oh, for the love of Cleavah." Vola raised her eyes to the heavens, but Cleavah herself didn't seem inclined to comment. "We're not stabling it here," she told the bartender. She turned back to her party, holding the beast as far away as possible. She was already missing enough chunks because of this thing. "We'll take it with us. Maybe we'll find a cheaper option along the way."

"Or maybe it will be good for intimidating witnesses," Sorrel said.

The Verdant district of Brisbene lay up the hill past a row of banks, each one bigger and grander than the last. The hospital sat smack in the middle of a grand park with sprawling green lawns and topiary that would make a better mount than the swamp beast.

Nurses in pristine white robes wheeled a couple of patients

around the grounds as Vola and her party crunched up the gravel driveway.

Vola eyed the columned portico and then took a moment to tie the swamp beast to a railing out of reach of the door.

Huge bronze double doors guarded the interior, carved with a relief of a woman with short curling hair, who stood on one leg. She was missing most of the other leg along with her left arm, and scars obscured the left half of her face. Flames crawled up the doors behind her, almost like wings.

The Broken. Greater Virtue of Righteousness. The rest of the pantheon had cast her out, worried that righteousness could rule over all the Virtues and Obstacles if she wanted. But mortals still worshiped her as a paragon of justice, honor, and healing.

Vola had always thought she deserved a few paladins of her own, just like Maxim and Ona. But she'd never chosen any. Not since she'd fallen.

Inside the doors, marble columns soared to a vaulted ceiling and a massive skylight showed off the brilliant blue sky. The clean open space reminded Vola more of the rich temples down in the city than the clinics where she'd learned most of Cleavah's healing spells.

Vola expected someone to greet them right away. Their weapons and armor clearly didn't belong in a place like this. But no one seemed to notice them as figures rushed back and forth. Nurses and healers, all dressed in the pristine white robes hurried as if someone's life depended on their actions. Actually, it probably did.

Vola jerked her chin at Sorrel, who gave her a swift nod.

The halfling was far better than Vola at talking to people and as long as she wasn't trying to intimidate a possible bad guy, she usually got people to talk to her. The best Vola could hope for was that no one would scream when they saw her.

Sorrel marched up to the nearest white figure and tugged on the woman's sleeve. "Excuse me, ma'am—"

"I'm sorry, but you'll have to wait your turn in triage, just like everyone else." The woman gestured absently through an archway to their left and hurried away.

Sorrel was left standing there with her mouth open. She tried again, planting herself in front of another doctor. "Excuse me—"

"Oh, no. We have another one," the doctor called to his colleagues. Then he herded Sorrel toward the archway. "Please step this way to our triage room. Someone will be with you shortly, and if you feel the need to vomit, please do so in the provided receptacles. Thank you."

"Hey wait!" Sorrel cried.

Vola exchanged a look with Lillie and Talon and hurried to follow.

"Excuse me, she's not sick," Vola said.

They stepped through the archway and found the triage room, which was just a large hall lined with chairs. Or at least it would be, normally. Right now, it was lined with gnomes, all of them varying shades of ill.

The doctor pushed Sorrel down beside a gnome who had his head in a bucket before he swept away down the hall.

"What on earth do you suppose is happening here?" Lillie said.

"Sick people," Talon growled and drew back into a corner, pulling in their elbows as if to keep from accidentally touching anyone.

"Yup. Sick people are happening here," Vola said. "We need to find someone in charge. Ah, there."

Another woman in the white smock of a healer headed toward them. She had her hair tied back and wore the simple silver circlet of an acolyte on her brow. Streaks of green and brown stained her clothing, and she wore her sleeves rolled up.

"Please take a seat. We'll get to everyone, eventually. But our healers are exhausted, and I'm afraid we don't have enough tonic to dose you and all of your fellows yet. You'll just have to wait until the next batch is ready."

"My fellows?" Sorrel glanced around in consternation. "I'm not a gnome!"

"There's been a mistake," Vola said. "Sorrel's not sick. We just need to talk to someone for our investigation."

The woman blew out her breath in exasperation as someone retched behind her, the noise echoing up the high walls. "Not sick? Then we don't have time for whatever questions you have. Can't you see we're swamped?"

"I can see you don't know the difference between a gnome and a halfling," Sorrel grumbled half under her breath. She crossed her arms and her feet swung wildly over the edge of the chair. "Makes me worry about how good a doctor you are. Remind me to go elsewhere next time I'm actually sick."

"Are you sure you can't spare just a minute?" Lillie said. "This won't take long."

"I'm afraid not." The woman pushed strands of her brown hair behind her ear. "It was the gnomish New Years yesterday, and I think every gnome in the city managed to get a handful of bad jaja root. They sprinkle it over their pies, you know. Only this batch had a fungus. So much food poisoning."

"So much vomit," Talon said from the corner.

Vola took a step away from her party, chewing her lip as she surveyed the hall. Gnomes lay on the floor moaning or slumped in the chairs. Gnomes were generally built a bit sturdier than halflings, taller with more girth and bigger bone structure. But these looked like they could blow away in a stiff breeze and their normally swarthy complexions were pale and slack.

Misery pulsed in the air and Vola winced. She glanced back at her party, fingers twitching. Back in Arthorel's manor, Cleavah had told her to practice. The only way the goddess could heal was through a follower, and the strength of that healing depended entirely on Vola.

Lillie noticed her glance and raised an eyebrow.

Vola had withheld the goddess's gift once before. And she lived with that regret daily. There really wasn't any reason to hesitate now.

Vola knelt beside the nearest gnome and put her hand on his shoulder. She bowed her head and took a deep breath.

"Lady bless," she whispered. "Your power through me, so be it."

"So be it," a voice like rushing wind breathed in her ear.

The healing washed out of her—a tidal wave compared to the calm flow of water she normally felt. As if her lady stood behind her with her hands on Vola's shoulders, pushing through her into the world.

And it didn't stop with the gnome in front of her.

Vola took the pain and nausea and the poison that flowed through everyone in the room and transferred it to herself. Her stomach roiled and burned, and she fell to her hands and knees, losing her grip on the nearest gnome's shoulder.

She concentrated on breathing—in, out, in, out—as the shared nausea faded, and Cleavah healed the food poisoning in her blood.

"Hey," the gnome beside her said. "Hey, I don't feel sick anymore."

Vola blinked as the gnomes began shifting, stretching, tentatively moving to see if they could do so without barfing.

Lillie stepped forward to put a cool hand under her elbow. Vola let her help her to her feet as the others stared. The acolyte gaped, her mouth hanging open as she surveyed the hall.

"I didn't know you could heal more than one person at a time," Sorrel said, quietly.

"I don't think I could until just now," Vola said.

"Would you explain that, please?" Lillie said, unhooking her spell book from her hip. "So I can take notes."

Vola's mouth twisted. "Do we have time?"

"There's always time for learning."

"I, too, would like to know what you did," the acolyte said. "If you wouldn't mind. Are you a healer?"

Vola rubbed her belly. The nausea and cramping faded with every clear breath she took, but the echo remained. "I'm a paladin," she said. "I was chosen by one of the Lesser Virtues. I get the power to heal from her. It's never been this…" She gestured around the hall. "This big before."

"Did you learn a new spell?" Lillie asked.

"I don't really learn spells like you. My lady told me to practice, so I did. I think she decides when I deserve new gifts."

"And who is your lady?" the acolyte asked.

Vola dropped her gaze and shuffled her feet. "Nobody as important as the Broken," she said and gestured around them at the temple-like hospital.

The acolyte cocked her head. "I only ask because it's unusual for one of the lesser gods to bestow so much healing power on a fighter. I wonder what she sees in your future."

"Death and dismemberment, apparently," Sorrel said, hopping down from her chair. "Goody. Now, about our questions. It seems you have some time now." Sorrel smiled up at her innocently.

The acolyte gave her a deep bow. "It appears I'm at loose ends. What would you like to know?"

"We're looking for a woman named Rilla." Sorrel glanced at Lillie.

Lillie checked her notes. "Dark skin, brown eyes. And she was wearing a green and gold jacket."

"Of course, I remember Rilla," the acolyte said. "She was investigating the theft."

"What theft would that be?" Vola asked, settling against the wall. Finally, they were getting somewhere. "Did someone break in to steal medicine or supplies?"

"Maybe a holy relic or two?" Sorrel added.

"No," the acolyte said. "No, they were just after bodies."

Vola's eyebrows went up. "Bodies?"

"Yes. We keep all the deceased in our morgue in the basement. Many of the corpses were stolen a week and a half ago. Rilla was investigating the theft."

Vola tapped her fingernail against her sword hilt. Stolen corpses. Gods, what a mess.

"Why would anyone want dead bodies?" Sorrel said with a grimace.

Lillie bit her lip, her brow furrowed in thought, and Vola made a note to ask her what she was thinking after they'd left.

"We have no idea," the acolyte said. "But Rilla seemed to have some ideas. She even had a suspect she was going to question. But we haven't heard from her in a week." Her face fell. "Nothing's happened to her, has it?"

"That's what we're trying to find out," Vola said gently. She pushed off the wall. "You said she had a suspect."

"I'm sorry. I don't have a name. I got the impression it was someone unsavory."

"If they were stealing bodies for some nefarious reason, that would fit," Sorrel said.

The acolyte's mouth pinched. "I hope Rilla didn't run into trouble."

"Thank you," Vola said.

"No, thank you." The acolyte gestured to the gnomes who were still milling about. Some were drifting toward the doorways, looking like they didn't entirely trust their stomachs, yet. "This was very selfless of you."

Vola shrugged self-consciously. It hadn't cost her much. Just a few moments of disorientation and nausea. She wouldn't be able to do much healing any time soon, but this investigation seemed to be a lot of walking and talking so far.

They made their way out to the front of the hospital where the swamp beast had eaten halfway through a column. They looked at the damage, looked at each other, and then gathered the creature up and hurried away before anyone could notice.

"So, how do we find Rilla?" Lillie asked. "If this is where her trail goes cold?"

Talon thumped a boot against the gravel. "I don't like cities. There're no tracks to follow."

"Well, we could take up her investigation," Vola said. "Go around to all the hospitals and see if they've had…body thefts."

Lillie sighed. "It's not exactly a dead end, but there are many, many hospitals in this city. It will take a while."

Sorrel dug around in her pocket. "It's not like we only have one option." She produced the receipt she'd brought from Water's Edge as they stepped from the gravel driveway back onto solid cobblestones. "We can track two leads at once. While we look for Rilla, we can also look for Myron Vidal. He's got Maxim's Warhammer. And maybe the Warhammer can help us."

"The Warhammer can help?" Vola said, screwing up her face. "Are you sure you aren't just saying that so we'll go do your thing?"

Sorrel's mouth fell open. "Would I do that? Besides, it belongs to a god. Anything's possible." She tapped her teeth. "The trick will be finding Myron. We don't have an address."

"Oh, that's the easy part," Lillie said. "We just visit the registry."

The rest of them stared at the wizard, who flushed under their scrutiny.

"What?" she said. "Every city has one. All citizens living in the city have an entry in the registry. It's all very organized and official. If the address isn't on the receipt, it *will* be in the registry."

Of course, in Vola's experience, nothing was as easy as it should be.

After several hours of trying to convince the ancient lizard who manned the front desk that they weren't there to lay siege to the registry building, they found that there was no entry for a Myron Vidal in the city.

"This doesn't make sense," Lillie said as they returned to the inn for a late lunch. "Every legal citizen has an entry. It's a law. Why wouldn't we be able to find him?"

"Maybe he isn't a legal citizen," Sorrel said.

Lillie blinked at her. "I don't understand."

"Maybe he's here illegally," Talon growled.

"That's not…You can't do that. It's against the rules." Lillie stopped short in the middle of the street.

"Yeah," Vola said, tilting her head. "It's called breaking the law. People do it all the time. You know how Lord Arthorel was kidnapping and selling his people to slavers?"

Lillie's shoulders drooped. "I had no idea it was so common."

Vola rolled her eyes and noticed the sign above the inn door had changed again. Now, when she squinted, it read "The Leering Lynx."

"Going off our track record, we'd be out of a job if everyone followed the law," Sorrel said as they pushed inside.

The common room was mostly empty with just a few lone adventurers scattered around with their lunch plates.

"I have no idea how to find someone who isn't registered legally," Lillie said in a small voice as she plopped down on a barstool. "How will we find Myron without an entry in the registry?"

"Underground," a deep voice said, interrupting them.

They turned to look. The deep-chested barbarian who wore a

red and purple kilt sat at the end of the bar sipping from a ceramic mug.

"What?" Vola said.

"You need to find someone or something that's not exactly legal, you go to the Underground. Everybody knows that."

Vola leaned an elbow on the bar and gave the bald barbarian her full attention. "Assume we're not everybody."

He blew on his drink. "Well, then I'd tell you to head to the Varnassi Exchange and tell the man behind the counter you're looking for 'Zelstrano's 19th edition.'"

Vola looked back at her party.

"I don't know," Lillie whispered. "This place doesn't sound like it's exactly above board."

"Of course it's not," Sorrel whispered back. "It's called the Underground. Not the above ground."

Vola glanced at Talon.

The ranger shrugged. "Take the shot."

SEVEN

"IT'S A BOOKSHOP," Vola said, hands planted on her hips while she looked up at the shop front. A cart driver shouted at her to move before he took a second look at her and went around.

Lillie pressed her hands to her cheeks, eyes shining. "It is. Oh, it's so beautiful."

"The Underground is under a book shop?" Talon said.

"It's not exactly…atmospheric is it?" Sorrel said, her head cocked.

"No, but it is secret," Vola said. "Who would think to look here?"

"Let's go in," Lillie said, then grabbed Vola's hand to drag her off the street and through the front door.

The inside was about what she'd expected, dim light illuminating rows and rows of bookshelves crowded with leather-bound volumes.

A copper lantern swung over a counter set along the back wall where a shopkeeper in a leather apron more suited to a butcher waited.

Lillie skipped along the shelves, making embarrassing little noises under her breath as her fingers skimmed the books.

Vola wasted no time stepping up to the counter.

"Um, we're looking for Velstrano's 18th edition?" She wished it hadn't sounded like a question but it was too late to take it back now.

The man gazed at her from behind his spectacles, unfazed.

Wasn't he supposed to open up a secret trapdoor or something?

The man bent, shuffled under the counter, and whomped a huge leather-bound tome onto the counter. Dust puffed into the air.

"Oh," Lillie said, dragging the word out in appreciation as she limped to the counter. She ran her hands over the cover.

Vola made a face. How was a book supposed to get them into the Underground?

"I'm pretty sure it was supposed to be the 19th edition," Sorrel whispered to Vola.

"Right, um. Actually, could we see the 19th edition?" Vola asked the shopkeeper.

His expression remained fixed as he reached under the counter. There was a clunk and a bookcase against the back wall slid aside revealing a passage into the back alley.

"Oh. Right. Thank you," Vola said.

Lillie bit her lip. "But, couldn't we just…"

"We don't have money for books, Lillie." Vola grabbed the back of Lillie's bodice to drag the wizard away. "Where's Talon?"

A book snapped shut behind them, and Vola turned in time to see Talon placing a slim volume back on the shelf.

Vola jerked her head, and they shuffled through the passageway.

"What were you reading?" Lillie asked Talon.

The hooded figure shrugged. "Romance."

Lillie paused long enough to blink before they stepped through into the open air again.

"Oh, wow," Vola said. She was tempted to just stop and stare for a moment.

Here, behind the bookshop, a network of alleyways were crowded with booths and little shacks. Fortune tellers gestured for them to come closer, thieves lounged in the shadows, eying their limp purses, and fighters in varieties of armor hulked down the narrow passages.

Vola craned her neck to peer down a dead end, noting the entire system was cut off from the rest of the city through a series of barricades and collapsed buildings.

"It's like a city within the city." She licked her lips and angled toward a stall displaying a variety of edged weapons.

"Etruvian darksteel, adventurer," the dealer said with a sly grin. "Three times cheaper than you'll find out there."

Vola's mouth watered.

Sorrel cast a look at the quarterstaff hanging over her shoulder and snorted.

Lillie took Vola's arm in a gentle but firm grip. "We don't have money for swords, Volagra."

Sorrel scowled up at the sky. "It's not underground," she said. "I thought it would at least be in the sewers. You're disappointing me here." She shook her head at the alley.

"We need to find an information broker," Vola said. "I mean there has to be one here among all the other vendors. Excuse me." She leaned back over the weapon stall. "Who do we talk to if we need to find someone specific?"

"Talk to Fang. She runs the place. Runs all the information, too."

"Where?"

"Down at the end. Next to the pit."

Lillie pulled a face. "The pit?"

"That's more like it," Sorrel said, perking up.

The pit was as easy to find as it sounded. They just followed the sound of cheering and roars of pain. Backed up against a dead-end alley, a scaffold presided over an actual pit dug into the street. The misplaced cobblestones had been piled high around it in a knee-high wall.

In the bottom, a couple of big, burly types wrestled half-heartedly in the dirt.

Vola made her way toward the scaffold where a couple of figures watched the fight. At the bottom of the steps, an orc in a leather harness and not much else stood blocking the way.

"We're here to talk to Fang," Vola said, trying to catch a look past him.

"Nobody just talks to Fang," the bouncer grated out. He sounded like he talked through a mouthful of marbles. Considering the size of the tusks curving up from his lower jaw, that wasn't surprising.

"Well then, good sir, may we converse with her?" Lillie said. "Engage in discourse. Repartee?"

"You think making fun of me will get you in?" The orc crossed his arms, making the leather over his chest creak.

"She really isn't making fun of you," Sorrel said from near the orc's knee. "That's just how she talks normally."

The orc spit, and Sorrel sprang out of the way. "You want to talk to Fang, you gotta catch her eye." He pointed to the pit.

"Oh, come on, don't you have any fellow feeling for another orc?" Sorrel asked.

"Half-orc," Lillie said under her breath.

"You know, like brotherhood. Camaraderie."

"Must be a little people thing," the orc said. "We just have people we kill and people we don't kill."

Vola opened her mouth to argue that it was more nuanced

than that but—well, on a level deeper than intelligent thought, he wasn't wrong.

"Looking at all the options here," Sorrel said, tapping her chin. "There is a lot of space between your legs and I am very small. What if I just whipped right past you?"

"Then I do this." The orc picked Sorrel up with one hand and lobbed her toward the pit.

Vola started to yell and then sighed instead. "I guess that answers that question. Come on," she told Talon and Lillie.

"Thank you for your time," Lillie threw over her shoulder as they sprinted for the wall.

In the pit, the two fighters scattered as Sorrel hit the dirt rolling. They scrambled up the walls out of the way as Sorrel sprang to her feet, staff out. "That wasn't very nice," she called to the orc.

Vola vaulted the wall and slid down the side of the pit to land beside Sorrel. Talon leaped and rolled so they came up with their knives out.

"Where's Gruff?" Vola asked.

"I'm holding him in reserve. In case this goes badly."

"I'm sure this is a wonderful idea," Lillie called. "But you're on your own because I'm stuck!"

Vola spun to find Lillie hanging over the wall, feet dangling, wide butt in the air. She stomped to the wizard and grabbed a flailing foot.

"Thank you—oof." Lillie twisted in midair and landed halfway across Vola's shoulders.

"Uh, guys," Sorrel said just as the crowd around the pit roared with approval.

A low snarl traveled all the way down Vola's spine. She dropped Lillie and whirled around. Lillie wobbled and fell on her butt just as a dragon swarmed over the wall and down into the pit with them.

"Is that an actual dragon?" Vola said, mouth hanging open.

"Draconis minimus, actually," Lillie said, dusting off her backside. "Notice how it's only about as big as a horse. Draconis maximus wouldn't fit in this alley."

"Trust me, I'm noticing." Vola dove to the side to carry Lillie out of range of the spout of fire that arced toward them.

"Of course, they're just as impressive with breath weapons as their larger cousins."

"Lillie!"

"Oh, right. Try noise. They don't like that."

"Don't forget you work with fire, too."

Vola stepped away from Lillie. Now the wizard had her feet under her, she didn't need Vola crowding her so close she couldn't cast.

The dragon—red and gold and lithe as crap—raised membranous wings and dove for Sorrel.

The halfling planted one end of her staff and swung so the dragon's attack sailed past without so much as singing her tunic.

Noise. Lillie had said noise.

Vola drew her sword and swung her shield onto her arm. She roared at the top of her lungs and clanged her sword against her shield, making an awful racket.

Talon caught onto the idea and sprinted to the other side of the creature, where they yelled incoherently.

The dragon hissed and swung its head back and forth as if it couldn't focus between the two of them. It spun in a circle, its tail whipping around so fast it whistled.

Vola ducked and turned her shoulder so the wicked tail tip just glanced off her round shield. She thrust out with her shield arm and launched upward to slice into the scales just as the tail tried to dart away again.

The dragon screamed as she struck. Its jaws lunged for her.

A gray blur struck the side of the dragon's face, and the teeth snapped shut just inches from Vola. Sorrel landed on both feet and spun kicked the dragon in the throat.

It gurgled just as a crack and a boom made them all duck. A streak of lightning struck the dragon's back and arced over its wings with a crackle.

"Now!" Lillie called, hands high as she held onto the spell.

Vola was already lunging upright. She launched herself into the air and brought her blade down on the dragon's head. Right between the eyes.

The dragon yelped and thrashed away, Vola's blow leaving a slice as long as Gruff's tail in its forehead.

The dragon scampered away and wound itself in a complicated knot at the other end of the pit, protecting its head and throat.

"Not sure how official this all is, but I believe that round went to us," Vola said, standing and cleaning her sword before returning it to its sheath.

Talon stood, shuddering, their hands shaking so bad light flashed along the edges of their knives.

"You all right?" Vola asked.

"Yeah." They shook their head. "Yeah. It's just…it reminded me for a second. Of my pack. Of my home."

Vola's gut clenched. That's right. Talon had lost their pack to a dragon.

"Was it one like this?" Vola asked them quietly.

Talon glanced at her, and their hood had fallen back enough Vola could see their startled blue eyes. "No. No, it was one of the big ones. And it won't be hurting anyone again."

Vola shook her head and stepped back. Then she caught a flash of light hair. "Lillie, what the heck are you doing?" The wizard wasn't the one she'd thought she had to worry about.

Lillie approached the dragon, hands outstretched in a calming gesture. "The poor thing. They're keeping him here just to entertain them with this bloodbath. We have to help free him."

"Get off me, lady," came a gravelly voice, and the dragon lifted its head to glare at the wizard until she skipped back a step. "I get paid for every bout whether I win or lose. And I'm a she. Not that you even bothered asking."

"Oh, oh I'm dreadfully sorry," Lillie stammered.

The dragon blew out a puff of air that smelled of sulfur and exasperation. "Assumptions aren't polite for any species."

"Er, just out of curiosity," Sorrel said, leaning on her staff. "How much do you get paid?"

The dragon snorted. "Enough to pay for my drinks. But don't you think about poaching on my territory. This is my pit."

Sorrel held up her hands. "Right, if we want to go into business as bounty fighters, we'll find our own pit."

"Good." The dragon surged to its—her—feet as the crowd around the pit settled bets and money changed hands. "I have to get this slice taken care of before some other big shot adventurer thinks it'd be fun to impress Fang."

The dragon lumbered to the edge of the pit and swarmed up the side. She perched on the repurposed cobblestones for a moment. "Thanks for a good fight. It was fun. You deserve a bone. So, for future reference, lightning stings, but it's more effective if I'm in the air. It's why dragons don't fly in thunderstorms."

I'll just log that away for the next time we fight a dragon, Vola thought, but Lillie was already jotting a note in her book.

Talon and Sorrel climbed out of the pit, and Vola stooped to give Lillie a leg up. This time the wizard swung a knee over the wall and fell down the other side.

Talon leaned down to give Vola a hand so she could walk up the side of the pit and hop over the wall.

The bouncer stood at the bottom of the scaffold with his mouth open.

Vola raised her eyebrows. "Eye-catching enough?" she said.

The orc shook his head to clear it and stepped aside, gesturing up the steps. As the party passed, he cleared his throat. "You, uh, you free later?" he asked Vola.

Vola blinked as Sorrel muffled a snort in her elbow.

"Maybe for dinner," she said after a moment's hesitation.

"Did you really just pick up a date in a pit fight?" Lillie whispered as they headed up the scaffold.

"How else are we going to eat tonight?" Vola said, lips twisted in a self-deprecating smile. "What's so funny?"

Sorrel chortled out loud. "Orc flirting is bashing something over the head so well it doesn't get back up again."

Vola growled.

"Half-orc flirting." Sorrel held her hands up in capitulation. "Three-quarter orc flirting? If you're half and he's whole, then together…" She started ticking numbers off on her fingers.

"Don't hurt yourself," Vola said, then focused ahead of them where they would presumably find Fang.

Cages full of exotic creatures lined the scaffolding. Birds with flaming feathers, a white fox who sizzled against the bars, varying lizards, and dragons even smaller than the one they'd just fought. Vola could only assume these didn't talk back since they didn't seem to mind their cages too much.

In the center of the platform, a figure in a gray tunic and trousers stood with his hands on his hips. He stood just a little taller than Lillie and had a grizzled beard, though his back wasn't bent at all with his age.

The stranger faced a tall slender elf dressed head to toe in sleek black leather. Vola counted at least twenty knife hilts and she was sure she was only seeing the ones the elf wanted her to see. Long, black hair cascaded down her back, and Vola tossed her own ratty braid over her shoulder with a huff. Trust an elf to get away with loose hair in a fight.

"Fang?" Sorrel mouthed to the rest of them.

"This is ridiculous," the man said. "You'd rather stay here playing King of the Hill than help your family."

"You're too young to be my family," a querulous voice said.

Vola shifted her weight and craned her neck to see around both the stranger and the deadly looking elf. An ancient halfling leaned on a gnarled staff. Stark white hair fell around her shoulders in thick dreadlocks, and her skin was so thin that Vola could see nearly every vein in her face and neck.

The stranger in front of them threw out their hands. "You must feel some loyalty to us. We raised you."

The halfling chuckled, lips pulling back from her one yellow tooth. "I left before you were even a lusty thought in your father's head," she lisped through her bare gums. "Do not tell me what I feel and what I don't feel."

"But Fang—"

"Enough."

Vola blinked and almost missed what happened next. The old halfling flickered and moved, faster than Vola's eyes could track, and suddenly she was behind the stranger. She lashed out, her hand extended flat in front of her. Her palm had barely made contact when the stranger went flying and hit the rough planks of the scaffolding with a yelp.

The old halfling dusted off her hands—the gnarled staff lay forgotten at the tall elf's feet—and then shooed the man away as if he was no more than a large bug.

"If you want to leave with all your bones intact, I suggest you do it now. I don't give second chances."

The stranger picked himself off the floor. He hesitated a moment while the old halfling stared, unfazed. Then he slunk back toward the scaffolding stairs. As he passed Vola and her party, he nearly ran into Sorrel.

He did a double-take, glancing down at her gray tunic, almost a direct match for his. He frowned and hurried away.

"Friend of yours?" Vola asked Sorrel.

"No," she said, eyes narrowed. "I don't think so. But then I don't know every single monk sworn to Maxim, so…"

Vola turned back to the leather-clad elf and the ancient halfling who made her tremulous way back to her abandoned staff.

"Fang?" she said.

"Yup," the halfling said.

"We had a question we hoped you could help us with."

"Can you teach me that?" Lillie said, limping forward.

"Although that wasn't it," Vola said under her breath, following Lillie.

"Teach you what, my dear?"

"The way you just teleported. Is it a spell? Could I learn it with practice? Could you teach me?"

Vola rubbed her temples.

Fang chuckled as she bent to retrieve her staff, then used it to push herself back up again. "Ask your friend there." She gestured to Sorrel, who looked taken aback. "She'll be able to teach you."

Sorrel glanced between Fang and Lillie. "Uh, what?"

"Your tunic. You come from one of Maxim's monasteries, right?" Fang spit. The elf beside her grimaced and stepped out of the way. "That's where I learned it in the first place."

Sorrel's mouth fell open.

"You monks never used to leave your monasteries. Now you're crawling out of the woodwork everywhere." The old halfling settled herself once more. "Now, what did you want? You bashed poor Hurren good enough to catch my attention. I'll at least hear you out."

"We're looking for a man named Myron Vidal," Sorrel said. "We can't find him using the normal means. We thought he might be into something more up your alley." Her expression brightened. "Get it? Up your —"

Vola pushed Sorrel behind her.

Fang's eyes thinned and her lip curled in the barest trace of a smile. "Well, isn't that interesting," she murmured.

"Why?" Vola said.

"You're the second person today to ask about him."

Vola cocked a thumb over her shoulder. "Was that what you were arguing about?"

Fang waved an airy hand. "Information isn't free."

Vola sighed. "Of course it isn't. We don't have anything of value to trade you."

"Well, then I don't have anything to tell you."

"Please, it's for a good cause," Lillie said with a glance at Sorrel. "He has something that…doesn't belong to him."

"So does everyone within half a mile of you, right now. Seems like you'd better come up with something of value if you want to find him," Fang said, examining her fingernails.

Vola threw up her hands. "We literally walked into this city with nothing but ourselves and a…" She froze, hands in the air, gaze fixed on the cages around them as a niggling idea made its way through her mind. A roar went up from the spectators around the pit but it barely registered for Vola.

Fang stared at her, waiting for the rest. Her party waited as well.

Vola let her hands drop slowly and cleared her throat. "You, uh, you seem to have a thriving exotics trade going on here. Are you a collector or a dealer?"

Fang's mouth worked like she was chewing something except she had no teeth. "Dealer," she finally said. "There's always a buyer somewhere."

Vola's stance relaxed as she stood with her weight over one

foot, hip cocked. "We maybe have one thing you'd be interested in. A very rare swamp equine."

Sorrel squeaked behind Vola's legs.

"Very hardy. Lots of great features like shiny scales, wonderful personality, and it can forage in just about any terrain."

Lillie's eyebrows went up, then her mouth dropped open in an o. She drew herself up and clasped her hands over her heart. "You can't sell Millford," she said in a voice wrought with drama. "He's the only one of his kind! He's priceless."

Vola bit down on her tongue hard. She put a hand on Lillie's shoulder as if to comfort her. "Do you want to find Myron or not?" She turned back to Fang, palm out. "We would be willing to trade the creature for say the price of Myron Vidal's location."

Fang worked her mouth some more, eyes narrowed before she finally gave a sharp nod. "Okay. But I have my own spell casters. If there are any illusions on this creature, the deal's off and I come after your hide myself. With a pair of blunt scissors."

Vola winced. "Fair enough."

Fang snapped her fingers at the elven bodyguard.

"The mon—er—creature is tied up outside the bookshop," Vola told her before she sauntered off the scaffolding.

"There's a Myron Vidal who's making my life a little harder," Fang said. "Seems like that might be a theme with him if that's your man as well. He's been trying to smuggle dead bodies out of a warehouse on the east docks."

Lillie sucked in a breath, and Vola perked up. "Dead bodies?"

Fang held up her free hand while the other clutched the staff. "I don't deal in dead bodies. It angers too many of the gods to be profitable. So, I've told all my smugglers to stay out of it. But Myron's still going. He must have a partner I don't control."

Sorrel elbowed Vola in the knee. "See, see? I told you if we just worked the Myron angle, the Rilla investigation would fall into place."

"Somehow, I doubt you saw that connection coming," Talon said.

"And you know where he is?" Vola asked Fang.

"I do." Fang waved her fingers as if casting a spell. "And if Myron Vidal disappeared during your investigation, I wouldn't cry."

EIGHT

ACCORDING TO FANG, Myron Vidal rented the upstairs room over a primer school run by a cadre of priests from the Lesser Virtues.

"We use the rent to keep the school running," the head priest said, leading them up the back steps which creaked as they climbed. "Charitable donations only go so far."

"And how is Myron as a tenant?" Vola asked.

The priest sniffed and eyed her sidelong. He'd made it clear he'd prefer to do anything else besides talk to an orc, but Vola's party wasn't giving him much of an option. He glanced at the others, but Sorrel and Lillie just gazed back at him with equally polite expressions and Talon was silent under their hood.

"He doesn't give us any trouble," the priest said. "We'd like to keep it that way."

"We'll keep the bloodbath to a minimum," Vola said with a snort.

The priest's lips thinned. "See that you do," he said, completely missing the sarcasm.

He left them at a door painted a cheerful pink and hurried down the stairs again.

"I just love that people like that are in charge of teaching children," Lillie said, voice flat as she stared at the white bunnies cavorting along the walls.

Vola knocked on the door, a little harder than necessary, and the cheap wood cracked.

Someone hauled it open far enough to peek out. Half of a pasty face and a pair of spectacles peered through the gap. Then he noticed the crack.

"Hey," he said, voice high and breathy. "You broke my door."

"Er, sorry," Vola said. "Are you Myron Vidal?"

"Yes, who are you?"

"I'm Vola. And this is Sorrel, Lillie, and Talon. We're here to ask you some questions. Would you mind if we came in?"

The half face brightened. "Questions? What kind of questions? Physics? Biology? Magic?" He seemed most excited by the last prospect.

Vola glanced at Sorrel and the others and considered their options. "Magic," she said. And it probably wasn't even a lie.

"Come in. Come in." Myron disappeared from the opening and the door swung wide.

Vola pushed through into a sunny room crowded with several tables covered with an assortment of glassware and brass equipment that steamed in the light.

Myron stood in the middle of the room, hands on hips, frowning as if he'd forgotten something.

Vola had always envied elves for their ability to look effortlessly beautiful, no matter what. Take Lillie for example. Or Fang's bodyguard.

But Myron had snagged the elven traits of tall and slender with pointed ears and apparently nothing else.

He'd obviously cut his wheat blond hair himself, without a

mirror, and he blinked watery gray eyes behind his thick spectacles and a monocle. His shoulders hunched as if he leaned over a desk even while he stood in the middle of the room.

Vola glanced into the corners, but there weren't any warhammers or dead bodies just lying about. Nor was there any evidence of Rilla.

Not that she'd expected it to be that easy.

"Hi," Sorrel said before Vola could really take the lead. But that was probably better. The halfling presented a much less intimidating front than the armored orc. At least to those who didn't know them.

"Um, what's with the glasses and the monocle?" she said. "Don't people usually use one or the other?"

"If one is good, both are better, right?"

"Okay, good point."

The elf tipped his head. "You mentioned magic."

"Yes. You purchased a warhammer from a woman named Astrid," Sorrel said, pulling the receipt from her pocket. "Do you still have it?"

"Warhammer?" Myron said, brow furrowing. "What would I do with a warhammer?"

Sorrel hesitated. "Uh, usually hit people with it."

"You don't remember buying it?" Vola said. "There was a swamp with a big hill coming out of it. Astrid lived at the top."

Recognition lit in his eyes. "You mean my staff. Yes, I bought my staff in a swamp."

"Yeah, the Warhammer would look like a staff without its head," Sorrel said. "Do you still have it?"

"I use it for my work," Myron said. "Why?"

"Would you be willing to part with it?" Lillie asked.

Myron's mouth screwed up in a tight pout. "I just said I'm using it for my work."

"It's very important," Vola said. "Maybe we could buy it from you."

"With what?" Talon muttered.

Vola glared at them.

Myron's eyes darted between them. "I need it. What I'm doing is important, too. You…you're trying to steal my research, aren't you? Everyone's always trying to steal my research."

Lillie made a gesture down by her leg, telling them to back off. She limped toward Myron. "No. No, of course not. I can see the value of what you have here, but I promise we're not interested in taking it. How did you contain a motile, semi-self-aware liquid without causing an adverse reaction?" She pointed to one of the bits of glass bubbling away near the window.

"You understand basic fluid dynamagic?" Myron said, his face opening up again.

Sorrel made an impatient noise in the back of her throat but Vola gripped her shoulder. "Give her a second," she whispered.

Lillie shrugged humbly. "I took a beginner course at the university as part of my curriculum. But does anyone really understand fluid dynamagic, or do we just observe the complexity of the universe and make notes?"

Myron beamed. "That's what I've always said." His eyes narrowed. "Are you sure you're not here to steal my work?"

Lillie shook her head. "I'm quite happy where I am, thank you. I enjoy thinking about magical problems, but I prefer practical applications as opposed to theoretical ones."

"But that's exactly what I'm doing," Myron said, waving his arms around. "A practical solution to the conundrum of terminality processes." He dropped his arms and glanced at Lillie out of the corner of his eye. "Would you…would you like to see some of my work?"

She placed her fingertips on his arm. "I would love to."

He drew her along his tables describing each bit of paraphernalia in detail while Lillie nodded and looked fascinated and the rest of them tried to shift their weight without interrupting whatever this was. Vola was pretty sure on anyone else she'd call it flirting. But on Lillie, it was mostly by accident. She wouldn't have the first clue how to flirt her way out of a bar full of interested men.

Myron finally ended beside a large chest in the corner where a winding set of tubes crawled in and out of the wood sides.

With a flourish, he threw back the lid and presented the contents to Lillie the way a paramour would present a bouquet.

"Oh," Lillie said, her hand going to her mouth, her eyes round and unblinking. "Oh, my."

"I think I'm nearly there," he said. "Just a few finishing touches, now."

"Yes. It's a lovely corpse, Myron. Thank you for sharing it with me."

Vola's hand flew to her sword hilt, but Lillie gave her a little head shake as she firmed her lips and removed her hand from her mouth.

"I definitely see the value of what you're doing." Lillie bit her lip. "Did a woman named Rilla come by to ask about your research, as well?"

Good job, Vola thought.

"She didn't want to talk about my research. She just wanted to yell at me about ethics. Why can't people understand that the end result makes the method worth it?"

"Some people can be so close-minded."

"She wanted to take my bodies away. She would have ruined my research."

Vola's feet twitched, but she forced herself still. What had Rilla gotten herself into? And what had Myron done to her?

"What did you tell her?" Lillie asked gently as Vola held her breath.

"Nothing. People like that never listen to reason. I just got rid of her."

Vola gripped her sword hilt, preparing to draw.

The door burst open and three gray-clad figures rushed into the room, crowding Vola and Sorrel back. Talon unsheathed their knives in a smooth movement.

"What the—" Vola started, but Myron cried out and pointed at Lillie.

"You *are* here to steal my research, aren't you? Just like Rilla!"

"No! Wait—"

Myron raised his hand toward the ceiling and pulled down. A long staff decorated with intricate carvings of knots followed his fingers out of thin air. Light flickered over its surface as if reacting to the room, and Vola noticed Sorrel straighten up with a gasp.

"Holy Maxim," the halfling said.

One of the intruders hissed through her teeth. "Get it!"

"No!" Sorrel cried.

The first stranger sprang for Myron and Sorrel leaped to intercept them. They fell in a tangle of limbs, Sorrel deliberately putting her foot in the figure's back as she tackled them.

"Out of my way!" the stranger cried.

"I saw it first!"

Vola lunged for Myron. "Don't let him get away."

Myron was the last person to see Rilla alive. They couldn't afford to lose this lead.

One of the strangers turned and threw himself at Vola's feet, tripping her so she ran headfirst into the wall. She bit her tongue on a curse. What the hell was happening? For once, everything had been going well.

Lillie raised her hands to form a spell and the third and last stranger leaped on her. Vola's heart leaped to her throat, but she was still tangled with her own enemy.

No one had thought to tackle Talon. The ranger spun and pried the stranger off Lillie before throwing them into the opposite wall.

Sorrel puffed as she climbed to her feet and flung herself at Myron.

Behind her, the first stranger pushed up on her elbows and spat. "Geez, Sorrel. You're screwing everything up. Again."

Sorrel froze, face going slack in shock. Vola sucked in a breath.

Myron took the moment of surprise to raise the staff and swing it against the wall. A swirling vortex of black and purple energy whirled into existence, peeling the plaster back.

Wind rushed past Vola, pulling at the edges of her shirt and making it flap. She twisted and planted her elbow in her assailant's gut and lunged for Myron.

Her fingers brushed the hem of his robe as he stepped through the portal.

Talon threw a knife in his direction and Lillie spat out a counterspell, but it sizzled against the bare floorboards as the portal shrank and disappeared. Leaving Talon's blade vibrating in the blank wall.

NINE

"He got away," Vola growled and spun to glare at the gray-clad newcomers. "What the hell is wrong with you?"

A little lightning bolt streaked from the ceiling and struck the floorboards at Vola's feet, completely ignoring the fact that they were inside and protected from any of the usual weather.

The stranger who'd tangled with Sorrel climbed to her feet and brushed off her knees. She was human with brown hair cut so short it barely brushed her ears and frown lines marring her otherwise smooth forehead. She wore a wraparound tunic identical to Sorrel's.

"Tallah," Sorrel said, voice flat.

"So this is where you ran off to." The woman surveyed the room with narrow eyes and then swept her gaze up and down Sorrel, paying special attention to the stains and rips in the halfling's tunic.

Sorrel's lips thinned, and her fingers curled into fists.

"I'm sorry, but who are you?" Vola said, crossing her arms over her chest. Normally when this protective urge rose inside her, there was something to hit or swing her sword at. She'd always hated having to defend against words.

"I'm the abbess of Maxim's monastery up on Half-moon Peak."

Sorrel's monastery. Although Vola could have guessed that from the halfling's reaction.

The other two monks straightened up. One was the old man they'd seen arguing with Fang. He scratched his nose self-consciously. The other, a younger female dwarf with thick red-brown hair tied back in a tail, glanced at Sorrel.

Sorrel glanced back. Her shoulders relaxed a smidge but the skin around her eyes went tight and pinched.

"Sorrel, as your abbess—"

"I don't recognize you as my anything," Sorrel said.

Tallah drew herself up, but the dwarf stepped in, sliding between them as if she'd had lots of practice. "Sorrel, you know what Father Naemon said. We're honoring his last wishes, and Tallah is our leader now."

Sorrel stared at the dwarf. She didn't say anything but slowly shook her head.

"You need to stand aside, Sorrel," the dwarf said. "This is more important than your petty grudge."

Sorrel's shoulders jerked as she blew out the breath she'd been holding and then sucked in another. "Petty grudge," Sorrel said, voice more quiet and deadly than anything Vola had heard from her before.

Without thinking too hard about it, Vola sidestepped until she stood beside Sorrel. Talon didn't bother masking their movement as they stalked to the wall where Myron had disappeared and yanked their blade from the plaster. Lillie wasn't even paying attention. The wizard scribbled frantically in her spell book while Sorrel glared daggers at her fellow monks.

Tallah sneered over the dwarf's head. "Don't bother, Hazel.

Her incompetence screwed up our mission. We could have had him and been back at the monastery before lunch—"

"Excuse me?" Vola made sure to pull back her lip so her tusks looked bigger. "You barged into our investigation and scared off our lead suspect. A woman's life is at stake and you bungled the whole job."

"We're not here about some woman. We came for—"

"Maxim's Warhammer," Sorrel said. "I'd recognize it anywhere."

"Well at least you remember your lessons," Tallah said, rolling her eyes. "All those ancient texts told us how important this is, too."

"I didn't recognize it because of a text," Sorrel said and then snapped her mouth shut on whatever else she had to say.

The dwarf's gaze caught on her, but Tallah sneered.

"You were the one talking to Fang," Vola said, glancing at the older monk. "She told you where to find Myron."

"She was a monk once. She owed us that information at least. Even if she's another one who has forgotten her vows of loyalty." Tallah sniffed at Sorrel. "Just stay out of our way from now on."

"Stay out of your way?" Vola said. "You interrupted us! We would have had Myron and the staff if you hadn't scared him off. Why can't you just trust Sorrel? She's been tracking the Warhammer down since you sent her after it."

Beside Vola, Sorrel flinched. "Um," she said.

"Trust Sorrel?" Tallah said and laughed out loud.

Vola's brow furrowed. Oh, shoot. Sorrel hadn't ever said she was sent, had she? Vola had just assumed that part. She'd just assumed Sorrel was in good standing with her order, unlike Vola.

"We didn't send Sorrel anywhere," the dwarf, Hazel, said quickly. "She just disappeared one day after Tallah took over. We all assumed...well, we assumed she'd run away."

"There's a difference between running away and leaving in protest," Sorrel said with a growl that was almost worthy of Vola.

Tallah waved a hand. "That's just word choice."

"Word choice is very important," Lillie said. She bent over to squint at one of Myron's bubbling glass baubles. "It's the difference between calling someone a sissy and a sycophant."

Sorrel snorted. "Tallah wouldn't know the difference."

Lillie clicked her tongue in disapproval, and Tallah's face went red.

"Enough." The abbess's hand slashed through the air. "You'll stay out of our way while we retrieve the staff or we'll treat you as the enemy and take you down faster than you fled the monastery."

Sorrel's face went white with rage. "You didn't bring enough monks to make that threat."

Tallah's lip lifted in a sneer, and she swung around to stride from Myron's rented room, taking the silent old man with her.

The dwarf wrung her hands and looked between Sorrel and the door where her abbess had disappeared. "You could come back, you know," she told Sorrel breathlessly. "You could come back and everything could be just the way it was. You wouldn't even have to apologize. I would make sure she didn't ask you to"

"I wouldn't have to apologize because I didn't do anything wrong," Sorrel said. "Maxim knows *my* conscience is clear."

Sorrel's steady gaze made the dwarf flush.

"Hazel!" Tallah's voice snapped from the hallway.

The dwarf jumped and left the room, casting one last look over her shoulder at Sorrel.

It was late by the time they returned to their inn, now bearing the name "The Cozy Cottage" scrawled over the first couple of attempts. The lanterns sent flickering light over the adventurers crowded around the common room tables.

An orc leaning against the bar caught sight of them as soon as they entered and gave Vola a twitchy grin. He slouched toward them, his hands bunched in his leather pants.

"You ready for dinner?"

Talon snorted behind them as Vola recognized the bouncer from Fang's alley.

"Uh," Vola said. Oh gods, she'd forgotten about her date.

Sorrel pushed past her hip with a grumble and stalked through the crowded common room.

"Could you give us a sec?" Vola told the other orc. "I think I have to handle something first."

His smile turned sappy. "No worries. I was an adventurer before Fang hired me. I know how things can crop up. I'll wait."

With a wink, he made his way back to the bar, where he sat beside the barbarian in the kilt.

"Well, that was nice of him," Lillie said.

Vola rubbed the back of her neck. "Come on."

They caught up to Sorrel, who approached a booth crowded with rogues. Their knives lay close to hand as they tossed dice across the stained table.

Sorrel stepped up and tapped the end of the wood with her finger. "I need this table," she said, low and flat.

Vola gulped and hurried to back up the halfling who glared across at the rogues, each one at least twice as big as she was. But the rogue on the end took one look at Sorrel's expression and swallowed his laugh.

"Sure thing," he said and hurried his fellows out of the booth.

"Handy," Talon said as Sorrel slid into the vacated space.

The rest of them plopped down onto the split leather and scooted in.

Sorrel traced the jagged circle of a mug stain on the wood but didn't seem to be in the mood to chat.

Vola wanted to ask "what the hell happened back there?" but she couldn't help remembering the way the other monks had talked down to the halfling. The way fierce Sorrel had gone sullen and defensive in response.

"Do you want to talk about it?" Vola asked instead.

Sorrel opened her mouth. Then closed it. "No." The halfling's jaw twitched as if she ground her teeth.

Vola had never seen Sorrel actually angry before. She always ran into battle with a grin, and she was the one who made them smile in the face of treacherous employers and carnivorous swamp blossoms.

"Then we don't have to talk," Lillie said.

Vola snorted. "Lillie wasn't even listening."

Lillie gave her a hurt look. "I knew you were handling the altercation. You would be a poor paladin if you couldn't keep us safe from three monks who didn't even want to hurt us. Just like I would be a poor wizard if I couldn't take notes and listen at the same time."

The wizard hesitated, eyes darting to each of their faces. "I think we can all agree that there are things in our pasts that we would prefer remain in the past."

Vola started to protest and found she didn't have anything to say. She would have said she trusted her party implicitly, but there were plenty of things she didn't want to talk about with them. Things that had happened at the academy and before that she'd rather not dig up. She shut her mouth with a click.

The others nodded warily.

"Good." Lillie clapped her hands.

A platter thunked down on the table full of mashed potatoes and half a roast chicken. A pea rolled away from the mountain of veggies beside them.

Vola gaped up at the bartender. "What—"

"The orc at the bar. Said good plans need good food otherwise brains don't work."

Vola leaned around him to stare back toward the bar. The orc wiggled his fingers at her.

She hid a smile. "Tell him thanks."

"I do like smart men," Lillie said, beaming at the bartender.

He clunked a mug down in front of her. "That one's for you."

"What? Not again."

The bartender shrugged. "As long as he keeps buying them, I'll keep delivering them."

Lillie blinked as the bartender returned to his post through the throng.

"Who is he talking about?"

"The skinny one at the bar," Vola said, tearing off a leg of chicken. "Three seats down from the bouncer wearing the red and gold tunic. I figure he's the one that's been sending you the drinks."

Lillie glanced at the mug, face going slack with a sort of wordless horror. "I-I didn't know. That's where they're coming from?"

"It's how men let a woman know they're interested."

Lillie looked up, mouth agape.

"Don't look at me," Talon said. "Wolves just sniff each other's butts. It's more polite."

Lillie glanced at Sorrel, who gave her a curt nod.

"What do I do about it?" Lillie whispered.

Vola frowned. "You don't know?"

"No, I don't know! Why would you assume that I know?"

Because she looked the way she did. But Vola was trying to be better about the assumptions she made.

"You have two options. You can flirt with him. Or you can tell him no."

The blood drained from Lillie's face. "Both of those would require talking to him."

"Well, yeah." Vola refrained from rolling her eyes, trying to remember she wasn't that confident about the date waiting for her at the bar. "You were pretty good at flirting with Myron."

Lillie sputtered. "That wasn't flirting. That was holding an intelligent conversation with an interesting person."

"That can be flirting, too," Vola said. "Bonus points if it gets you information."

"Negative points if the guy turns out to have kidnapped a woman," Sorrel finally said, breaking her silence.

"Hmm." Lillie slid her new drink in front of Sorrel. "I guess I'm probably sitting at zero then. Myron definitely made Rilla disappear."

Sorrel pushed the mug away.

The rest of the party stared at her.

"What exactly was he studying?" Talon finally asked.

"Reanimation of the dead," Lillie whispered. "Necromancy. About the worst possibility I thought of when we learned dead bodies were missing."

"So, he's making them walk around?" Talon said. "So what?"

"Besides the fact that it's very, very illegal and deeply upsetting to the families of those dead bodies?" Lillie glared at Talon.

"You lop their heads off, they die again, don't they?"

Lillie opened her mouth and Vola interrupted.

"I'm sure you figured that out right away," she said. "What else were you writing? He showed you all sorts of things."

Lillie bit her lip. "Yes, he was looking at many different reanimation techniques, not just magic. But I think there's more than that. There were pieces of some other plan there, but I could only see the edges from what he showed me. And I'm convinced that wasn't his actual laboratory. There were too many fragments of his studies. It was just a smaller space with room for auxiliary experiments."

"So, we're still chasing him," Vola said, sitting back in the booth. It felt good to have a clear goal. Even if it was the same one as before. "We'll need to find his real laboratory. Maybe we'll find other people he's murdered."

"I don't think he's truly a murderer." Lillie shifted in her seat. "He steals all his bodies."

Vola raised an eyebrow at her. "You don't think he's capable of killing someone who gets too close to his research? Like Rilla."

Lillie looked down at her hands.

"She might not be dead," Talon said. "Who knows what he can do with that staff."

They all carefully didn't look at Sorrel.

Sorrel sighed. "Probably anything. It's definitely Maxim's."

"Do you know anything about it?" Lillie said, reaching for her spell book.

"Beyond who it belongs to? No." She rubbed her forehead. "I wasn't sent. I don't have all the books and scrolls on it. I came on my own."

"Because of what happened at the monastery?" Vola said.

"Yes. But it doesn't matter what happened," Sorrel said. "We can't leave that staff in his hands. With it, he wields the power of a god. We have to get it back."

"Of course we do," Vola said, calmly folding her hands in front of her.

Sorrel, halfway into a breath for another argument, deflated.

"And we must do it before those self-righteous monks get to it," Lillie added, raising her chin. "If only for the principle of the thing."

Talon examined the tip of their knife. "He's the lead suspect in Rilla's disappearance and that is a job we got fair and square."

Sorrel looked between them, eyes wide.

"We trust you," Vola told her quietly. "We believe you. If it's a choice between trusting you and trusting a group of strange monks who don't know how to knock, of course we're going to trust you."

Finally, Sorrel laughed.

"Now," Vola said and pushed herself from the booth.

"Where are you going?" Lillie asked.

"I have a date. And we still have a necromancer to find. So, I'm going to see if he knows anything about graverobbing."

"Sounds like a fun evening," Sorrel said as Vola walked toward the bar.

TEN

"Your date gave you a list of graveyards?" Sorrel said, walking backward so she could wiggle her eyebrows at Vola.

Vola sighed. "And burial sites and tombs. There's a necropolis somewhere outside the city, too, in case Myron gets really ambitious."

"Uh huh," Sorrel said, and without looking, she dodged a farmer bringing his cow to market. "What happened after that…"

"After that, nothing," Vola said with a glare. "We talked. Mostly about work. We shared a piece of chocolate cake and traded the best ways to sharpen a blade."

"Sounds like he could have been more lively." Sorrel nudged Talon, who walked beside her. "Get it? Cause they talked about dead guys."

Talon didn't respond.

"But did you enjoy yourself?" Lillie asked, eyebrows scrunched. "Isn't that what people do on dates? I don't think they're supposed to talk about work so much."

"Honestly, it was kind of nice to talk to another orc who recognizes that it doesn't always have to be 'smash your enemies' and 'mount their heads on our spikes.' I get enough of that from complete strangers. This was very pleasant and civil."

"Pleasant and civil is not going to get you any action from your boyfriend," Sorrel said.

"You're one to talk," Vola said with a snort. "Aren't you celibate?"

"Doesn't mean I can't make fun of everyone else's love life. That's the best part."

"I didn't know Maxim required celibacy," Lillie said. "Is that a specific of your order?"

"I follow Maxim, not the order," Sorrel said with a frown. "Not anymore. And I'm celibate because I choose to be celibate. Mostly, I just don't want to mess with all that love and sex stuff. I'm just not interested. But for some reason, when you try to explain that, people get all weird and try to convince you other-wise. 'Oh, you just haven't met the right person' or 'you'll get there one day.' Right, and how's that tenth husband working out for you, Martha?" Sorrel shook her head. "It's easier to just say I'm celibate and then everyone assumes it's a vow or a geas and I don't have a choice in the matter. People accept it much more readily if they think it's not my choice."

"Huh," Lillie said, smooth forehead creased in thought.

Vola passed a wrought-iron fence and stopped before the gate. Sorrel leaped to the top of the fence where she balanced with one hand, covering her eyes.

The morning light speared through the clouds illuminating the graveyard nearest the inn. There wasn't any sort of signage or official gravekeeper's shack. There was just this empty green space between two ramshackle houses, crowded with headstones nestled in the grass. More sunlight made it to the ground here where the buildings stepped back, illuminating the morning dew and making individual blades of grass shine.

It would have been picturesque except for the black gouges in the earth where someone had dug up the graves.

"So, what's creepier than a graveyard?" Sorrel said, tilting her head.

"A graveyard with no bodies," Lillie responded with a shudder.

"I don't know," Talon said. "I think it's kind of peaceful."

"All right, so Myron's been here," Vola said. "Let's see if he left us anything to work with."

Talon sent Gruff along the edges to sniff out any traces of Myron while the rest of them minced their way between dug up graves.

Vola stopped beside a hole. The dark soil mounded beside them smelled wet and loamy. Not altogether unpleasant as long as you ignored the half-rotten casket in the bottom of the hole.

"Lovely," Sorrel said, stopping beside her. "It makes this spot so much more pleasant. Hey Vola, maybe you should bring your boyfriend here next time."

Vola reached out and pushed Sorrel.

She fell in the hole with a whumph as Vola turned to survey the rest of the graveyard.

"I'm fine," Sorrel called up. "Ew. Worms."

Talon prowled the ground between the graves, hooded head down as if studying the dirt while Gruff ranged outside the fence. Three graves down from Vola, Lillie pursed her lips and then knelt very carefully in the loose soil. She pulled out her notebook and started scribbling, pausing now and then to read the tombstones.

"Anything?" Vola called.

Talon's hood came up, but they shook it back and forth.

"Lillie?"

Lillie held up a finger but didn't look up. "Maybe. But I'm not sure yet."

Sorrel clambered out of the hole at Vola's feet and hopped up to sit on the smooth crest of a tombstone.

"I'm not really sure what I'm looking for," Vola confessed to the halfling who swung her legs back and forth.

Sorrel shrugged. "Neither am I, but then we're not really the ones on point for this."

Vola gave her a look. "What do you mean?"

Sorrel pointed at Vola's chest. "You're our tactics and healer." She pointed to Talon then Lillie. "There's our tracker. And our brains. Tracker and brains are what we need for this. Don't worry, we'll be on point again soon."

Vola gave Sorrel a lopsided grin. "And what are you, then?"

Sorrel gave Vola a look like that was a silly question. "I'm the muscle. Duh."

"Right," Vola said as Sorrel hopped off the tombstone.

With the sun bright in the sky, the graveyard wasn't an unpleasant place to wait, but Vola's palms itched for something to do.

As she turned to stalk around the perimeter with Gruff, a flash of color along the fence line caught her eye.

Ivy grew between the wrought-iron posts of the fence, twining with the cross pieces. Vola pulled back the dark, shiny leaves to find clusters of flowers all along the fence.

Red and yellow blooms dominated the area, but now and then there was a blue blossom with the petals fading to white toward the center.

Vola reached in her belt pouch with a twinge of guilt and pulled out the flower Cleavah's devotee had given her. After two days in the dark recesses it should have been crushed and limp. But it sat on her palm as pristine as the hour it had been handed to her.

Broken Grace.

Vola rubbed the back of her neck and cast a glance at the sky. "Okay, okay, I get it. Hey, Sorrel." She raised her voice to the halfling. "Wanna help me pick some flowers?"

In the end, they found several handfuls of the blooms Cleavah's devotee had requested. Not enough to fulfill the job, but enough to ease Vola's guilt. By the time they'd reached the gate again, Talon had joined Gruff and Lillie was standing, dusting off her pants.

"Well?" Sorrel asked.

Talon shook their head. "Gruff couldn't find his trail. He was here, but he didn't come in or out through the gate or by any of the neighboring streets."

Vola chewed her lip. "If he used that staff, he could have just teleported in here."

"That doesn't help."

"I might have found something that will," Lillie said, glancing down at her book. "But I'll need more evidence."

"More evidence like more robbed graveyards?" Sorrel said.

"What are you looking for?" Vola said.

"Patterns," Lillie responded. "But it's not a pattern yet with this small of a sample size. I need more to be sure. Lots more."

They went down the list Vola's date had given her. Every race in the city had their own burial customs, their own spaces, and traditions. The gnomes, who made up the city's largest non-human population, preferred to inter their dead in mounds like they did out in the countryside. The gnome graveyards they found had mounds split open at the top, like a cake that had been baked too long.

Dwarves always built elaborate tombs for their dead. The doors of which had been smashed open and the slabs inside emptied.

And elves burned their dead in intricate ceremonies on tall

piers outside the walls, and the orcs sent their loved ones to the afterlife in boats floating out into the ocean. So, they couldn't check if any of those bodies had been stolen.

By noon they'd searched through seven human, gnome, and dwarven grave sites, and ended in a large graveyard that catered to those too poor to be picky. Here all the races mingled, gnome mounds standing beside dwarf tombs and human headstones.

Along the edge, just like in every site they'd visited that morning, Broken Grace grew among the ivy. Vola and Sorrel had picked enough by now to fulfill Cleavah's need. And Vola had made a mental note to look up what association Broken Grace had with burial sites.

Lillie stood among the disturbed graves, her hands on her hips, lip between her teeth.

"Do you have enough evidence now?" Vola asked.

"More than enough," Lillie snapped, but not like she was angry. More like she'd found a puzzle and was annoyed when she couldn't immediately solve it.

"He's stealing spell casters."

"I thought he was stealing bodies," Sorrel said, leaning against an open tomb.

"Dead spell casters." Lillie opened her book and ran her finger down a list of names. "It's not about race. He's stolen someone from every single one as far as I can tell. It's about ability. Every grave that's been desecrated belonged to someone who had at least some trace of magic. Wizards, sorcerers, even bards and rangers who have their own spells." Lillie gestured at Talon who nodded back.

"But…what's that mean?" Vola said.

Lillie threw her hands in the air. "The hell if I know."

Vola blinked and fought the urge to hold out her hands in defense. If the wizard was cursing, you knew things were bad.

"Normally, necromancers just raise whoever is nearby and convenient." Lillie paced back and forth between the graves, her limp more pronounced with her agitation. "Zombies, skeletons, ghouls. It doesn't actually matter because death strips us of the abilities we had in life. The only ability they have is given by the necromancer when they are raised."

She stopped and rubbed her forehead, leaving a streak of grave dirt in the sweat across her forehead.

Vola held out her hands. "Okay, okay. Take a step back, for a second. Why do necromancers do what they do?"

"Some start with good intentions. They want to raise their dead loved ones to have a little more time with them, though it hardly ever works that way. Some just don't care. They're fighters and it's a lot more exciting to fight with an undead army at your side."

"What about Myron?" Vola stopped the wizard with a hand on her shoulder. When Lillie blinked up at her in confusion, Vola pulled a large, clean handkerchief from her pocket and handed it to her, gesturing at her forehead as she did so. The wizard rubbed at her skin, grimaced at the dirt smeared on the clean linen, then scrubbed some more.

"Myron is in it for the challenge," Lillie said, handing back the handkerchief. "He was looking into different ways to reanimate the dead. Besides magic, he'd been looking at chemistry and steam and electricity. But whatever his greater purpose is—whatever it is that I could only see the edges of—has something to do with spell casters."

"And did it leave you any clues to find him with?" Sorrel gestured around at the disturbed grave sites.

Lillie shook her head. "We're looking in the wrong place."

"What?" Sorrel cried. "All this waiting and this isn't where we'll find him?"

"We're not finding Myron because we've been searching the places where he's already been. We need to find a graveyard he hasn't harvested yet. We wait there. We wait there long enough and we might catch him at it."

Sorrel winced. "I wish you hadn't said 'harvested.'"

ELEVEN

LILLIE SPENT hours that afternoon sifting through city records to find the local graveyards with the most concentrated populations of buried spell casters, which she then cross-referenced with the list of sites they'd already searched and they knew Myron had been to.

In the end, they ended up in one of the graveyards where several races buried their dead. Vola hunkered down beside a gnomish mound, using it's bulk to hide the gleam of her chainmail. There were torches lit at the gate but nothing deeper in. Most people didn't come to visit their deceased loved ones in the middle of the night.

Unfortunately, the rest of them couldn't disappear as well as Talon and Gruff. Vola trusted they were there somewhere, but the ranger might as well have been invisible.

Sorrel's small stature gave her an advantage, but she kept twitching and standing up to peer toward the graveyard entrance.

Vola dug in the dirt with the toe of her boot. It hadn't rained in the last couple days but somehow all these graveyards still seemed damp.

Lillie pulled out a ragged towel she'd brought from the inn.

"What's that for?" Vola whispered.

"I need to concentrate on casting so we have some warning when Myron comes, and I don't want to sit in grave dirt." She carefully laid out her towel and sat in the middle, keeping her limbs tucked away from the damp earth. Then she closed her eyes and began tracing lines in the air while her lips moved with an incantation.

Vola raised her head and peered around the darkened graveyard, searching for anything new. Nothing yet, and the night was quiet. Just some late-night revelers coming down the street, their boots clunking against the cobbles.

Vola's eyes narrowed. She slouched a bit to stay hidden, but kept her gaze trained on the entrance.

The men on the street spoke aloud to each other as if they didn't have any reason to hide what they were doing this late at night, but they carried shovels and wheelbarrows that clattered. They stopped beside the gate to the graveyard. More than late-night revelers it seemed.

"Lillie?" Vola said. "Is that almost ready?"

The wizard finished whispering and drew her hands apart, then let them drop to her sides. "Done."

When she looked up, her eyes reflected the moonlight almost like a cat's, but the sheen that caught the light was blue instead of green or yellow. The spell would allow her to detect any magic used in the area and hopefully identify its source.

"Good, because I think something's happening."

Sorrel had knelt to peer around the mound. She didn't care about the grave dirt on the knees of her loose breeches.

"Myron's not with them," she said, squinting into the dark.

"No, but…here they come."

The group of men, dressed in nondescript jackets with patches over the worn spots, grabbed the torches from the gateway and started into the graveyard.

"There. Divine magic." Lillie swung around on her towel and pointed toward the back corner of the graveyard where a cluster of dwarfish tombs reflected the moonlight.

"The staff?" Sorrel scrambled around to face the way Lillie had indicated.

Vola squinted. Her orc half was trying to give her human half a better time seeing in the dark, but the moonlight was throwing her off. She could walk through a pitch-black room better than she could navigate a moonlit graveyard.

The air shimmered ahead of them. Like the reflection on the surface of a pond, the tombs wavered and Myron stepped into the graveyard.

The men didn't even bother to greet him except for a couple of nods. They just parked their wheelbarrows and dropped their shovels beside them. A couple of them with crowbars stepped up to the dwarven tombs and started to work the cover stone loose.

"All right, move out," Vola said under her breath. "And remember the plan. Don't scare him off."

The three of them flowed out from around the gnomish mound, trusting Talon to be following along from the shadows with Gruff.

They didn't try to mask their approach, but they did hurry across the damp ground, Vola down the center with Sorrel and Lillie spreading out to either side of her.

"Myron," Vola said softly as they approached.

The necromancer's head jerked up from where he'd been watching the graverobbers work, his mouth a dark o under the sheen of his spectacles.

"You!"

Vola held up her hands as Myron brought up his staff. "We don't want to fight you. We just want to talk. Where's Rilla?"

The grave robbers had frozen, staring back and forth between the party as it approached and Myron, who probably held the purse strings.

Myron shook his head making his lank blond hair sway across his forehead. "You just want to steal my research. Like Rilla did."

Sorrel sighed on Vola's left. "We're really, really not interested in taking your corpses. Like negatively interested."

Myron stepped back once, and a growl rumbled through the air near his feet.

Gruff leaped a headstone and crouched, neck and shoulder muscles bunched as if to pounce. Talon, visible now as if they'd dropped a cloak of shadows, nonchalantly swung their bow up with an arrow cocked.

"Myron, we're the type of people who make dead bodies," Lillie said quietly. "We don't need to raise them."

It was a great line, which was immediately ruined when Lillie tripped over a crooked headstone and landed on her face with an "oof."

One of the men moved very slowly, crouching to pick up his shovel.

Vola fixed him with a glare. "Don't do something stupid."

The man gave her a sickly grin and spread his hands. "You've caught us robbing graves. Do you know what the punishment is for that?"

"As long as everyone stays calm, no one has to get arrested for anything tonight," Vola said.

Lillie pushed herself to her feet, her eyes reflecting the light with that blue-green shine as she scanned the graveyard. She sucked in a breath.

"Vola, magic to the right."

Vola drew her sword and settled her shield on her arm. "What kind?"

Lillie opened her mouth, but a gray-clad monk came flying

over the top of a mound, feet aimed for the wizard. Vola stepped into his trajectory, catching his blow on her shield. She flung him aside as battle cries rose around them.

"Loyalty and strength!"

"For the monastery!"

"For Maxim!"

Sorrel hesitated a moment, mouth hanging open. "Hey, that's my line!" Then she leaped to intercept one of the monks.

Half a dozen of them had come over the headstones and mounds to converge on the dwarven tombs.

The grave robbers leaped for their shovels and crowbars and had no trouble defending themselves from the monks who seemed determined to screw up Vola's operation.

"Get the staff!" one of them yelled, and Vola recognized Tallah's short hair and pinched expression.

"Oh, no you don't," Sorrel growled.

Three of the monks broke off from the fray to converge on Myron. But Sorrel dashed in front of them, swinging her own quarterstaff around. They ducked back a step.

"Stand down, Sorrel," the monk in front said. It was the dwarf Tallah had called Hazel. "You're making a big mistake. Again."

"The only mistake here is how long it took me to see that you betrayed me."

Hazel jerked back another step, face stricken.

One of the grave robbers fell with a cry under Tallah's fists. The other monks were engaged, trying to get through the robbers to Myron, who dithered between the two groups as if wondering who to attack first.

"Lillie, do you have anything non-lethal?" Vola called. She wasn't in the business of slaughtering monks but this was ridiculous.

Lillie's mouth set in a firm line. She gave Vola a nod and started pulling together a spell.

Vola's gaze darted between Sorrel's monks and the grave robbers. She didn't want to kill any of them. Or at least she didn't have a contract to kill any of them. She wouldn't have minded knocking a few stupid heads together hard enough to bleed, but that was strictly personal.

A cry made her spin.

Myron shook his foot, trying to dislodge Gruff's teeth from his ankle while Talon had an arm around his throat and a grip on his staff. The ranger tried to yank the staff away from Myron, but Myron choked out a spell. A little zing of lightning zapped Talon's arm, and they tore away with a curse. Gruff yelped and let go.

Vola had a clear target now. She launched herself at Myron and the staff, which had started doing its glowing thing again.

"They're going for the staff!" Tallah yelled behind her. "Engage."

Before Vola reached the two of them, Myron began an incantation and reached for the ground.

The earth under Vola's boots rolled, and she stumbled mid-charge. The headstone in front of her fell and cracked, making her spin to avoid getting her toes crushed.

I need some better boots if I'm afraid of getting squished by headstones, Vola thought.

Lillie finished her spell and shot it at Tallah. The abbess tripped, fell to one knee, and her head lolled. Like she thought a nap in the middle of battle was a great idea.

The abbess's eyes fluttered closed, and she tipped forward.

One of the other monks grabbed her before she fell headlong over a headstone and shook her awake. Tallah rubbed her eyes, then glared at Lillie.

Lillie glared back. "Drat."

Vola could think of a few better words. If Tallah had gone down, Vola had a sneaking suspicion most of the fight would have gone out of the monks.

The ground shook, making the soles of Vola's feet tingle, and she grimaced at the dirt. What the…?

"Oh, bloody hell." They were fighting a necromancer. In a graveyard.

Vola had just enough time to dance back as a hand dark with dirt and rot shot out of the ground where she'd been standing. A bolt of lightning struck, just missing the rotting fingers.

"Geez."

All around them, the dead scratched their way to the surface like swimmers in a pool of mud, pushing through the damp earth until their mouths yawned in the night air.

"Oh, nasty." Sorrel darted out of the way as dead hands crawled toward her feet. She leaped up onto a headstone and balanced there as her fellow monks looked around in horror.

"He's desecrating the dead," Hazel said, hand creeping up to cover her mouth.

"Yeah, that's what he does. Do your homework next time."

Vola danced out of the way and swung her sword in an arc as the dead rose and turned their attentions on the living. She cast around, taking stock of her companions. Sorrel hopped from tombstone to tombstone, staying out of reach of the grasping hands. Lillie sprayed fire in a circle around her, keeping the zombies at bay.

Talon was surrounded. The zombies were too close for their bow so Talon had drawn their knives. Gruff growled from the perimeter, lunging and tearing down zombies as he came to them, but he wouldn't reach Talon quickly or without injury.

Myron stood in the clear for the first time since they'd approached. The staff in his hands glowed, and his narrowed gaze darted around the fight as if assessing his options.

With a growl, Vola headed for Talon. As much as she hated it, Myron could wait.

She charged, shield lowered and sword ready to swing. With a heave, she bowled her way through the dead, tossing them aside with her shield and slicing through half-rotted tissue.

Talon cried out and went down under a pile of bodies. Gruff howled.

Vola saw red.

It closed in on her from the sides, seeping into her vision until everything was painted in blood. She knew from experience that it would take over. The lust and the rage would overwhelm the world until everyone and everything was dead, or she was.

Kill, kill, kill, the voice prodded in the back of her head.

She fought it with a growl, pushing at it until the red receded enough for her to work. She used the rage without letting it swamp her. With nothing more than will, she changed it to say, *protect, protect, protect.*

She needed a free hand. Sword or shield? Henri's first lesson had been to never drop your weapon. But the thought of letting go of the shield he'd given her made her stomach drop.

She chose the sword and sent it spinning away to pin a zombie to a tree like an ugly butterfly.

With her free hand, she grabbed zombies, tearing through them and flinging them aside until she found the black-clad figure underneath.

Talon's hood had fallen, leaving their pale face bare. Glassy blue eyes stared up at Vola.

A zombie grabbed her belt pouch and yanked, probably hoping to throw her off-balance, but the cheap stitching parted and the flowers they'd collected that morning spilled out onto the ground around Talon.

The zombies hissed and stumbled back as if the petals stung. Vola caught the movement, and she used their hesitance to clear the area.

Then she planted her shield between Talon and the hoard of the undead.

As if she'd been waiting for just that, Lillie's voice rang out through the graveyard. "Everyone down." Calm and authoritative, like a general ordering a firing squad to shoot.

Vola knew that tone and the spell that went with it. She trusted Sorrel recognized it as well, and she ducked her head, covering Talon's vulnerable form even as Gruff dove behind the shield.

A wash of intense heat blew over them, making Vola's ears pop and hair curl. Talon winced and curled into Vola's side.

Lillie created pockets of safety around them, but it always felt like standing a little too close to a furnace in full heat.

The flames whooshed out as quickly as they'd come, leaving behind nothing more than the wash of cool night air, the smell of burning flesh and hair, and little fires fed by now de-animated dead bodies.

Vola peeked out from behind her shield.

The graveyard finally lay still. Flames flickered from the ragged clothes and flesh of the corpses lying in the dirt instead of shambling around in a parody of life. Sorrel sat on a headstone, legs swinging, lips pressed thin and tight so that the skin around her mouth turned white.

Monks picked themselves up off the ground, batting at the little flames that licked their clothes.

"You threw a fireball at us," Tallah said, pointing an accusing finger at Lillie.

Lillie examined her fingernails, standing in a perfect circle of burned earth. "I did tell you to get down. I cannot be held responsible for your incompetence. Nor can I shield everyone who blunders into our investigation. I had to make a choice, and I chose those I could trust."

Tallah seethed while Vola glanced around, trying to find Myron.

"Gone," Sorrel said, voice clipped. "Portalled out the moment he saw his zombies could only hold us off for a moment or two."

"Great," Tallah said, hands on hips. "How will we find him now?"

"That would have been easy if you'd left any of the grave robbers alive," Vola said. "Beginner's mistake." She stood and swung her hand to indicate the grave robbers lying among the smoking dead. They weren't on fire, telling Vola they'd gone down before Lillie's fireball scoured the area. "We could have questioned one of them." Vola shook her head. "Useless."

She could have gotten to Myron herself, too. But she'd made a choice just like Lillie, and she couldn't find it in herself to regret it.

She knelt beside Talon again, taking stock of their injuries.

Hazel hurried forward. "Is he all right?" She hesitated. "Or, um, she?"

"They," Vola said shortly, pretending not to notice Talon's furious flush. The ranger snatched their hood and pulled it up to hide their face once more.

Vola tried to be quick, running her hands lightly over Talon's limbs, finding the bite marks and deep scratches left by undead teeth and nails.

"Don't worry," Sorrel said, kneeling on Talon's other side. "That doesn't look bad. Unless…do you think they'll turn into a zombie?" Sorrel whispered to Vola.

"It doesn't work that way," Lillie said, coming to stand over Vola's shoulder.

"It doesn't?" Sorrel said.

"Only in bad novels."

"Could everyone just shut up a minute," Vola said with a sigh.

"I have bandages," Hazel said, craning to see.

Vola glared up at the dwarf. "You've done enough. Now step back."

The monk flushed and retreated while Vola found the last of the damage.

It had been a full day and a half since the incident at the hospital. All the energy Vola had spent there had returned, filling the well until Vola felt like a dam ready to burst.

She placed one hand on Talon's arm and another on their shin. "Lady bless."

Light poured out between her hands. She spared none of it. They'd go home and rest after this and even though Lillie said it didn't work that way, Vola wanted to be sure to burn out all the filth and rot dirty teeth and nails might have left in Talon's blood.

The power seared through the ranger, making them hiss, but they didn't pull away. Every bite and scratch transferred to Vola's skin, but she gritted her teeth and pushed through the pain until Talon sat there whole.

As the last of the wounds closed, Talon pulled away and Vola let them. They'd be fine now, but Vola knew personally that pride always hurt worse than any other blow. It might take a few minutes for Talon to forget that feeling of lying vulnerable in the dirt.

Vola turned to scoop up the flowers that had fallen scattered on the ground. The ones that hadn't burned that is. She stroked the soft edges of the petals. The dead had reacted to the flower almost as violently as they'd reacted to the fire.

"Hazel, come away," Tallah called. "This is a dead end."

Sorrel blew out her breath in a huff and clambered to her feet as if to lunge after them, but Lillie put a calming hand on her arm.

"Let them go," she said.

Vola couldn't imagine that quiet tone would work, but something in Lillie's face made Sorrel back down from the fight, and they watched as the monks retreated from the graveyard. Tallah cast one scathing look back at them before they disappeared down the street.

Talon picked themselves up off the dirt and dusted off their pants as Gruff wound around their legs, whining.

The flowers wouldn't stay in her torn pouch, so Vola searched for a new place to stash them. Finally she shoved them down the front of her shirt under her chainmail. Cleavah's devotee would just have to handle getting them smelling of sweat and metal.

Lillie was walking amongst the dead, biting her lip as she tiptoed between the corpses.

"Lillie?" Sorrel said.

Vola recognized that look as well. "What are you thinking?"

Lillie stopped over one of the grave robbers—the one that looked the least beat up—and tapped her lip. "I'm thinking this isn't a complete dead end." She turned to give Vola a look. "Do you think you could carry this for me?"

Vola glanced between the body and Lillie, eyebrows drawn tight until it finally dawned on her.

"Oh my goddess," she groaned, covering her eyes.

TWELVE

THE DEAD GUY'S head thunked up each step to their room in the inn, despite the care Vola took to keep him from dragging.

"Shh," Sorrel whispered. "Don't wake anyone up."

"Probably too late for that," Talon muttered.

"There must be some people in this part of town who aren't familiar with the sounds of a dead guy getting dragged up the stairs," Vola huffed. "So long as no one pokes their head out their door, we should be fine." Theoretically. Vola herself had decided she'd need a much stronger tea after this.

Sorrel darted ahead of them on the creaky stairs to open their door while Talon stooped to pick up the guy's head.

Vola ducked into their tiny rented room and winced when there was a meaty clunk behind her.

"He's okay," Talon said and kicked the door shut behind them.

"He's dead," Sorrel said. "He's a little far past okay."

"That's my point," Talon said.

Vola didn't bother with niceties. She dumped the corpse in the middle of their floor. He wasn't leaking any fluids yet, but she wasn't going to take any chances on not getting their deposit back.

There weren't a whole lot of other options, anyway. The room they'd rented had one bed that wasn't exactly big enough for two but they'd made work anyway, and there was a rickety chair in the corner. They'd been taking turns sleeping in the bed while the other two slept on the floor. Vola still wasn't sure that it was worth the money they'd spent on it. They could have just camped outside the city if they hadn't had to trek in every morning.

"All right, what exactly are we going to do with him?" Vola asked.

Lillie had rushed to her pack on the floor at the foot of the bed, and she rummaged through it. "You wanted to question him, right?"

Vola narrowed her eyes. "Yes. But I recall you saying something about this being very, very illegal."

"Don't worry, I'm not going to reanimate him." Lillie pulled out three books Vola didn't know she'd had. "We're just going to talk to him."

"So, this isn't necromancy?"

"It falls in that gray area right before you actually get to illegal. There are plenty of law-abiding citizens who contact their dead loved ones through seances."

"The only difference here is that we stole him," Sorrel said. "Great. Now we're body thieves, too."

Vola rubbed her forehead and wondered how thin the walls were. It was the middle of the night but in a place like this, it was just as likely their neighbors were still awake as well.

"Let me guess," she said. "You have a spell for this."

"Yes, of course," Lillie said, lifting a book in each hand and squinting at their covers. "My father believed in being prepared for anything."

The wizard flinched, and Vola carefully looked at the wall and pretended she hadn't heard anything. Lillie very rarely mentioned anything that had happened to her before they'd met. And she'd never slipped up far enough to mention a family.

"I just have to find it," Lillie continued with only the slightest hitch. "And make the preparations. Spells for speaking to the dead aren't usually simple. But it shouldn't take long." She cracked open one of the books there on her lap as she knelt on the floor.

Vola's eyes slid to the dead guy taking up much of their floor space and then flicked away.

Talon sat in the corner by the door, knees pulled to their chest.

"You all right?" Vola asked them. They didn't seem to be bouncing back from the fight in the graveyard as quickly as Vola had been expecting.

"Fine," Talon grated out. But the hood was ducked as if to avoid Vola's gaze.

After the healing, there couldn't be anything wrong physically, Vola thought. But there were plenty of other things that could be wrong inside Talon's head. They didn't seem to mind the dead guy on the floor, so that wasn't it.

Sorrel paced between the corpse and the window in the wall opposite the door. Her movements were frenetic and jerky, like a puppet with an inexpert handler.

Vola glanced between the two of them. Talon noticed and waved her toward Sorrel. "Go," they grated. "You can do something about her."

Vola sighed and stepped over the dead body to plop down on the bed. She watched Sorrel pace, making her regard clear.

On the fifth pass beside the bed, Sorrel glanced at Vola, noticed her gaze, and flushed. Finally, the halfling hopped up onto the cheap straw mattress. Then she scooted until her back pressed against the wall.

"The monks want that staff pretty bad," Vola said.

Sorrel stiffened. "For all the same reasons we do," Sorrel said, chin in the air.

Vola examined her profile. "Maybe not all the same reasons," she said. Sorrel clearly had something to prove by getting to the staff first. "Hazel doesn't seem so bad."

Sorrel snorted, but it didn't sound like mirth. It sounded like resignation. Or just a weary acceptance. "You know, we were friends because we were both short. But it's the ones that aren't that bad that end up being the worst. They convince themselves that what they're doing is for the best and then end up turning a blind eye on everything that might be wrong with it."

Vola's lips twisted. Sorrel's hurt stank of betrayed friendship. From the way they interacted, Vola would put all their meager savings on it being related to Tallah. Hazel had chosen Tallah over Sorrel somehow.

Lillie cleared her throat quietly. "This is ready."

Talon stood from their place in the corner and stalked to the dead guy. They huffed and bent to haul the man upright before setting him in the chair by the window.

Lillie examined him.

"Was that really necessary?" Sorrel asked.

Talon glanced between them and the corpse and then shrugged. "It seemed more polite than leaving him on the floor."

Vola nodded, conceding the point.

Sorrel and Vola slipped off the bed to stand. That seemed more polite, too.

"How's this work?" Vola asked Lillie. "Should we tie him down?"

Lillie shook her head. "I'm not doing anything except letting him talk. He won't be able to move. I don't think he'll even be aware of his body. Although that part is just an assumption since I've never actually been dead before." Lillie tapped her lips as if in thought. "I'll have to concentrate on this, though."

"All right, you cast," Vola said. "I'll ask questions."

With whatever preparations Lillie had made, the actual spell only took a few minutes. A glow emanated from the grave robber's head where it lolled against the back of the chair.

Vola glanced from the steady light to the door, chewing her lip.

Talon followed her look and went to stuff a towel in the crack under the door. At least now, no one would come to investigate any strange lights.

Then the man's lips began to move and air seeped out in a hiss.

Sorrel's mouth screwed up. "Oh, ew, ew, ew."

Lillie closed her eyes to concentrate.

"Do you want to know where Myron and the staff are or not?" Vola whispered to Sorrel.

Sorrel shut up, but the disgust on her face didn't abate.

"Is it working?" Vola asked Lillie.

"Ask your questions," Lille said, sweat popping out on her brow.

Right, quickly then. For Lillie's sake and not just to get it over with. "Um, can you hear me?" Vola said.

A pause, then a voice that could have been a man's but with an echo-y quality behind it said, "I hear."

"Hello," Sorrel said, voice forced in the quiet room, then she gulped.

"Are you the grave robber we—I mean are you the grave robber who was—" Bleh, how did you ask someone if they knew how they'd died? "Were you a grave robber in life?"

The man's mouth moved. "Yes."

"Were you hired by Myron Vidal?"

"Yes."

"What were you doing in the graveyard?"

"Digging."

Vola rolled her eyes. Ghosts weren't that talkative, apparently. "Digging for what?"

"Bodies."

"Okay," Vola said. "Do you know where Myron is now?"

"No."

Vola blew out her breath. "Do you know who might know how to find him?"

"His mother."

"Do you know his mother?" Sorrel said, perking up.

"No."

She sagged again. "Oh."

"He's pretty literal," Vola said.

"What's your name?" Talon said unexpectedly.

A pause. "Bruno."

Vola rubbed the back of her neck. "Bruno, who hired you to dig up bodies?"

"Mister Vidal."

"Where did he find you?" Vola said.

Another pause. "He said he was looking for gravediggers."

"Aren't gravediggers supposed to put bodies in the ground, not take them back out again?"

"We do both. Who else would know the best place to dig them up but the men who put them there?"

"Well that makes a weird sort of sense," Sorrel said.

"Bruno, do you know where Mister Vidal takes the bodies?" Vola asked.

"No. That was my boss's job."

"And where's your boss?"

"Dead. The monks killed him before they got me."

Vola rubbed her eyes. Wonderful. She glanced at Sorrel.

"Bruno, do you know anything about the staff Mister Vidal uses?"

"No."

Before Vola could think of another question, Bruno's head snapped up.

"Whoa." Vola skipped back a pace, her hand going to her sword hilt.

"Creepy, creepy, creepy," Sorrel whispered.

"Who are you?" Bruno's voice had changed. It wasn't as deep, and it had lost some of the echo. "What are you doing with this man?"

"Uhh," Vola glanced between Lillie and Bruno's corpse.

Bruno turned his head to survey the room, and his whole body sat forward with a slump as if it was trying to remember what muscles were.

"I thought it wasn't supposed to do that?" Sorrel hissed at Lillie.

"It's not," Lillie hissed back. The blood had drained from her face, leaving her pale with the sweat standing out on her brow. "I'm not doing this."

"Oh, no," Vola said.

Then Bruno stood up, spine unfolding in a series of twitches.

Someone gulped. Vola was pretty sure it was Talon.

"You!" Bruno said, then pointed to Lillie with a finger that wavered back and forth.

"It's Myron," Talon said.

"You think?" Vola said and jumped back as the dead puppet took a swing at her.

Bruno windmilled his arms, lunging in for the attack and the four of them tried to scatter. Which was difficult in a room no bigger than an outhouse.

"Ouch!"

"Oof."

"This room is not big enough for this fight. Just jump on him."

"I told you we should have tied him down."

"You did not! That was my idea."

Vola couldn't draw her sword in the space, it was too tight. She had a three in four chance of hitting one of her friends instead of the enemy. But her shield was still strapped to her back, so she swung it down onto her arm and bashed Bruno across the face with it.

The walking corpse didn't even pause. He didn't seem to feel pain or even notice that his head hung at a funny angle, his nose pointed at the ceiling now.

"Lillie, how do you kill zombies?" she called.

"Fire," Lillie said. "But I can't in here. I'll just burn down the inn."

Sorrel leaped to the bed and used it as a springboard to plant both feet in Bruno's chest.

The zombie stumbled back into Talon, who spun him around and stabbed their knife through his arm. Anchoring him to the wall. Whatever funk they'd been in before didn't keep them from fighting back now.

"Great," Vola said. "Now we can just figure out how to break Myron's connection…" Vola trailed off as Bruno looked down at his pinned arm and then casually ripped himself free at the shoulder, leaving his stump leaking all over the floor.

"Well, we're not getting our deposit back," Sorrel said.

Then Bruno reached back, pulled the knife from the wall, and then swung his severed arm around like a club.

"Great!" Vola said while ducking. "We gave him a weapon."

Bruno lurched for Lillie.

The wizard squeaked and threw out her arms. A thunderclap sounded and a wall of air shoved Bruno back. He staggered into the opposite wall.

And crashed straight through the crumbling plaster.

A family of gnomes on the other side, popped up, eyes wide over the edge of their blankets.

"Sorry," Lillie called. "I'm so sorry."

Talon followed Bruno and spun him to crash through the gnomes' door into the hallway.

Vola groaned. So much for being quiet.

Gnomish curses filled the air as she and Sorrel and Lillie clambered through their own door to see Talon racing down the steps. Bruno followed, tripped on the first step, and tumbled down the rest.

"Sleep tight," Lillie called over her shoulder to the gnome family.

They staggered to a halt at the bottom of the steps to see Talon facing off against Bruno as he lurched to his feet in the common room.

Ah, now Vola had room to work. She drew her sword and charged.

The bartender stuck his head out his door. He surveyed the fight with a sigh.

Lillie whispered a cantrip, and the arm Bruno held caught fire. The zombie dropped it with a wordless cry.

Sorrel used a table as a springboard and leaped onto the zombie's back. He staggered in a circle, moaning as Sorrel pummeled the top of his head.

"Bring him down," Talon shouted. "Take his head off."

Vola got close enough and stuck out her leg. Bruno went down with a wet smack, and Sorrel rolled free. Vola brought her blade down on the zombie's neck, severing its head.

Finally, the body lay still.

After a moment's hesitation, Sorrel climbed up a barstool and raised her finger at the bartender still gawking in the doorway.

"A lager, please."

THIRTEEN

"I FEEL like it was kind of mean of him to kick us out." Sorrel sat on the top of the fence that separated a small overgrown city park from the ill-lit street. "I mean we did save him and all the other people in the inn from Bruno."

"I don't think he appreciated the blood on the common room floor," Lillie said. She didn't do anything so uncouth as slouch, but she had dark circles under her blue-green eyes.

None of them had slept. Talon had given up trying to fight it and had curled up in the corner of the park with Gruff. Vola leaned against the fence and kept having to right herself when she dozed off between blinks.

"Necromancy and destruction of property," Vola said. "That's what he cited as his reasons to evict us."

"It wasn't our necromancy." Sorrel swung her feet so her sandals clunked against the fence slats. "It was Myron's."

"It was our destruction of property, though," Lillie said with a wince. "It's hard to argue with holes in the wall."

Sorrel pursed her lips, but she didn't seem to have anything to say to that. Vola squinted up at the sun which had finally climbed high enough to see over the houses.

Her companions were exhausted. And their sideways necromancy hadn't given them a new lead. They were going to have to track down more dubious gravediggers themselves. But they wouldn't be able to without rest. And there wasn't an inn in the city that would take them without payment.

Vola glanced down at her belt pouch and sighed. She'd stuffed the ruined leather into one of her extra shirts and tied it off to her belt. Time to swallow her pride for the sake of her party.

"What?" Sorrel said.

"Stay here." Vola pushed off from the fence. "Watch each other's backs. I'm going to find us a place to stay." Or rent money. Whichever came first.

She plodded through the city, head down, letting that inner sense of Cleavah lead her where she had to go so she didn't have to think too hard about it. The goddess had to know how bad things were for them, but it was completely humiliating to have to admit it out loud. And Cleavah wasn't exactly the kind of goddess who was overflowing with wealth and opportunities. She protected the weak and the helpless, but Vola was neither. She was supposed to be the one doing the goddess's work, not the one who needed her help.

New graffiti marred the door declaring "Cleeva's a limp biskit" and one of the boarded-up windows had been smashed through. Vola checked the street then hurried across to push the door open.

She'd expected the place to be empty. Cleavah wasn't exactly popular, and it wasn't a holy day.

But she stepped across the threshold to find a crowd camped in the front room. Families huddled together around candles, mothers carrying babies, fathers holding hysterical children. There were blankets spread across the cold flagstones where children played or napped. One ancient woman sat in the corner, rocking back and forth, knitting needles clicking in her hands.

Vola blinked at the noise. They weren't disruptive. There was a clear path to the altar which was heaped with pitiful offerings. There were just a whole lot of bodies crowded into a space meant to hold a couple at a time.

Vola spotted the devotee wading through the families, her hands full with a basket and several jars. Worry lines creased her forehead and her limp was more pronounced, but her gold skin still glowed with health and her curling hair was tied back as neatly as it had been the first time.

Vola made her way over and took the basket without asking. "Mistress," she said. "What's going on?"

"Vola. Oh, good you've returned. I trust you've come with the Broken Grace? It's become a little desperate in here."

"I can see that. What is all this?"

"Dead have been rising all over the city. I knew it was coming, but I didn't expect it to be quite so bad this soon."

"The dead…" Vola said, then her lips thinned. Myron. He must have been stepping up his operations now he knew they were coming after him.

"Wait," Vola said. "How did you know this was going to happen?"

The devotee gave her a look before stooping to hand a man one of the jars. "How do you think?"

Vola's teeth clenched. Cleavah must have told her.

The devotee spoke to the man who examined his jar of blue liquid. "Paint your windowsills and the threshold of your doors with this. Don't leave any inch uncovered. The dead can't pass it. It will keep you and your family safe after nightfall."

"Thank you, mistress," the man said, bending over her hand so that his greasy hair fell in his eyes.

Someone at Vola's feet stood up. A woman, the size of a carthorse. She loomed over the devotee.

"I need one," she said.

The devotee nodded. "I know. I'm trying to get to everyone in the order they've come in."

The woman glanced at the basket. "You won't have enough. Give me mine, now."

The devotee's eyebrows arched. "Please sit down, or you will start a riot," she said quietly.

Vola's hand slid toward her sword hilt.

The woman causing the disruption sneered. "I'm not waiting here till you forget about me. I need one of those, and I'm taking it."

She pressed forward, meaty fists bunched at her waist.

Before Vola could decide to draw on a civilian, the devotee had stepped forward to meet the brute. A flash of light gleamed along a metal edge, and suddenly, the devotee had a long, curved fish knife pressed against the woman's thick neck.

"The lady of sharp implements bids you sit and bids you be quiet. I will get to everyone, but anyone causing a scene or trying to go out of turn will find out how sharp my lady's implements are. Understand?"

The carthorse opened her mouth as if to protest, but the devotee's hand twitched and a trickle of blood welled and spilled down to drip on her collarbone.

"And anyone seeking asylum from Cleavah would do well to remember that the lady does not forget."

"Yes, mistress," the woman whispered, eyes wide.

The devotee stepped back and flicked the knife so droplets of blood splattered the flagstones under their feet. "Now. Why don't you have a nice little rest while you wait?"

The woman's eyes fluttered, and she slumped to the ground, taking a nap right there.

The devotee bent and arranged the woman's limbs so the lit candle wouldn't catch her clothing, and then she straightened. She glanced at Vola's hand on her hilt and raised her eyebrows.

"Thank you, but I don't think that will be necessary. You have the flowers, yes?" She pressed a hand to her temple before looking at Vola intently.

Vola cleared her throat and let her hand drop to her side. "Yes."

She pulled the knotted shirt from her belt as the devotee passed into the back room. Vola followed and unfolded the shirt to reveal the ruined belt pouch and the tumble of flowers inside. She could see clearly in her mind the way the zombies had fled from the fallen blossoms. "They repel the undead, don't they?"

"Yes." The devotee took the flowers from Vola and dropped them into a large bowl on a table in the back. There wasn't much in the room except the worktable and a cot in the corner. "They work naturally by themselves, which is why they're planted around graveyards and necropoli. But it's even better if you can make them into a salve or paint."

"And spread it on your windows and doors to keep them out," Vola finished for her.

Vola stepped back to the door while the devotee worked, and she looked out at the families camped on the flagstones. Many had left after they'd gotten their paint but there were still too many waiting. Here, in a dingy little temple off a forgotten side street. They hadn't flocked to the greater temples on the hill. They weren't crowding around the Greater Virtues begging for help.

Probably because they knew they wouldn't get any.

The Greater Virtues were flashier, sure. But they were also silent. Uncaring. You didn't see Maxim stepping down off his pedestal to serve the masses. Or Ona or anyone else. They weren't helping anyone. Maxim sat back in his temples while his monks ran around the city getting in Vola's way.

"I'd like to help," Vola said, gripping the door frame. "Do you need more flowers? Or help making the paint?" She didn't serve one of those silent gods. And for the first time, that thought didn't make her gut squirm unpleasantly.

"The best thing would be to get rid of the cause," the devotee said, intent on her work smashing petals.

"Myron," Vola said. "We're working on that. We just…we needed a moment to catch our breath." It seemed silly to admit now with the weight of their investigation growing.

But the devotee was nodding. "Yes. Your instincts are correct," she said. "Your job as a paladin is to protect them. That comes first. So that together you can protect others. You don't have to second guess that."

Vola shuffled her feet.

The devotee pointed to a little stool beside the door. "Your payment."

Vola took the pouch that had been resting on it. "Thank you."

"There is one more thing," the devotee said, meeting her eyes. "The one you're supposed to protect next. Rilla. You must find her quickly."

Vola's head jerked up. "She's alive?"

The devotee dipped her chin. "She is."

"Where?"

She shook her head. "That's the part Cleavah doesn't know."

Vola rolled her lip between her tusks. "Why didn't she tell me? She used to…" *She used to talk to me.*

The devotee tilted her head with a little smile. "Did you ask?"

Vola's cheeks warmed with a flush.

"Sometimes she'll give you the answer," the devotee said. "Sometimes she won't. And sometimes the answer will be to wait. But if you don't ask, the answer will always be no."

FOURTEEN

Vola left the temple over an hour later. The devotee was nearly hip-deep in blue paint now, and hopefully, she'd have enough to distribute to everyone who'd sought shelter and out to the rest of the neighborhood as well. Vola made a mental note to find more flowers.

And to learn what the devotee's name was. Odd that she hadn't thought to ask.

A couple of city guards dressed in shining breastplates and crimson cloaks loitered across the street. They straightened when she appeared and her muscles went tight and alert. She kept her hand from her sword—nothing good came from drawing on the city guard—but her eyes tracked their movement across the street as they made for her.

They didn't move like the lumbering city guards that were common in cities everywhere, all swinging arms and planted feet. Good for holding steady in a charging mob but with no finesse.

These moved light on their feet. Their weapons were higher grade than a guard's pay would cover and they looked well-used.

"You Lightbringer?" one of them asked as they came closer.

He had the face of a young god and the voice of a sailor roughened by wind and salt.

"I am," Vola said. "Volagra Lightbringer. Knight paladin of the Whiteshield Academy." It was a mouthful, but it was a subtle threat in case they doubted an orc with a shield.

The other guard spat. He rubbed his red nose. "Your employer wants a word with you."

Vola frowned. "My employer? I'm pretty sure I'd remember if anyone was actually paying me."

"Fine, *our* employer wants a word." He pulled out a long cloth. "You'll need to go blindfolded. He's particular about who knows where he lives."

Vola shifted her feet, giving herself a wider, more balanced stance. "We're going to have problems if you try to put that on me."

"Problems we can handle," the first one said.

He came at her.

She ducked and put her shoulder into his gut. It didn't have quite the impact she'd hoped for since he was wearing plate and she just had chain mail. But she followed it up by lifting and sending him over her back to tumble to the street.

The red-nosed guard moved to punch her in the gut, but when she jerked, he used her reaction to plant his other fist in her face. A clever feint that caught her off guard for a moment. She growled and kicked his knee, unwilling to draw steel just yet. She didn't think these two were actually city guards but if they were, she'd be in even bigger trouble if she drew blood.

Red-nose staggered back as the other guard swept her feet out from under her. Vola twisted as she fell and reached to yank his booted feet out from under him. He landed next to her. The breath left his lungs with an oof and she turned to pin him to the street. His grin sharpened only inches from her face and he did something with his knee that levered her considerable weight off his chest and tossed her back so her mail scraped the cobbles.

She was surprised enough she didn't see the kick aimed for her chin until it snapped her head back against the stone and she saw stars.

The red-nosed guard hauled her up by the collar. "Your companions put up a fight, too."

Vola froze, ice trickling down her spine as her head spun. "What did you do to them?" she growled.

"Nothing bad," the younger guard said, dragging himself off the ground. "But we have them. If you don't cooperate, then you'll be left here and they'll be…with us."

Her breath came faster, and red licked at the edges of her vision. She forced herself to stop gasping and fought down a twitch as the blindfold was tied over her face. It smelled like sweat.

The two guards manhandled her down the street for what felt like a block. After that, there was a wagon that smelled like fresh straw. The swaying made her head spin and pound and she concentrated on not barfing. It was impossible to tell how far they'd gone but when they hauled her from the wagon, there were smooth flagstones under her feet.

Up a flight of stairs. Across something that felt like thick carpet under the soles of her boots and another flight of stairs.

Voices caught her attention, and she unwittingly turned her head toward the sound. There was the higher-pitched string of Sorrel chattering and the low rumble of Talon answering her. Vola didn't relax but the muscles in her shoulders went from waiting to ready.

The guards must have sensed the difference. The hands on her arms tightened and then suddenly they pushed and let go. Caught off guard, she stumbled across the edge of a thick carpet and fell to one knee.

"I think she sprained my wrist," the rough voice of the younger guard said.

"Serves you right for jumping a paladin," Sorrel snapped from Vola's left. "You're lucky she didn't break your face."

Someone touched Vola's elbow, and she flinched away, hand going to her weapon. Which they hadn't bothered to confiscate. Idiots.

"Shh," Lillie's voice said in her ear. "It's me. I'm going to take this blindfold off now."

Lillie's hands pulled the cloth from her eyes, and Vola blinked in the sudden sunlight. She found herself on her knees in a wide room lined with tall windows. The entire inn where they were no longer welcome would have fit under the vaulted ceiling.

"Are you all right?" Lillie asked quietly.

Vola flexed her fingers against the plush red carpet and pushed herself to her feet. She braced her hands on her knees while she waited for her head to stop throbbing.

"I'm fine," she finally said when she felt like she could say it without lying. "Where are we?"

"I...have a guess. This is someone's receiving room," Lillie said under her breath. "There's not enough furniture to be an office or a parlor. It's meant to intimidate us." Her eyes kept moving around the room cataloging everything from the curtains to the patterns in the wood paneling.

"That makes me feel loads better," Vola grumbled. She glanced around, taking stock of the room and her party.

Sorrel stood in the middle of the carpet, fists planted on her hips as she scowled at the gilding climbing up the walls. Talon's hood shifted from guard to guard, who stood between the windows.

They showed signs of a fight. One had a brand-new black eye, shining and red, and Vola imagined she could make out the shape of Sorrel's fist in the bruise. The guy next to him had blackened armor, singed by flames. And the next one down the line pinched his mouth in what looked like extreme pain but there wasn't a mark on him. At least not anyplace Vola could see.

"Are they all accounted for?" the red-nosed guard said behind her.

"All except the wolf," one of the others replied. "We're still trying to bring him in."

"I hope he bites you," Talon said, fingering their knives.

The ornate door at the end of the hall opened with a click and a man walked through. His perfectly combed brown hair glinted in the sunlight and it took Vola a second to recognize him.

"Oh," she said. "That employer."

He looked much more comfortable in a red and gold jacket and sleek black pants than in the fisherman's waders he'd been wearing the last time they'd seen him.

With a practiced gesture, he snapped, and the guards all turned as one and filed out the doors. Lillie tilted her head and Vola knew that look. Puzzle pieces were clicking into place over there. Vola waited. She could be patient enough to wait until Lillie presented them with the whole picture.

The man planted himself in front of them and crossed his arms over his chest. His narrow eyes surveyed them and he opened his mouth to speak.

"You kidnapped us off the street just to have a word with us?" Vola snapped before he could.

"Do you know how rude that is?" Sorrel said.

"I needed to talk to you," he said.

Lillie shook her head, eyes full of censure. "You could have just sent a note."

"You can't know where we are," he said, his eyes darting to each of their faces. "You had to be blindfolded."

Lillie snorted and rolled her eyes. "Then you should have

drawn the curtains." She gestured airily at the windows. "The view from Cliffside Palace is especially striking, isn't it?

His mouth dropped open. "How do you know that? Have you been here before?"

Lillie's cheeks went a slightly darker shade of pink. "I read, you imbecile."

"Not to mention this is a step up from anything in the city," Sorrel said, digging her toe into the carpet.

The man's lips thinned and he dropped his hands to his sides. "Well, enjoy it now. Because this is the last time you'll see it. You're fired."

Vola raised her eyebrows and took the chance to cross her own arms. "Oh, you found your…girlfriend, wasn't it? Rilla?"

He flushed and glanced at the door the guards had left through. "No," he said, quite a bit quieter. "But I've had reliable intel that your team is incompetent. And considering how long it's taking you to find her, I'm inclined to agree."

"Incompetent?" Talon said, low and compelling. And from the way the man straightened, he'd felt it in the base of his spine.

"Yes," he stammered. "You've let your culprit escape twice now."

Vola tapped her finger against her upper arm. "You've been talking to some monks, haven't you?"

He took a step back, then raised his chin. "Well, yes. They are here on official business for Maxim, and they've offered to help."

"Out of the kindness of their hearts," Vola said with a smirk. She exchanged a look with the others. Sorrel scowled and Lillie rolled her eyes. Talon flat out laughed, a grating sound that made the man jump.

"Now who's being incompetent?" they said.

"What?"

"Did you do any research at all on your new friends? Or on us for that matter?"

"Why do you think they offered to help?" Vola asked the man.

"Because it's the right thing to do. They're the type of people who would know that. They don't need to be paid to rescue a woman."

"Wrong," Vola said, raising a finger to point it at him. "They're here on official business for Maxim. That's what you said, right?" *Maxim who just sits on his ass,* Vola thought to herself.

"If you knew anything about them," Sorrel said, "You'd know that Maxim's will trumps everything else."

"They only offered to help because it gets them closer to Myron's staff," Vola said. "That's it. Once they have it, they'll run back to their monastery and be done. If they actually cared about Rilla, they wouldn't have attacked Myron—twice now—blowing any chance of learning Rilla's location. If they actually cared about her, they wouldn't have risked her life by angering him."

"Here's the deal," Sorrel said, stepping up to the man and wagging her finger in his face. "You're going to let us keep looking for her. And you're going to pay us really, really well when we do find her."

"Why would I do that?"

Lillie raised her chin. "Because you're desperate. We're not looking for your girlfriend. We're looking for a princess, am I right?"

He blinked and his mouth fell open as he gaped.

"The Princess Allellarilla of the Dagger Throne, to be exact," Lillie said quietly. "One of the fifteen ruling princesses."

Yup, that was the whole picture. All the pieces fit. The guards who didn't move like regular guards. The secrecy. The man with his soft hands and frantic eyes.

No one spoke while they stared at him, waiting for his reaction.

He finally smoothed the front of his jacket with trembling fingers. "That is extremely confidential information. No one can know that the princess is missing, possibly dead. Especially not now when her disappearance is linked to a necromancer."

"She's alive," Vola said into the still air.

The man looked at her sharply. "How do you know?"

"A goddess told me. Now suppose you tell us who we're actually working for."

The man drew himself up so the gold on his jacket glinted. "I am Princess Alellarilla's steward. You may call me James."

"Really?" Talon said. "That's what you're going with?"

"What? It's my name."

Talon huffed as if they didn't believe him.

"If secrecy is so important, why are we looking for her instead of the royal guard?" Vola asked.

"I have them investigating foreign leads. But if they start poking around Brisbene, they'll draw attention. And once the locals know, the whole country will know."

"Why was a princess going after a necromancer anyway?"

"You think she consults me before haring off?" James snapped.

Lillie spread her hands. "The Princess of the Dagger Throne protects Southglen from internal threats. She must have thought it was worth it."

"It wasn't if it costs us her life." James shook his head. "Either you or the monks better pay off or Southglen is in serious trouble."

"We'll find her, James," Sorrel said. "You'll have your princess back alive and well."

She spun on her heel before Vola could wince. She wasn't sure she'd have made that promise.

"I'm still going use the monks," James said behind her. "I need all the help I can get."

Sorrel paused. "Go ahead. It won't make any difference. Because we're going to find her first."

Vola shot a glance at Talon, who shrugged, and Lillie, who raised her eyebrows. They both turned to follow Sorrel.

"We'll show ourselves out this time," Vola said. "The front door's this way, right?" She strode after her party.

Outside the long room, a hallway led to a flight of stairs leading down. Paintings lined the walls between leaded windows casting little diamonds of light on the floor as Lillie rushed to catch up with Sorrel and Talon.

"You need to know something," she was saying, voice coming in quick gasps. "Slow down, this is important."

"What?" Sorrel said, pausing at the top of the stairs.

"We really do have to find her now," Lillie said. "There isn't another option. If we don't, they'll have us executed. They can't risk anyone knowing the Dagger Throne is empty. Not yet."

Sorrel turned on her. "Would you rather we just forgot about her? Would you rather I hadn't made that promise?"

"No," Lillie said and grasped the halfling's arm. "No, of course not. We wanted to find her even before we knew who she was. And what if Myron kills her and does the same thing he did with Bruno last night? He could put his own undead puppet on the Throne. No, we have to find her, like you said. I just wanted you to know everything I know."

Sorrel glanced up, lips going white. "Is that a suggestion? You think I should spill my guts about myself just because you told us this?"

Lillie stepped back a pace. "No. That's not what I meant. I just meant that the monks aren't just risking Rilla's life now. They're risking our lives and the entire country."

"Fine," Sorrel said and crossed her arms over her chest. "Then we do what I promised and we find her first. It's our only option."

She stormed away down the steps.

Someone hissed behind them, and Vola glanced over her

shoulder to see a familiar figure against the wall. She blew out her breath and signaled Talon to follow Sorrel.

"Watch her back," she said. "Lillie, with me."

Talon didn't question the order. They hurried after Sorrel while Vola strode across the hallway to Hazel, who shifted from foot to foot outside the room where they'd met with James.

"Why do you think I'd want to talk to you?" Vola said, low and even.

The dwarf flinched and avoided Vola's gaze. "I know you don't think very well of us, but we're trying to do the right thing."

"The right thing is getting in our way and endangering other people?"

"No. We're trying to recover a very dangerous divine artifact. It has nothing to do with anything personal. It's more important than our lives."

"Right," Vola snorted. "So that gives you the right to tromp all over people?"

Hazel looked up at them with sad eyes. "Whatever Sorrel has told you about us is a lie. We're not as bad as she says."

"Maybe you're not aware that calling someone a liar is a grave insult where I come from," Lillie said quietly.

Hazel glanced at her. "She's done it before. It's why she's not at the monastery anymore. She spouted a bunch of lies about Tallah. It would have gotten her kicked out and exiled if she hadn't run away first."

Vola gripped the dwarf's tunic and in one smooth move, lifted her, and slammed her against the wall.

Hazel yelped.

Lillie gasped but didn't intervene.

"Do you know what I am?" she said, voice deceptively calm.

Hazel's eyes flicked between Vola's swarthy features and her mail and finally settled on the shield on her back. "A paladin?" she squeaked.

"A holy warrior," Vola said. "I right wrongs with the power of the divine at my back. Do you think I give my trust lightly?"

"She's not who you think she is," Hazel gasped, hands clutching Vola's clenched fist.

"Is she Sorrel Thornbough?"

"Yes—"

"Then she is exactly who I think she is."

"She's an oathbreaker."

Vola froze. Then slowly her fingers tightened and Hazel choked.

"Volagra." Lillie placed her hand on Vola's arm, eyes wide.

Vola took a deep breath and loosened her grip.

"You're a paladin," Hazel gasped out. "Your oaths bind you but they also define you. How do you feel about someone who breaks them?"

Vola opened her fist and Hazel fell to the floor in a heap.

Oathbreaker.

The word rang through her head, hitting every sharp corner in the process. But it was just a word. Words meant different things. Her own vows had been words. And as much as Vola loved to swing her sword and cut down her enemies, she'd promised to right wrongs even when they didn't require swords.

"Sorrel is fierce," she said, staring at the wall over Hazel's head. "She is impulsive. She is fast and strong and likes a good drink. And I've never met anyone more honorable."

Now Vola pinned Hazel to the floor with her gaze. "If she lied to you, if she broke her oaths to you, it's because you broke her first."

Hazel blinked away tears and glanced away. But she swiped her nose on her sleeve and raised her chin. "That's not an excuse."

"It's not," Vola said. "It's an explanation. And I trust her enough to wait for her to tell me her excuses herself."

Vola turned away, but Hazel climbed to her feet using the wall for support. "You don't understand."

Vola spun back, and Hazel flinched against the wall. "No, you don't understand. You abandoned her. I don't need to know why. Because nothing is enough to justify that." Vola took a couple of deep breaths then deliberately stepped back to give Hazel some more room. "Sorrel's not yours anymore. She's ours." She gestured between herself and Lillie. "And if you try to hurt her again, you'll have the rest of us to deal with as well."

Lillie raised her chin and Vola half expected lightning to crackle between her fingers, but the wizard kept her agitation hidden a lot better than Vola did.

Hazel gaped at them, mouth working, but no sound coming out.

And when Vola turned to head down the stairs, only Lillie followed her.

"Sorry if I put words in your mouth," Vola said quietly.

Sorrel and Talon waited at the foot of the stairs. The monk looked up at them, brow furrowed.

"No," Lillie said just as quietly. "As with Sorrel's promise, I would not have done anything differently."

FIFTEEN

THE MAN behind the counter in the bookshop barely glanced at them as they gave him the password that would let them into the Underground.

"Do you really think we'll find gravediggers here?" Lillie asked as they crossed the threshold into the crowded alley. Mid-afternoon sun cascaded down around them.

"Grave robbing is illegal," Vola said. "Where else would you find people willing to break the law for some extra gold?"

"Everywhere," Talon said.

Vola paused to consider. "Okay, where else would you find the greatest concentration of people willing to break the law?"

"And it's our only lead," Sorrel said. "Unless knowing Rilla's a princess changes anything." She glanced at Lillie.

Lillie bit her lip. "It actually opens up a lot more avenues worth exploring. This could be entirely political disguised as something more mundane. The fifteen princesses that rule the country of Southglen are widely acknowledged as some of the most powerful in the world. This could be an attack by a foreign nation. Or it could be the first salvo in a revolution."

"Great, more options," Vola said. "How about we stick with this one since it's closest to what we know?"

"And we know Myron was the last one to see her alive," Sorrel said, ticking it off on her fingers. "And her man James seemed to think this was worthy of investigation."

Lillie nodded. "I agree."

Talon didn't add anything. They stepped out of the way of a group of gnomes, hood moving frenetically, trying to keep track of everything at once.

Vola sidled closer. "You all right?" she asked quietly.

"Fine," Talon grated out.

Vola frowned. "You know you can tell me if you're not."

"I'm fine, Vola."

Vola backed off with a wince. "All right."

"Isn't it just like a princess to be kidnapped by someone like Myron?" Sorrel said with a snort.

"Actually, I think it says more about Myron," Lillie said. "The princess who sits on the Dagger Throne is in charge of rooting out threats to the kingdom. She is Southglen's first line of defense against invasion and insurrection. She isn't always a fighter, but she is always deadly."

Vola raised her eyebrows. "That doesn't bode well for us."

They strode down the alley, ignoring the booths selling weapons and armor this time. Along the wall where another alley bisected theirs, someone had set up a bar open to the sky and air. Vola made a straight line for the bartender. If the Underground was anything like the inn formerly known as The Snuggly Bunny, this would be the hub for anyone looking for work. Even questionable work.

Of course, everyone else had the same idea.

Vola tried to squeeze between a couple of ill-dressed thieves to catch the bartender's eye, but the thieves cast one glance at her and put their shoulders together, effectively walling her off.

Vola exchanged a look with the others.

Sorrel winked. "Let me handle this." The halfling shimmied between another two barstools, squeezing in like a greased pig.

And then she shot out again and landed on her butt.

"Funny. That usually works." The monk hopped up and planted her hands on her hips. "How's a girl supposed to get a drink around here?"

Talon tapped Vola on the shoulder and pointed down the bar at a familiar red and gold hide.

Vola grinned and made her way to the dragon they'd fought just a few days before. She sat draped over two barstools with a bowl of something that steamed.

"Hi," Vola said.

The dragon glanced at her and away and then jerked back. "Oh, hey. The adventurer with a kick that can move mountains."

"I'm Volagra," Vola said, extending a hand.

The dragon shook it gently with her claw. "Hurren."

"That's a pretty name," Lillie said.

"Not half as pretty as you," the dragon said, leaning her scaled elbow on the bar. It creaked. "It means Skyfire. You're a wizard. You like fire, don't you?" the dragon crooned.

Lillie's face went red, and she stammered.

The dragon glanced at Vola. "Did I read that wrong?"

Vola rubbed her lips, unsuccessfully hiding a smile. "I think that was just Lillie being polite."

"What about you? Are you just being polite?"

Vola tilted her head. "Do you flirt with everyone who kicks your butt?"

Hurren shrugged, making her scales ripple in the light. "Pretty much. I like fighters. Especially fighters strong enough to kick me around the ring. What harm is there in a little light flirting between opponents?"

The dragon surveyed the others. Talon didn't move but Gruff saw the look and his lip lifted in a growl.

"That's a no," Hurren said. She glanced at Sorrel.

Sorrel shrugged. "I'm game. As long as you keep your hands to yourself and you know this isn't going to go anywhere."

Hurren grinned, showing off canines as long as Talon's knives, and she nudged the man on the stool next to her. Smoke curled from her nostrils and the man vacated the stool faster than if he'd sat on a bee.

Sorrel scrambled up to the empty seat. "We wanted to talk to someone who knew more about this place than us."

"Mmhmm." Hurren planted her chin on one claw. She batted her eyelids. Dragons didn't really have eyelashes.

Vola just stood back and crossed her arms, trying to keep from outright grinning. Lillie looked on with something akin to fascination and confusion. Vola half expected her to pull out her pen and start taking notes. Talon's hood was drawn over their as if the ranger's mind was somewhere else completely.

Vola scanned the crowd. With Sorrel taking point and Lillie and Talon distracted it was Vola's job to watch the perimeter.

She was glad she did. Two stalls over, between a man selling decks of rigged cards and a fortune-teller who may or may not have been a real down on their luck prophet, Vola glimpsed a gray tunic. The bearded monk from Myron's quarters was watching them.

Vola shifted to plant herself squarely between the monk and her party. She made sure she met his eyes and put her hand on her sword hilt in a gesture well known throughout the world.

The monk glanced at them, then up and down the alley. Finally, he stepped away and faded into the crowds of the underground.

Vola relaxed a fraction. Of course they were being followed. They were going to have to figure that one out soon.

When she turned back toward the bar, the dragon was saying, "Rumors were going around there for a while that someone was paying good money for dead bodies, stolen or otherwise. But Fang made it pretty clear anyone who started working for Myron Vidal wouldn't be welcome back here. I think he's working with her rival."

Sorrel tapped her teeth, thinking. "So, no one around here would have taken the job."

Hurren shook her long head. "Nope. Though there are plenty of gravediggers who moonlight as grave robbers outside of Fang's influence. Try Dodson over in the Narrows. He's into some shady shit."

"And he wouldn't have minded angering Fang?"

"That ship sailed a long while ago." Hurren's spine spikes flattened as she glanced over her shoulder. "Speaking of..." The dragon slipped off her barstool and patted Sorrel's hand. "It's above my pay grade to tangle with Fang. And she's headed right for you."

Hurren dropped to all fours and snaked her way through the crowd toward the pit just as Fang stomped up to Vola, trailing her elven bodyguard.

"You," Fang said, waving her finger. It barely made it to Vola's waist.

"Me," Vola said.

"I heard you were back in the Underground. You tricked me."

Vola plastered a politely confused look on her face. "Tricked you? Tricked you how?"

"Don't play dumb. That monster, that swampy thing you saddled me with. You knew what it was all along?"

"A swamp monster?" Vola said, stroking her chin. "Yes. We knew it was a swamp monster. But you accepted it as payment."

"That wasn't payment," Fang spat. "That was a scam."

"We did say we didn't have anything worth selling to you,"

Lillie said politely. She sat on the vacated bar stool. "Strictly the truth if you were paying attention. And there were no illusions on it."

Fang spluttered. "You're going to take it back."

Vola fought to keep a straight face. "Why would we do that?"

"It ate my merchandise," Fang said, and now that Vola glanced down the alley to the scaffolding on the end, she could see that all the cages were empty. "The exotics. It ate them."

"What? All of them?" Lillie said.

"All of them."

"You need better handlers," Talon said.

"It tried to eat the handlers, too." Fang waved her wrinkled hands in the air. "At least two of them have sizable chunks missing."

Vola froze for half a second as an idea flitted through her head. "You were a monk, weren't you, Fang?" she said softly.

Fang hesitated with her mouth open. Then she dropped her hands and crossed her arms. "I said I trained at the monastery. I didn't say I was a monk."

"No, we guessed that part," Vola said.

"The monks who came to you right before us," Sorrel said. "You told them where to find Myron Vidal as well, didn't you?"

"They paid for the information," Fang said, her gaze flitting between them.

"But not anything else. You were arguing about not helping them. What else did they want?"

"They were calling on my loyalty." Fang's eyes narrowing. "As if I owe them any after they refused to listen to me. They kicked me out for not upholding the tenets of Maxim and then expected me to fall in line as soon as they showed their faces in my domain."

Sorrel crossed her legs in a very calculated gesture. "Sounds familiar."

Fang's gaze sharpened on her.

Vola examined her fingernails. "I'm willing to do something for you, Fang. We can take the swamp monster back in return for one small favor. You keep the monks off of us. You keep them distracted so they can't follow us. And I guarantee they won't get what they came here for."

"Because you'll have it," Fang said.

"Sorrel will." Vola gestured to the monk who sat quiet and focused. "I have no stake in this. The...object...belongs to Maxim, so Sorrel decides what to do with it."

"Done," Fang said, barely pausing. "I'll keep them off your tail and you take that wretched beast with you. And make sure they don't get what they want."

"Done." Vola held out her hand, and Fang shook it. Then she pointed around the alley. "There are one or two floating around here already."

"I'll handle it. You wait here for delivery of your monster."

Vola leaned on the bar between Sorrel and Lillie, chuckling to herself as Fang bustled away. "Two for one," she said. "We got something out of the swamp monster twice, now, and we didn't have to deal with it for two whole days."

"Yeah, but we'll have to deal with it now," Talon said.

"I will need a drink before that," Sorrel said, trying to catch the bartender's eye. "Shouldn't Hurren have bought me one? I thought that was part of the whole flirting thing."

Vola shook her head. It was really something when, out of the four of them, Vola was the one with the most romantic experience.

A man down at the other end of the bar was eying Lillie.

Sorrel eyed him back.

Fang's bodyguard appeared through the crowd, leading the swamp monster at arm's length. The beast tried to take a bite out of a passerby, who yelped.

Lillie sighed. "I'll take it this time, but it will be someone else's turn in an hour." She hopped off the stool.

The man at the end of the bar watched as she walked away. Sorrel pursed her lips as if thinking.

"No, Sorrel," Vola said. "You may not trade Lillie's favors for a beer."

"Oh, come on," Sorrel screwed up her face. "I've had a bad day."

"No."

The man saw them talking and sidled up beside them. "Hello, what does your fair friend like to drink?"

"Beer," Sorrel chimed in before Vola could answer.

"Not okay, Sorrel," Talon said over her shoulder.

Sorrel shrugged. "It was worth a shot."

Vola's eyes narrowed. This looked like the same man from the inn. The one who'd been sending Lillie drinks all week. Had he followed them here? Or was it just dumb luck?

"Do you really like her?" Vola asked. "She's never even spoken to you, has she?"

The man shrugged. "I...I'd at least like the chance to say hello. And I'm not very good at talking to girls. I thought maybe if I could give her something she likes..."

Vola tried to relax. He sounded genuine enough. And someone with less confidence might be just what Lillie needed. Maybe. Or maybe she just needed to be left alone. Either way, Vola couldn't make that decision for her.

"She likes wine," Vola told the man. "Red, preferably. But it's not going to go well. I promise."

He gave Vola a rueful grin. "That would be okay, too. She could just come tell me no and I'll stop."

By the time Lillie returned to the bar trailing an angry-looking swamp monster, there was a glass of something red sitting in front of her stool.

"What?" Lillie said. "Not again."

"It's that one down there," Vola said, pointing.

The man twiddled his fingers when he saw Lillie looking.

"Oh for heaven's sake," Lillie said, turning her shoulder and hiding her face behind her hand.

"I did try to tell him no. He might take it better from you."

"I tried to tell him beer, but Talon and Vola wouldn't let me," Sorrel moped from the seat beside her.

"Do I drink it?" Lillie said, eying the glass as if it would bite.

"That depends," Sorrel said with a thoughtful look. "Are you thirsty?"

"I mean, would he take that as an invitation?"

"It was a gift. Why shouldn't you drink it?" Talon said.

"You're overthinking this," Vola said.

"Of course I am," Lillie said, covering her face. "I overthink everything."

The bartender finally appeared before them. "What else can I get you, ladies?"

Talon made a little noise in the back of their throat, and Vola glanced at them in concern. They said nothing.

"A stout, please," Sorrel said, raising a finger. "And my friend will have a—"

"Tea," Vola said.

Sorrel rolled her eyes.

"And for you, sir?" the bartender said, turning to Talon. "Or ma'am?"

"Them," Vola corrected.

"No," the rough voice came from the hood.

"No drink?"

Talon shook their head, and Gruff stood, hackles rising. "No. That's enough. I can't... Just no."

Vola's stomach clenched. She'd never heard that tone from Talon before. Granted, they didn't hear a lot coming from Talon, ever, but when they did speak, it was always with confidence. Humor, anger, exasperation, too, but always confidence. This sounded strangled.

Vola straightened up from the bar. "Talon—"

"Can we leave?" Talon said. "Go find this Dodson? I don't like it here. Too many eyes. Too many questions."

Vola tried to meet Talon's gaze, but their hood was firmly turned away. Back in the swamp, back when they'd first met, Talon had said they wore the hood to deflect questions. With more time together and more experience, Vola still didn't have all the answers to the mysteries Talon presented. But she was starting to see the shape of what was wrong. Just the barest outline.

"Of course," she said.

Sorrel didn't even argue about leaving before she got her beer.

SIXTEEN

THE NARROWS TURNED out to be an old, dry canal where several shady businesses had set up their offices. They climbed down the steps still stained from algae and who knew what else into the dried-out bed where hairline cracks ran through the stone. The steep walls rose over them, cutting off the late afternoon sun, casting the canal in deep twilit shadows.

Three signs jutted out from the wall, indicating the storefronts set into the old drainage grates that dotted the stone. Lillie squinted up at the names and led them to the third door.

"Dodson and Associates. Gravediggers for hire," Lillie read.

Vola peered around the narrow space before pushing the grate open. No gray-clad monks followed them so Fang must be doing her job.

Inside, the skinny tunnel was lit with a couple of flickering oil lanterns, and Vola ducked to keep from smashing her skull on the low ceiling.

She led the others back to where someone had carved a room out of the old canal wall. Here sat a desk and a chair upholstered in cracked leather. Stuffing poked through the cracks.

A man sat at the desk with his feet up. His boots sat on the ground beside him.

Vola's nose wrinkled, and she blinked watering eyes. Lillie choked and held her hand over her mouth.

Vola sure hoped that smell was the man's feet and nothing else.

"Are you Dodson?" she managed to say. *Just don't breathe and you'll be fine*, she tried to tell herself.

The man dug around in the back of his mouth with a dirty finger before he pulled it out, examined the tip, and flicked whatever he'd found in their direction.

"That's me," he said. "You need a grave dug?"

"Actually, we heard you might be interested in some business on the side," Lillie said.

At the sound of her voice, Dodson sat up, knocking over an empty bottle as he swung his feet to the floor. "Well, hey there, beautiful. Didn't see you back there. Step into my office and we'll talk."

He gestured to the chair, and Lillie crept toward it uncertainly.

Vola frowned and made certain she loomed just behind the wizard. Sorrel drifted to the far wall where a schedule hung written in an illegible hand, and Vola caught sight of Talon edging toward a door in the back.

Lillie sat gingerly.

Dodson came around to sit on the edge of the desk directly in front of her. "Now sweetheart, what's your name?"

Lillie's eyes narrowed. "I...well, I'm Lillie, but what I'd like to do is discuss your business—"

"Yeah, yeah, sure, honey. But isn't that a little over your head? I can explain it all if you'd like, somewhere private."

He reached out to stroke Lillie's knee.

Vola's hand flew to her sword hilt, but the change in Lillie's posture stopped her. The half-elf had stiffened and a rare fire lit behind her eyes.

Vola'd only seen it once or twice, but it paid to remember what made the wizard angry.

"Remove your hand from my person or I will remove it from your arm."

"There's no reason to get tetchy. You're the one in my offic—"

Lillie grabbed Dodson's wrist and a bolt of lightning sparked between them. It blew Dodson back into his desk, and he fell over it with a scream and a thud.

Smoke rose over the edge of the desk.

"Now why didn't you do that with the guy at the bar?" Sorrel asked curiously from her spot by the wall.

"I-I didn't want to be impolite," Lillie stammered.

Vola raised an eyebrow.

"He was just, I don't know, saying hello. This…this was entirely different."

"Clearly," Vola said. She tapped Lillie's shoulder and jerked her thumb.

Lillie vacated the chair, and Vola plopped down in her place just as Dodson climbed back to his feet, groaning. He used the desk for support.

"You bitch—" He raised his gaze to the chair and found Vola's tusked smile instead of Lillie's.

Talon stepped up behind him and placed both hands on his shoulders.

"You were saying?" Vola made sure to grin widely.

Dodson snapped his mouth shut.

"Now," Vola said. "Let's try this again. Since you find my companion distracting, you'll be dealing directly with me."

Lillie growled from over her shoulder, and Vola nearly choked on a laugh.

Dodson's eyes darted between her and Lillie.

"We were asking about your side business," Vola said, leaning forward to fold her hands on the desk. "The one that isn't on the sign outside."

Talon pressed down and Dodson sat abruptly. "You want a body buried somewhere no one will ever find it?"

Vola paused with her mouth open. "No. But I will remember that for future need. We're looking for Myron Vidal, and you've been working for him."

"So? What do you want from me?"

"You know where he is. You have a drop-off point, don't you? A place where you leave his…merchandise."

"So?"

"So, tell us," Talon grated from behind his ear.

He shook his head. "Nuh-uh, that's how people disappear. You don't anger the guy who collects dead bodies. He'll just add you to his collection."

Vola kind of doubted Myron was that cold-blooded, but they had seen him panic before. She could imagine him making a mistake when cornered. And he'd certainly made the princess disappear.

Dodson winced and cast a look back at Talon. "And you can stop pinching me, sir. It won't do any good."

Talon flinched back, hands jerking away from the man.

"So, threatening you won't make a difference, will it?" Vola said, just to make sure.

"Lady, if it's a choice between you killing me and him killing me, I choose you. You won't make my body dance after I'm dead."

"We don't have to kill you," Talon said just behind his ear. "We can make you hurt. Hurting can last a long time."

Vola eyed Talon, not entirely sure if the ranger was serious or not. It was…always hard to tell with Talon.

"What if you didn't tell us?" Lillie said, voice thoughtful. Everyone cast a glance at her, and she spread her hands out.

"What if you just added four more corpses to your next shipment?"

Vola froze, mind racing along the edges of a plan. "That could work."

"What's in it for me?" Dodson asked, beady eyes narrow.

"Pain," Talon said.

"No," Vola interrupted. She cast a look at Talon. "Stop that."

"We're not going to pay you," Sorrel said. "But do you need any chores done? Any pesky problems you need taken care of?"

"Now that you mention it," Dodson said, stroking his chin. Vola didn't like the look he was giving them.

"Within reason," she added.

"This is well within your skill set," he said. "There's a graveyard I like to…frequent. Only all the necromantic activity in the city recently has woken something unpleasant there. You clear the graveyard, and I'll take you to the drop site."

SEVENTEEN

THE SITE DODSON wanted cleared wasn't even that far. Vola didn't relish fighting in a graveyard at night again, but none of them wanted to wait until morning when they were so close.

They could be rescuing their princess by sunrise if they hurried.

Talon strode to the gate and kicked a wrought iron post.

"Does anyone else feel like this is turning into an endless trail of little chores?" Sorrel said as they stared through the bars.

"When this is over, I'm never setting foot in another graveyard again," Lillie said.

Vola just sighed and collected a couple of Broken Grace blooms that hung from the fence nearby.

"I don't want to go straight in there," Talon said abruptly. Their cloak flared as they planted their hands on their hips. "It doesn't feel right."

Vola eyed them. The ranger couldn't seem to stand still. They paced away from the fence and back again, hood drawn over their face as they concentrated on their feet.

"We can sweep the perimeter," Vola said. "Make sure nothing nasty is waiting to ambush us once we're in there."

"At least nothing nastier than the ghost Dodson wants us to get rid of," Sorrel said.

"Do we even know how to get rid of a ghost?" Lillie said. "I'm not familiar with exorcism."

"I guess we'll find out if steel works." Vola jerked her head at Lillie and Sorrel. "You two take the left. We'll take the right. Guard each other's backs. We'll meet in the middle on the other side. Yell if anything grabs you."

"I can't tell if she's being funny or serious," Sorrel grumbled as they stepped away, following the fence line.

Talon had already started off in the opposite direction, Gruff at their heels. Vola hurried to catch up. She cast her gaze up the slope that rose from the fence and back down into the graveyard while trying to keep an eye on Talon at the same time. The ranger stalked up the slope and back down, hands clenching around their elbows.

"What's wrong?" Vola said, quietly.

Talon's hood jerked and turned a little to glance at her.

She could see the shape of Talon's agitation. The way they flinched any time someone called them he or fumbled in confusion. But she didn't know what to do about it. She didn't know how to guard against this threat she couldn't see. She had the sneaking suspicion the threat was in Talon's head, and she didn't think she'd be able to defeat it while it lingered there.

"Dodson is a pig. You know that, right?" Vola said.

Talon shook their head. "It's not Dodson." Three times they reached up as if to draw their hood back and three times they decided against it, letting their hand fall back.

"Well, something's wrong," Vola finally said when it seemed like Talon wasn't able to start by themselves. "Something's been wrong in a way since we got to the city."

Talon's gait hitched and their hood jerked up.

"Tell me," Vola said.

Talon shook their head. But then Gruff pressed against their side, and their hand sank into his thick fur. It was hard to tell under the swathing cloak but Vola thought their breathing evened out a bit.

"All right. It's not *just* Dodson." Talon leaned into Gruff. "You know the best thing about animals?"

Vola tilted her head, inviting.

"They don't make assumptions. They don't just look at you and assume."

Vola breathed in sharply through her nose. This, this was the festering problem and somehow, she'd been feeding it. They all had.

"No?"

"Humans, elves—all the two-leggers—are the ones that assume. Because humans have to put everything in its box. And I'm really tired of sitting in the wrong box."

"All right," Vola said. Not because she knew what was going on, but because she knew it would be all right no matter what Talon said. It had to be. She'd *make* it all right if that's what it came down to.

"I think I'm going to have to leave," Talon said, sounding like they were strangling. "After we find Rilla, I have to go. I have to find somewhere I can start over. Where I don't have to explain everything, where I can just be me and I don't have to hide anymore."

Vola's hands clenched in reaction. Red flickered at the edge of her vision but she couldn't even tell where the anger was coming from. Was she angry at Talon, who was so miserable they felt like they had to abandon their party? Or was she angry at whatever it was that made Talon miserable?

Vola took a deep breath and pushed aside the formless rage

and desire to do something. "You can't be you here?" she said. "With us?"

"I want to," Talon said, their voice low. "But I started out wrong. Didn't know how to handle it and now it's all twisted up, and *I'm* wrong and I can't make it right here. Not without a lot of work. I just thought you should know, so it wasn't a surprise."

"What about you is something you can't be here?"

Talon didn't respond right away.

"Talon," Vola said, evenly. Firm but not pushy. "Just tell me."

Talon hesitated, then reached up with a shaky hand to push their hood back.

Freckles dusted their nose and patchy bits of sandy-colored beard bristled from their chin. The bits of bare skin gleamed red and raw like they'd scraped a razor over their face too fast and too hard. Their blue eyes wavered on Vola's face.

"You know I'm not a he. But I'm not a they, either. I'm a she."

Vola felt it was important not to blink like she really really wanted to. She kept her face calm, eyes fixed on Talon's.

Talon's face twisted before they—she—ducked her head and yanked her hood back up. She turned so Vola could only see her shoulders heaving.

"I'm a girl, but when people look at me, they see a boy."

"So you hide," Vola said quietly.

"It's easier than explaining. It's easier than changing everything."

"But you're ready to change."

Talon raised shaking hands to her face and rubbed, under the hood, before she finally turned. "No. I'm afraid. But I don't think the fear will ever go away unless I just do it. And I'm…tired. So tired. And I don't want to be tired anymore."

Vola leaned against the fence, crossing her arms. "And you think the best way to not be afraid and to not be tired anymore is to abandon us?"

Talon jerked up. "No. That's why I'm telling you now. I'm not abandoning you. Just leaving."

"I thought we were your pack," Vola said.

Talon's shoulders fell.

Vola pushed up straight and reached for Talon's hood. Talon flinched, and Vola paused. Then she very slowly pushed the hood back again.

She ignored the red-rimmed eyes and the raw skin under the patchy beard.

"I don't see a he," she said. "Or if I'm honest, a she. Not yet. But I do see Talon. If that's who you choose to be. You can leave if you want. If you think that's what will make you happy; if you think that's what you need. We won't hate you for it. We'll understand. But you don't *have* to leave. If you do, make sure it's because you want to. Not because you're afraid to stay. Change is hard. You're not wrong. But some people can make it easier. You just have to find the right people."

She very gently pulled the hood back up over Talon's head, covering her face. "And until then, you can keep hiding. It's all right. I won't tell anyone."

She turned to follow the fence some more, then paused. "But if you don't mind, I'm going to practice thinking of you as a her. Thank you for telling me."

"Thank you for listening," came the whispered reply behind her.

Vola hesitated a few steps away, long enough to swallow the lump in her throat and rub her nose.

All right, that happened. It had happened and…it wasn't terrible? It wasn't wonderful or comfortable either, not when it had been so long coming. But they'd get through it. As long as Talon chose to stay, they'd get through it, eventually.

A short, sharp cry made Vola's spine straighten. It sounded like Lillie.

Talon was already over the fence, Gruff flowing after her. Vola vaulted the wrought-iron and tried to draw her sword at the same time. She ended up caught halfway over and had to hop on one foot to free her stuck boot. Talon sprinted into the dark.

"Shit, wait!"

A lightning bolt lit the tombs with a brief flash of light, striking the fence right where Vola's boot was stuck. The leather sizzled and tore free, and Vola lurched away from the fence into the graveyard.

No one was yelling anymore. But the site wasn't that big and Vola was across it in about thirty seconds. Lillie crouched against the fence opposite them while Sorrel stood feet planted as a shape rose from the ground, all shifting shadows and gray mist.

"What the he—heck, guys? What are you doing on this side of the fence?" Vola hissed at the two of them. She tried to edge around the shape, closer to her people. She signaled Talon to flank from the other side.

"It wasn't on purpose," Sorrel said, swinging her staff back and forth, eyes trained on the looming figure. "I think it pulled us."

"Ghosts can't do that," Vola started.

Lillie shook her head violently. "That's not a ghost. Look out, Sorrel."

"What?" Sorrel turned.

The shadow creature caught her with a blow across the chest, and the halfling went flying. Across the graveyard, Sorrel skidded, rolled, and popped onto her feet. Clearly, she was fine, but now she was a million miles away.

Vola glanced between the creature and Lillie and charged for the creature. If she could keep its attention on her, she could absorb most of its damage while Lillie attacked from afar.

An arc of fire split around Vola and hit the creature square in the face. Vola shook off the searing heat and leaped with her sword ready.

And then hit the ground as if nothing was there.

Vola gaped from her knees and stared at her sword. What the hell just happened?

The creature spread its arms, draped in shredded death shrouds, and grinned, revealing decayed teeth.

"It's a wraith," Lillie called. "Vola, it's a wraith. Normal weapons won't work."

Neither would fire, it seemed. Damn Dodson to a dark, cold hell.

The wraith gathered itself.

"Lillie, move!" Vola called.

Lillie squeaked and ducked behind a headstone as Vola leaped between them and took the blow. It crashed her back into a fallen tree, and she gasped, all the breath leaving her lungs at once.

"For Maxim!" Sorrel sailed over Vola's head, staff slung over her back. The halfling punched at the wraith, fists glowing with white light.

That seemed to do something. At least, the wraith flinched and turned its attention on Sorrel. It snapped out and grasped her by the neck, then slammed her into the ground.

Sorrel choked and scrabbled at the wraith's misty hand.

A storm of arrows flew, each one striking the wraith's exposed back with a thud. The wraith didn't even seem to notice, but then the arrows sprouted thorns and the creature roared in pain. It let go of Sorrel and spun toward its unseen assailant while Sorrel scrambled backward.

"Now, Vola," Lillie called.

Vola snatched up her sword and planted her feet. "Lady, give me your anger," she whispered and closed her eyes. In her hands, her hilt grew warm to the touch.

Without looking, she leaped forward and plunged her sword into the wraith's back.

It screamed as light shot through the emptiness inside the creature and burst into a million glowing pieces.

Vola fell to one knee with a gasp, still clutching the hilt of her glowing sword.

Sorrel trotted to her side. "You all right?"

"I will be once I have a word with Dodson."

"Get in line," Lillie said, stepping up to them.

"Watch it!" Talon's voice called through the graveyard. "On your left."

Vola sprang to her feet to turn and found three more wraiths hauling themselves out of the ground.

"Oh, I'm definitely going to kill him now," Vola growled.

"How long does that glowy thing on your sword last?" Sorrel said, spinning to watch their backs.

Vola planted her feet. "Long enough."

By the time they returned to Dodson's office, Vola limped, Sorrel had white marks around her neck, and Lillie had a nasty scratch down her cheek. Talon seemed uninjured but they—she—had done the most to distract the creatures so the others could strike. Gruff walked beside them with his head down, panting.

Dodson waited with his feet up on the desk again.

Vola swept them off the top with a shove. "Your graveyard is clear, you bastard. And you could have mentioned it was wraiths, not ghosts."

Dodson grinned, revealing brown teeth. "You came out all right. Party like you a wraith won't even put a dent in."

"There were five. Believe me, there are dents, and I'm going to take them out on you."

Vola reached for his shirt but he jerked back and held up his hands. "Before I take you to the drop site? Bad tactics, there."

Vola growled and shoved him back. "Fine. You'll take us to the site, then?"

Dodson tapped his cheek then held up one finger. "One more little thing and then we can go."

Lillie glared at him, the cut on her cheek seeping a little. "What one more thing? We did what you wanted."

"Yes, but I have this very distracting problem. Not sure it will let me do my job."

"Spit it out," Talon said.

"You have a healer, right?"

The others glanced at Vola.

"I've got this pesky rash. It's getting in the way of my personal life. Very distracting. Shouldn't be a problem for you."

"I've heard that before," Vola grumbled.

She glanced at her party. They sagged where they stood. Everyone just wanted this over with so they could rescue Rilla.

She'd have to buy them all a vacation when this was done.

"Fine." She stepped forward to place her hands on his upper arms. "I hope she gives you warts in uncomfortable places. Lady bless."

He yelped as white light flashed under her hands. She grimaced, waiting for the mirrored sting of whatever rash he was complaining about but it never came. And when she drew her hands away, she left red burns on his skin in the shape of her palms.

Dodson rubbed his arms. "I don't know if that was worth it."

Vola grinned. "My lady is vindictive. I wouldn't complain too loudly if I were you. Now you'll take us to the drop site. No more chores, no more excuses."

"Give me three hours," he said. "We go with a load at

midnight. People ask fewer questions about loaded wagons after dark."

EIGHTEEN

WHILE SORREL and Talon rested in Dodson's back room, Vola hurried through the dark streets towards Cleavah's temple. Lillie had refused to let her go alone, and now the swamp monster took the opportunity every other turning to nip at her heels.

"Stop that, or I'll drop you off at a glue factory instead," Vola said, yanking on the lead rope. "And I won't bother to collect you afterward."

The swamp beast cast her a glare that practically glowed in the dark.

"You didn't have to come, you know," Vola told Lillie. "I'm hoping this will be quick."

Lillie rolled her eyes. "I finally realized you always make sure we have someone with us. Because we should have someone watching our back. That includes you. Sorrel and Talon can take care of each other. I'm going to make sure you make it to our date with Dodson."

She wasn't wrong. This *was* safer. But it seemed a little unnecessary. There was no one on the streets this late, but Vola wanted to be sure to catch the devotee before they headed to Dodson's drop-off point. She was hoping the devotee might have some more resources like the Broken Grace that would help them against the necromancer.

She also had an unpleasant favor to ask.

Vola wouldn't wish the swamp beast on anyone she considered a friend, but for the same reasons, she also didn't feel right unleashing the monster on the city without any sort of warning. Hopefully, Cleavah's devotee wouldn't mind stabling the beast for a couple of days.

Vola came around the corner and caught a young man with a dripping paint brush raised to finish the last e in "Cleevas hors live here."

"Oh, dear. What a crime," Lillie gasped.

Vola wasn't sure if she was talking about the vandalism or the spelling. She surged forward and caught the artist by the collar just as he turned to scream. She yanked him up so his shirt cut off his air.

"Do something better with your life," she growled in his face, then shoved him back.

He squeaked and stumbled before turning tail to run.

Vola kicked the bucket of paint to run harmlessly into the gutter.

"Are you all right?" Lillie asked quietly.

Vola shook her head, but she wasn't sure that was really an answer. "It's just…she's the only one doing anything. She's the only one in the pantheon who's helping people, and they treat her like this. Just because she's got a funny name, and her symbol is a fish knife. She needs guards."

Vola pushed through the door without waiting for Lillie's reply, leaving the swamp monster on the doorstep.

She'd expected to catch the devotee by surprise, since the woman obviously wasn't paying attention to what was going on outside, but the golden-skinned, dark-haired devotee stood beside the altar, her hands folded in front of her.

"Hello, Vola."

"You couldn't hear him?" Vola gestured to the boarded-up windows as Lillie passed through the door behind her.

"I could," the devotee said.

Vola's brow furrowed. "Then why didn't you do something? You wouldn't even have had to wave your knife. Just stuck your head out and yelled. Don't you care what they say about Cleavah?"

The woman blinked. "Why should I?"

"They make fun of her. They don't understand."

"Exactly. They don't understand who she is. But you and I do. Why does it matter so much to you what they say?"

"Because…because it's not right."

"No, it's not." The devotee spoke calmly, her voice steady. "But you will never convince everyone. You know the truth of who she is. And that should be enough. Unless you, too, doubt."

Vola took an involuntary step back. "I don't doubt," she said. Cleavah was the one who helped the weak and the powerless, exactly the way Vola did. Cleavah was the one who gave her the power to heal.

But what kind of goddess let herself be ridiculed and mocked? What kind of goddess didn't defend herself?

Vola dropped her eyes and found the pack at the devotee's feet. "Are you going somewhere?"

"The necromancer's stronghold."

"What?" Vola cried.

The devotee raised one delicate eyebrow. "I have a responsibility to the families under my protection. One of them lost a loved one recently, and Myron has stolen his body. Their sons wouldn't listen to reason, and they've decided to storm the necromancer's stronghold to retrieve him. They've been gone for two days."

"Oh, I'm sorry," Lillie said.

The devotee's gaze lighted on her with a welcoming smile. "You must be Lillie."

Lillie gasped. "How on earth did you—"

"She just does that," Vola said.

"My lady Cleavah tells me many things. She also said that you know where the necromancer hides now."

Vola shifted her feet. "Not exactly. But we have a way in."

"Then I will come with you and free the wayward boys."

Vola blinked. This woman, this minor priestess of a lesser goddess wanted to walk into a necromancer's lair and what? Wave her knife at him? She might have been able to wield that knife against angry supplicants, but fighting the undead was entirely different.

"I don't think that's such a good idea," Vola said. Lillie bit her lip in that way that meant she agreed, but she was too polite to say it out loud.

"Why not?" the devotee said, gaze clear and strong on Vola's.

Vola couldn't meet it head-on. She ducked her head and rubbed her neck. "I won't be able to protect you in there. I have to keep my party safe, and we have to rescue the princess. Look, I'll find the boys for you. I'll get them out."

"This is my task, Vola," the devotee said. The candles flickered, sending brief shadows stabbing up the walls. "You have your own."

"I'm not going to lead you into Myron's lair to get yourself killed." Vola's shoulders drooped. "Who would take care of all the people you do, then?"

The devotee was much better off here where she at least had walls.

"This is not a decision you can make for me," the devotee said as if she knew what Vola was thinking. Maybe Cleavah had told her that, too.

Vola's lips thinned and her breath hissed through her nose. "Watch me." She turned on her heel and pushed out the door, making Lillie scamper after her. She was a paladin. Her duty was to protect the weak and the helpless. Even when they refused her protection.

"Vola," Lillie said.

"We'll just have to take the swamp beast with us," she said, snatching its lead rope. "Maybe Dodson will have some ideas. Though I'm loath to trust anything he comes up with."

Behind her, Lillie squeaked.

Vola sighed and turned. "It's not that bad—" She gasped.

A man had grabbed hold of Lillie, his arm wrapped around her neck as he dragged her down off the step of the temple and across the street.

Vola dumped the swamp monster's lead rope and reached for her sword.

"Don't," the man said. He flicked his other wrist, the one that wasn't wrapped around Lillie's throat, and Vola caught the glint of steel in the moonlight.

Vola gritted her teeth, her stomach clenched. "What do you want?"

"Just her," he said. "My boss wants her alive. So, you just let us leave, and we can all go our separate ways without a fight."

"Your boss?" Vola squinted. The street wasn't well lit here, but she could make out a long nose and a mop of long brown hair. It was the man from the bar. The one who'd been buying Lillie all those drinks she hadn't known what to do with. He'd been stalking her this whole time. "So, Myron had you following us. He's more on top of it than I gave him credit for."

"Who the hell is Myron?" the bounty hunter said. "I work for

Lord Virvalim. He's been chasing this one all over the countryside."

Lillie stiffened, her wide eyes showing white in the dark. Vola's gaze snapped between them. How to pry Lillie away without hurting her?

"You know I'm not going to let you take her," she said.

He sighed like she'd merely stolen the last cupcake out from under him. "You should have just drunk your wine," he said in Lillie's ear. "Then I wouldn't have had to kill your friend here just to get to you."

"Your mistake is assuming she's the one to be afraid of," Lillie said, voice very soft.

Vola had enough time to shield her eyes.

Flames burst along Lillie's body, racing down her arms and legs and sending her hair upward in a wild torrent. Fire exploded out from her, blasting the bounty hunter back into the wall behind them, leaving a blackened outline against the brick.

He screamed as he burned, writhing against the cobbles. It only lasted a few seconds before he was nothing but a pile of ash, but Vola would hear those screams ringing in her ears for a long time to come.

She straightened and cleared her throat.

Lillie's flames sent light along the storefronts, illuminating the whole street until she doused them with a word and the fire retreated under her skin.

Vola blinked, trying to decide if the afterglow was real or just a leftover dazzle in her eyes.

She held her hand out to the wizard and was proud when it didn't shake. "You done?"

"Yes," Lillie said quietly. She took Vola's hand and let her draw her away from the outline on the wall and smear on the cobblestones.

Vola snagged the swamp beast, and they hurried back through the streets toward the Narrows and Dodson's shop.

Her heart still hammered in her chest, but she kept her expression neutral. Murder was a big no-no in the paladin handbook, but self-defense had a lot more wiggle room. Vola decided to lump immolation of a bounty hunter under self-defense.

"So, his name is Virvalim," Vola said carefully. "The man you're running from."

Lillie's lips went thin and white, and she looked away. "Yes."

Vola waited, but no more seemed forthcoming. "You know you'll have to tell us sometime. If only so we can protect you better."

Lillie jerked her chin up. "I think I just demonstrated I don't need it."

"That's not what I meant."

Lillie swallowed. "I know. I just…I don't want you to think less of me."

"Lillie."

Lillie finally met her eyes for a moment before looking away again. "Someday, Vola. All right? But not today."

Vola would let her keep her secrets for now. Sorrel had her fair share, it seemed. And Talon hadn't told the others about being a girl. Not that they didn't trust each other. But maybe the secrets were harder to share with someone you trusted. Someone whose opinion you cared about.

NINETEEN

Dodson wasn't too happy about hitching his wagon to the swamp monster, but Vola convinced him that this meant he wouldn't have to sacrifice a horse to their cause. Since she couldn't promise the wagon would come back intact, he finally agreed.

Just outside the dry canal, they strapped the swamp beast to a cart full of corpses, and Vola tugged its harness tight.

Lillie stepped up to swing a leg over the back of the wagon and grimaced.

"What's wrong?" Talon said, hauling herself up the side and into the pile of dead. "They're nice and quiet and some of them don't even smell."

"And they're not even moving," Sorrel said, hopping in. The halfling burrowed under the edge of the canvas Dodson used to cover his cargo.

Lillie dipped her toe into the pile. "Right, so this isn't traumatizing at all."

Vola climbed up, making the cart sway. She caught Lillie when she would have pitched over backward, then shifted a few bodies aside so the wizard could lie down along the length of the wagon without actually being buried. Sorrel and Talon disappeared beyond the pile on the other side, and Vola peeked to make sure they weren't visible.

Talon hadn't said anything since their—her—confession earlier. Vola kept telling herself that was because nothing had really changed. Talon was still Talon. Even if she'd been female this whole time and the rest of them hadn't known it. The only thing that was different was that Vola knew it, now. She would have preferred to talk it over quietly with Lillie and Sorrel, too, but Talon hadn't said if either of the other two knew, and Vola wasn't about to blow that secret if not.

"Keep your heads down," Dodson said. "Vidal's men will come collect the shipment and take it back to his headquarters. You just have to stay quiet for the ride."

Vola gave him a look as he pulled the canvas tarp up. "You don't have to worry about us. Just don't tip off his men."

Dodson snorted and yanked the canvas down, cutting them off from the night sky and the torch-lit city behind him.

Vola shifted down to lie beside Lillie, between her and the corpses. She placed her naked blade under her arm carefully. She wanted it close enough to grab but hidden in case anyone decided to check the wagon bed.

The wagon jerked, and they set off.

Vola held her breath most of the way, and not just because of the smell. But no one hailed them or stopped the cart. Either Dodson knew the path to take to avoid the city guards or he was right and no one cared what people hauled after midnight.

The clatter of wheels on the cobbles changed and softened until Vola guessed they'd moved onto packed dirt. From the angle of the wagon bed, they were moving uphill.

"Do you trust him?" Lillie whispered inches from Vola's ear. "Or will he betray us to Myron?"

Vola pursed her lips. "No, I don't trust him," she said. "But I don't think he'll betray us, either. Dodson's only interested in money, and I don't think Myron's thought of bribing people to stop us yet."

The wagon gave a jolt, and they stopped moving. It creaked and swayed as Dodson climbed down.

"Any minute now," he said under his breath beside the wall of the wagon.

It felt like much longer but barely five minutes later, an unfamiliar voice called to Dodson. "You have them?"

"Yeah. You've got my money?"

"Of course," the voice said. It was low and rough and Vola imagined it had seen many years at sea.

"Fine then. Take the bodies."

A hand threw back the edge of the tarp, and Vola froze, trying to look dead and rotting.

"Kind of a motley bunch this time," sea-voice said.

"I'm not paid to make them look pretty," Dodson said. "You want that, you go to a funeral parlor."

The tarp flipped back into place. "And I'm not paid to argue with the contractors. If Mister Vidal doesn't care what kind of bodies he gets, neither do I. See you next week, Dodson."

"See you."

Footsteps led away.

"Shawn, get the reins. I want to be back in time to put my money on Harold beating the crap out of Joon."

"You're risking everything on Harold?" another voice said. This one younger and higher than sea-voice. "He can't even tie his own — Yeaagh, what is that thing?"

"A horse?"

"No, it ain't. Look, it has scales. And its nose is dripping."

"Who cares what you call it? It's pulling the wagon, isn't it? Makes it a horse."

"I'm not getting near that thing."

"Just get up and drive. What do you think Mister Vidal is paying you for?"

"No, it just hissed at me. Did you hear it hiss at me?"

"It's attached to the wagon; it can't do anything to you. Look see, you just climb up like this and sit here where it can't reach."

The wagon swayed.

"Nuh-uh. Look at its neck. It could twist itself all around while I climbed up and get me in the—"

"You want to walk back, then? Over all those traps and barriers? I heard Mister Vidal's updated a few of them. He really doesn't want anyone to get in to steal his research."

The other voice grumbled and finally, a weight hauled itself over the back of the wagon and someone walked across the tarp-covered corpses to swing themselves over to the wagon bench.

"Sissy," the first voice said with a snort.

They started moving again, and Vola felt Lillie jerk next to her. After a second, she realized the wizard was smothering laughter.

After a while, the wheels thumped up onto a raised road and they trundled along that for a few miles. Something tingled over Vola's skin, making the hair along her arms stand up, and she flinched.

"Magic," Lillie breathed in her ear. "But the barrier let us through. They must have some sort of passkey."

They lurched to a stop, and Vola held her breath while the drivers paused. She shifted her hand to her sword hilt as quietly as she could.

"Unhitch the horse," the first voice said.

"There's no way it's a horse. I swear its eyes are glowing."

"Just unhitch it. Maybe Mister Vidal would like another dead body for his collection."

"He doesn't do animals," the younger voice grumbled. "Says they aren't what his boss is looking for."

"Then kill it and toss it in the woods. But whatever you do, stop whining."

The wagon shifted. "Fine, fine. Do you have a blade—Aaahhgh!"

"What's wrong?"

"It bit me. Oh my gods, I'm bleeding."

"Hold still, you sis—Holy fuck. It ate your finger."

"What? It what? Kill the godsdamned thing."

"Gladly, get behind me."

There was the shing of a blade being drawn, then an ominous hiss.

Someone screamed, and the wagon jerked again. Lillie clutched Vola's hand.

"Get it—"

"No, you get it."

"Just let it go die in the wilderness. Maybe something bigger and meaner will eat it.

The voices came closer around the end of the wagon, and Vola stiffened.

"You really want there to be something out there bigger and meaner than that?"

"Well, bigger, at least."

The tarp went back, and Vola kicked both feet at the nearest startled face.

A man went stumbling back, clutching his bloodied nose. The boy next to him gazed up at her with a face gone pale while he clutched his bleeding hand.

"Sorrel!" Vola called.

Without question, Sorrel leaped from the other side of the wagon, whipped around to smack the boy in the stomach with her staff, and then whumped him on the chest with her open palm.

The boy went down with a sigh.

Talon went for the man, who'd just managed to catch himself. She swept his feet out from under him and leveled her blade at his throat.

"Don't move," she growled.

Gruff appeared out of the darkness and slunk toward the man.

"Wolves and lizard beasts," the man said, then spat out blood. "I'm quitting. Mister Vidal is going to fire me, anyway."

"Probably a wise decision," Lillie said from the wagon. She tried to climb over the high side, slipped, and tumbled down to land on her feet. "Should we trust him to actually leave?" she asked Vola.

"Tie them up." Vola knelt to check on the boy. "Somewhere Myron won't find them. We'll come back for them when we're done." The boy's pulse beat strong against her fingertips. "Nice work," she told Sorrel.

"Stun strike," the monk said, leaning on her staff. "Kind of like what Fang did but not as lethal."

Vola cast a glance at the swamp monster which lingered near the tree line. A wide road stretched through the forest beside it.

She reached down to stretch out the boy's hand and winced. Then she blew out her breath. She hated to waste any healing this early on, but it wasn't the boy's fault he'd lost a finger. She could at least stop the bleeding for him.

She closed her eyes and put her hands on his. "Lady bless."

White light seared the night even behind her eyelids, and she bent over double in pain. Her hand ached so bad it curled in response. She'd never tried to heal a missing limb before and hadn't really considered whether she should. She blinked watering eyes and extended her fingers. One, two, three, four, five. They were all there even if it felt like she'd cut one off.

She turned the boy's hand over and sucked in a breath. She'd expected to see new skin covering the stump, but instead another finger stood out from the boy's knuckle.

One, two, three, four, five. Five fingers. Huh. And Cleavah's power still rolled gold and shining inside her. She'd have plenty as the night went on. Provided this didn't turn into a bloodbath.

Talon knelt to tie up their prisoners while the man gaped at Vola. "Why'd you do that?"

"I'm not in the habit of maiming children." She flexed her fingers. The ache was still there but fading. She'd be able to hold her sword in a minute. "What's he doing working for a necromancer, anyway?"

The man shrugged. "He's seventeen. You've gotta earn a living somehow. Mister Vidal's money is as good as anyone else's down in the city."

Vola finally took a chance to look around. They crouched outside a sprawling stone building that stood on a ridge above the city. Thick walls, sturdy doors, no windows. It would look like a fortress except it didn't have any battlements or weaponry.

"What is this place?" Lillie asked.

"Research facility," the man responded. "For the kingdom's wizards. They came up with new spells and techniques here until they lost their funding. Mister Vidal took over the abandoned building last year."

Vola turned back to the man. "Any idea what we can expect inside? Does he have more guards like you?"

The man scoffed. "We're not guards. We just handle the deliveries. There are five of us living. And we stay here on this side of the facility. The rest is for…is for them." He gestured his bound hands toward the wagonload of corpses.

"Would the rest of the living be willing to leave if we asked them?" Sorrel said. "This might get messy."

The man shrugged. "Probably not. We each need the money

for different reasons. Harold's got a sick kid. Joon wants to go to school to become a wizard. You know how it is."

"We know how it is," Vola agreed, thinking of her echoing purse. "We'll try not to kill them on our way to Myron."

"Fair enough. Inside, if you go right instead of left, you'll get to the undead instead of the living. If you'd like to avoid fighting them at all."

"Thanks," Vola said. "Now we're going to hide you in the bushes, okay?"

"Fine, fine. It'll be comfy. Just don't leave us anywhere near that monster." He glared at the swamp beast. Talon was already approaching it with her hands out.

"We won't," Vola said.

They settled the delivery man and boy far enough away from the door that no one would stumble over them, and they tethered the swamp monster far on the other side.

Vola gazed up at the door. "This is it," she said. "Rilla's in here somewhere."

"And Maxim's Warhammer," Sorrel said.

"Everyone ready?" Vola surveyed them. Sorrel stared at the door, lips tight. Lillie bit her lip but nodded. Talon's hood jerked, but then she nodded, too.

The door opened with the key the man had given them and they slipped inside. A long hallway stretched to either side of them.

Vola glanced at her party and shrugged. "Right, he said."

"So he did," Lillie said.

"Talon, scout ahead. Sorrel, take point. I'll take the rear."

Talon disappeared down the corridor, using the shadows between torch sconces to move unseen. Gruff padded after her.

The rest of them followed, slowly. Vola couldn't exactly sneak. She jingled too much. But she placed each foot carefully. There was no reason to alert Myron before they were ready. Unrelieved stone walls sent echoes back at alarming volumes. There weren't even any cracks to show where the stones had been fitted together.

Talon reappeared. "There's a room ahead. Full of bodies. Four are animated."

"The rest are just lying there?" Vola said.

Talon nodded. "Do we go ahead?"

Vola exchanged a look with Sorrel and shrugged. "There's only four. I say we go for it. If we take them out quiet, then we can keep sneaking."

"But Myron's a necromancer," Lillie said. "Four bodies will turn into more."

"Not unless he's there," Talon said. "And he's not if we hurry."

"Sounds good to me," Sorrel said.

They proceeded, and Talon gestured them through a door at the end of the hall.

They rushed through.

Four zombies, just like Talon had said. And piles and piles of dead bodies. This must have been where Myron stored them before he needed them for…whatever he was doing.

"Easy peasy," Sorrel said. Then she leaped forward, clearing the nearest pile by at least three feet. She landed on the far most zombie and whacked it on the head with her staff.

"Okay, then," Vola said. "Charge?"

She fit actions to words and charged for the nearest zombie as Lillie sent a stream of fire around her.

The zombie's mouth yawned wide as it screamed and went down under her sword, and the one next to it burst into flames. Arrows sprouted from the zombie on Vola's left.

"See?" Sorrel said, turning with a grin. "Easy enou—"

A moaning interrupted her, and the whole room shuddered.

"What was that?" Vola said, planting her feet and pulling her shield forward onto her arm.

"I don't—" Lillie started. Then she gasped. "Oh no."

"What oh no?"

"There's magic in the walls," she said. "It's—"

The bodies stirred.

"Oh no," Vola said.

"I already covered that," Lillie snapped.

Vola tried bashing a zombie before it had a chance to stand. Its legs went out from under it, but that didn't keep any of the other fifty from rising and shuffling forward.

The party closed in around each other, back to back. Lillie shot a fireball into the ground at their feet, warping the flames around them. The first line of zombies fell. The rest kept coming.

"It's a horde of undead," Sorrel said. "Of course, he has a horde of undead. Why wouldn't he? He's a necromancer."

"The man outside sent us in here," Talon said. "He knew we'd be outnumbered."

"Or he thought we might have been prepared for this," Lillie said. "Considering we thought it was a good idea to waltz into a necromancer's stronghold."

Vola stepped forward, swept her blade around to cut down three more zombies, then skipped back into place to keep her friends shielded.

"We *were* prepared," Sorrel said. "For Myron."

Lillie let the ranks get closer, then let loose another fireball.

"How many more of those do you have left?" Vola asked.

Lillie's lips twisted as she watched the inexorable press of the undead creep closer. "Not enough. Not if we haven't even found Myron, yet."

"Shouldn't there be some kind of limit to how many he can call at once?" Vola said. "*You* only have so many fireballs. I figured he'd have to be here to raise them."

Sorrel spun, kicking back another three. Vola cut down four.

Their remains shuddered and the bodies stood again, this time minus a few limbs.

"The facility itself is funneling magic into them," Lillie said. "It's a fascinating use of architecture—"

"Lillie," the other three shouted in unison.

"Oh, fine. It's an automated system. It will just keep animating them over and over again until either the intruders are dead or they lie in so many pieces they can't stand anymore. You can guess which one will come first."

"Fine with me," Sorrel said. "Come on!"

Talon's hood whipped around, and she seemed to focus on something. "Vola, can you clear a path to the wall?"

Vola glanced the way she indicated. "Maybe together with you."

"Sorrel, guard our backs. Lillie, take the flanks. I have an idea."

"Is the idea to kill as many of these suckers as possible before we die?" Sorrel said, wading into the fray, staff flying. "Because I like that idea."

Vola put her shoulder down and used her shield to barrel her way ahead. She flung aside a body already mangled beyond recognition. "I think the idea is to live."

Talon shot past her, knives out. There was a growl and a bark, and Gruff cut across their path, dragging another zombie. Its body acted like a broom, sweeping aside several more of the undead.

"Forward," Vola called, moving into the cleared space and preparing another push. Lillie fell in behind her, fire wreathing her hands, and Sorrel skipped along, whacking the dead fingers which reached for them.

Talon knelt against the wall, examining the grate set into the stone near the floor.

Vola caught on and turned to guard the ranger while Talon

fiddled with the fittings. She kept her breathing even, throttling down the panic her body insisted she should be feeling.

She caught a zombie across the face with her shield and ran another one through. That didn't work as well as she'd hoped. It pushed itself further up her sword, reaching with blackened cracked fingernails.

Vola's sword burst into flames, and the zombie threw up its arms. It screamed and slid off the end of her blade.

"Thanks," Vola said to Lillie.

"I didn't even know if that would work," Lillie said.

Talon got the grate open with a clang and she gestured Lillie inside.

"Go," Vola said.

The wizard dove inside without hesitation.

"Sorrel!"

Sorrel glanced over her shoulder, her staff holding back a half-rotten zombie. Her face hardened. "We're so close," she said. "Maxim's Warhammer is here. We just need to push through."

"This isn't defeat," Vola said. "This is strategic retreat."

She grabbed the back of Sorrel's tunic and ducked into the hole in the wall, dragging the halfling along, too.

Talon followed, letting the grate close behind her with a bang. The zombies piled against it, effectively blocking them in.

"It opens outward. Unless they smarten up and get everyone to back up, they'll just keep pushing it closed," Talon said.

"Will Gruff be okay out there?" Vola said.

"I would never have been able to get him in here. He doesn't like tight spaces. He'll just slip away and find another way to join us wherever we get to."

"I think we're lucky enough that we all fit," Lillie said, further down the stone tunnel. "This is actually rather cozy."

"Cozy for who?" Vola grumbled, folded over on herself so she fit in the tight shaft.

Sorrel tugged herself out of Vola's grasp. "We could have taken them," Sorrel said. She fit quite nicely. She didn't have to duck in order to sit in the tunnel.

"No, we couldn't," Vola said. "We might be ready for Myron, but I wasn't expecting a legion of undead he could command from afar. This is smarter. We're looking for Rilla and the necromancer. Nothing says we have to kill everything in our path."

"That's gotta be the first time an orc has ever said that," Sorrel huffed, but she uncrossed her arms and pulled her staff so it wouldn't catch on the walls or floor as they crawled.

"Half-orc," Talon said.

TWENTY

THE OTHERS all crawled on their hands and knees, Sorrel having the easiest time of it, obviously. But Vola had to shimmy through the vents on her elbows, and her sword and shield kept getting stuck on the ceiling until she ripped them from her back and pushed them ahead of her.

Thirty minutes in, she bashed her head on a low joint for the fifth time and growled an expletive. There was a bang that could have been a flash of lightning but it ricocheted off the stone walls of the tunnel and zipped around a corner and out of sight.

Lillie yelped.

"Sorry," Vola said.

"I thought we were trying to be quiet?" Sorrel said.

"We are." Vola rubbed her forehead and tried to take some calming breaths, but it was hard to convince herself that the walls weren't creeping in on her, pressing into her back and shoulders. "Lillie, have you seen anything promising yet?"

Vola really didn't like sending the wizard through first. They hadn't encountered any traps in the vents yet, but that didn't mean Myron hadn't thought to put any there at all. But Lillie had been the one to duck in first, then Vola, then Sorrel, then Talon. And Vola was wedged too tightly to squeeze past anyone which meant that was the order they had to stay in.

Lillie's butt thumped the floor, and she shimmied around to lean against the side of the vent. She dragged her notebook around so Vola could see the rough map sketched out on the page, and she realized that's why they'd been taking so long.

"Just storerooms and empty laboratories so far," Lillie said. "But I think I'm getting a feel for the shape of this place."

"Oh, I'm so glad," Vola snapped. "Is it a rhombus? Or a trapezoid? How about a parallelogram?"

Lillie leveled a look at her, and Vola ducked her head. "Sorry. I'm not a fan of being stuck in a vent."

There was a snuffling near Vola's ear, and she turned to find a wet snout pressed against a grate just like the one they'd used to get in here.

"Oh. Hey, Gruff."

Gruff snorted, then sat on his haunches and raised his snout to howl.

"Aw, crap. Talon?"

"I told you, he doesn't like cities. And he really doesn't like it if he can smell me and still can't get to me."

"Well, can you calm him down? He's going to blow everything."

"Gruff," Talon barked, and it rang against the narrow walls.

Gruff paused for a second. Then kept howling, long and mournful.

"He's going to get us all killed," Sorrel groaned.

"Gruff, stop that," Talon said. "Go on. I'll find you soon. Go. Go hunting."

Gruff's wail cut short with a disgruntled grumble. He snorted again and then disappeared past the grate and down the hall, leaving blissful silence in his wake.

Vola ducked her head and blew out her breath.

"Guys, listen," Sorrel said from beyond Vola's backside.

Vola paused.

Bells pealed over their heads, distant but definitely somewhere in the building.

"Did Myron raise the alarm?" Talon said.

"Maybe he wondered what a wolf was doing in his stronghold and put the pieces together," Vola snapped.

"Or maybe he found the zombies piled against the grate," Talon said.

Another sound joined the fray, duller but much closer. Footsteps trudged nearby. A lot of footsteps. Along with some shuffling and moaning.

"The zombies are on the move," Sorrel whispered.

"Yeah, but where to?" Vola said. "I don't see them yet."

Lillie worked herself around until she was facing forward and kept crawling. This time she stopped beside another metal grate and waved Vola forward.

Vola squeezed up behind her and peered through the bars.

Hundreds of feet marched just inches from their noses. Some wore ragged boots, others trailed moldering grave wrappings.

"I don't think they're looking for us," Lillie whispered. "They're not headed in the right direction. They're looking for someone else."

"Rilla?" Vola said.

"Maybe she was the one who set off the alarm, not Gruff."

"We should follow them," Sorrel said.

Vola shook her head. "No, we should get ahead of them. Get to the princess first."

Lillie held out her notebook. "Look, they're headed up that main passage. But the vents all cut across here. They don't follow the main line; they branch every which way. We can head them off and find whatever they're headed for first." She pointed to her squiggles as if they meant something.

Vola just gestured her on. "Go. I imagine we'll have to be quick."

Vola's shoulders burned as she crawled after Lillie through the tunnels. The vent angled up, steeply, and she took the moment to sit almost upright before hurrying to catch up to the wizard.

"Here," Lillie said, and something in her voice made Vola scramble to her side. "You'll want to see this. This is who they're headed for. And they'll find her soon."

"Is it Rilla?"

Vola crept up beside Lillie to peer through the grate, and her breath left her lungs with a whoosh.

Wide windows lined the wall opposite them, looking out onto a hallway. But between them and the glass under an empty table huddled three boys between fifteen and twenty. Young enough to be stupid and old enough to be clever about it.

And standing in front of them was a woman with golden skin and masses of dark hair curling down her shoulders and back. Cleavah's devotee.

"Crap," Vola said, deliberately trading the word she'd been thinking for something weaker. "She must have followed us here after I specifically told her not to."

Lillie bit her lip and glanced up as footsteps thundered down the passage. "They'll be here any minute, Vola."

And the devotee stood there in the room with a small smile tweaking her lips. As if inviting guests in from the cold.

Vola growled. "I can't leave her. Does this thing open from this side?"

The grate didn't budge when Vola tugged on it. She'd call back to Talon to see if the ranger could figure out how to open it from the inside, but it would take them forever to shuffle back up the tunnel so Talon could line up. Instead, Vola pushed Lillie ahead a few feet, then twisted inside the vent and kicked at the grate.

It gave way with a screech.

Vola stuck her feet through and dropped a couple of feet to the floor. This vent was almost halfway up the wall.

Cleavah's devotee glanced up at her with a warm grin. "Vola, right on time."

The boys blinked up at the armored half-orc with wide eyes.

"Mistress, what are you doing here?" Vola asked, retrieving her sword and shield from the floor as Lillie's butt shimmied into view through the grate.

"What do you think?" the devotee said. "I'm doing exactly what I said I would. Myron had them trapped here."

"The undead are coming." Vola strode to the nearest window. She peered around the corner. The zombie army was just coming into view.

"Yes, I know. Hello again, Lillie," the devotee said, holding out a hand to the wizard. Behind Lillie, Sorrel flipped out of the vent and landed on her feet. Talon slithered down the wall.

"And Talon and Sorrel. I'm so pleased to meet you at last."

"Talon, block the door," Vola called. "Lillie and Sorrel take care of the windows." She turned to the devotee. "Do you have any of that Broken Grace paste to keep them out?"

The devotee's plump lips pulled in a rueful smile. "I'm afraid it wouldn't hold them indefinitely. Not with so many. Once they start to pile up, they'll be able to walk right over their friends."

Lillie stepped up to the window and examined the edges. Her face blanched as the zombies outside caught sight of her and threw themselves at the glass. "Vola, this won't work. They'll just come right through."

The devotee handed Vola two vials, and Vola wasted no time tossing them to the others. "Here. Mistress, you should get out of here."

The devotee spread her hands, indicating the boys behind her. "Would you have me leave them?"

Vola speared her hands through her hair. "No, of course not. Take them through the vents. If we go now, we might all get out. If not…I'll…I'll hold off the dead here. For as long as I can."

Sorrel and Lillie shot alarmed glances at each other, but they didn't protest. It was too late now, anyway.

The devotee stepped up to Vola and put her palm to Vola's cheek. "Admirable. But stupid. You still don't know who I am, do you, Vola?"

Vola opened her mouth to argue, but the devotee was right. She didn't even know the woman's name to plead with her to go. Why had she never thought to ask her name?

Talon popped the cork on her vial and smeared the door's threshold and posts with it. The door thumped as zombies ran up against it.

Sorrel and Lillie did the same with the windows, smearing the blue paint along the edges. Sorrel yelped when the glass cracked.

Vola needed to concentrate on the looming threat, but something kept drawing her gaze back to the devotee. A niggling thought wormed its way through her mind that she was missing something. Something important.

"Mistress, why have I never asked your name?" Vola said, eyes narrowed. Something about the way the devotee was looking at her made bells go off in Vola's head. Like Henri used to when Vola was too thick to understand a lesson the first time. "That's not like me."

"I wanted you to recognize me on your own," the devotee said.

And now Vola heard the rush of wind in her voice. And the short, sharp shing of a blade being drawn. Vola knew that voice. Knew it so well she'd followed it through fire and swamp and down a long, lonely road that had ended with good friends who watched her back.

It was the same voice that had called her out of loneliness in the academy chapel. The same voice that answered when she healed. The same voice that had been missing for the last week. Because Vola hadn't asked for her help.

She didn't glow here in this abandoned room deep in Myron's lair, but Vola recognized her finally, anyway. Recognized her strength, her stubbornness, her kindness.

Vola dropped to one knee. "Lady."

"Vola, this isn't the time," Sorrel yelled. The door buckled under the weight of the undead. Sorrel threw herself at it, followed by Talon.

Vola gulped, glancing at them. "Lady, please, I can't protect you here."

Cleavah shook her head and reached to pull Vola to her feet. "Why are you so desperate to defend me, Vola?"

"I'm a paladin—"

"That is why I chose you, yes. But why defend *me*?"

Vola's chest heaved as she faced the thoughts tumbling through her head. She had to protect the weak and the helpless. And Cleavah couldn't even defend herself from vandals.

She hung her head.

Cleavah nodded. "Because you still don't know. Who. I. Am."

Who she was? Vola knew exactly who she was. Cleavah. Mother of sharp implements. Laughingstock of morons and savior of children and families. Goddess.

Oh.

Cleavah waited, face serene as the undead crashed against the door and the windows creaked and cracked.

Either she was a goddess or she wasn't. Either she was someone to be protected or she was Vola's source of power. Vola couldn't keep seeing her as one when she was so clearly the other.

Just because Cleavah chose not to defend herself that didn't mean she couldn't.

"Fall back," Vola told the others, voice quiet.

"What?" Sorrel cried.

Talon and Lillie stared.

"Fall back." Vola raised her head. "Trust me. I trust her."

"Yes," Cleavah said. "Now you do."

Vola didn't take her eyes off her goddess. Somewhere behind her, Sorrel heaved a giant sigh. Then she darted past to stand behind Cleavah and Vola. Lillie and Talon hurried to follow.

As soon as the others stepped behind Vola and Cleavah and the zombies doubled their pounding on the door, Cleavah folded Vola in her arms.

And waited.

As great as divinity was, Lesser Virtues could only use their powers through their followers. And Vola had been denying her that opportunity.

"Lady protect us," Vola whispered.

Light seared Vola's eyes just before she squeezed them shut. Behind her, glass shattered, but the sound was lost in a tremendous roar.

Vola's arms tightened around Cleavah, and she sucked in a breath as waves of heat washed over her, like standing too close to the sun, but she didn't dare pull away.

As the heat receded, Vola's skin tightened and tingled, sending goosebumps racing up and down her arms. Like Lillie's flames which bent around her friends, Vola felt like she stood in the middle of the furnace but nothing had touched her, even leaving her armor cool to the touch.

Vola blinked as Cleavah removed her arms and stepped back.

Big splotches of black obscured her vision for a second before she finally was able to clear them and glance around. The others all huddled on the floor, breathing but stunned. The boys still had their eyes squinched shut.

Vola spun. Broken glass littered the floor, mingling with ash bleached a pure white.

She stepped to the edge of the destruction and stooped to touch the ash. "Are they all gone?"

"Just the ones in this corridor. I am…only allowed to do so much through my followers. I'm only a minor goddess, after all." She gave Vola pointed smile and Vola flinched.

"There is nothing minor about you, lady," Vola said and meant it.

"No, but there are politics at play here." The goddess's eyes flicked upward for a split second before she stepped forward and touched Vola's chest.

The emblem she always wore but kept tucked hidden under her chain mail swung free and flashed in the light. A little fish knife hung on a chain.

"For remembrance," Cleavah said.

Vola's cheeks stung. "I won't forget now, my lady." And it wasn't just for remembrance. It was her link, her physical connection to Cleavah as well.

"See that you don't."

The others stirred.

"Lady, do you know where Rilla is?" Vola said.

Cleavah's expression darkened, her brows drawing down. "I do not. And it worries me I cannot see her. There is divine magic at work here. Greater than my own."

"The Warhammer," Sorrel said with a groan and pulled herself to her feet. She reached to help Lillie. Vola stepped to give Talon a hand. "I don't know how he's able to abuse its power like this. It shouldn't obey him."

"The necromancy corrupts it, I'm sure. Not a permanent change, but it is keeping my sight clouded." Cleavah glanced at them, then back to Vola. "Find her, Vola."

She reached to gather the three boys into her arms and disappeared in another flash of light.

"Soo," Sorrel said. "That was your goddess."

"Yes." Vola still stared at the empty space where she'd been.

Sorrel sighed. "I wish Maxim would talk to me"

"You…didn't recognize her?" Lillie said.

Vola's lips thinned. "She's never let me see her before. I guess because I was too busy underestimating her."

"Why would she reveal herself now?" Talon said. "To prove herself to you?"

Vola straightened and jerked her chin up. "No. She was just being herself. Exactly as she's always been. This was just the first time I let myself see who she really is."

TWENTY-ONE

"I cannot believe we're back in the vents." Vola scootched along the too-small space.

Lillie crawled in front again since she was the one with the map and the ability to use it.

"So far this is the safest route through this place," Talon said. "Why mess with something that's working?"

"Lillie, tell me you have some idea of where to look," Vola said, hanging her head between her aching shoulder blades.

Lillie stopped and flipped through her notebook again, chewing her lip. "I have been looking, Vola. She's not in any of the laboratories like Cleavah was. That seems like the most likely place to keep a prisoner. Unless he's holding her somewhere else. Somewhere closer to his work."

"Where else do we have to look?"

"There are only a couple of options left," Lillie said. "Just ahead is what I believe to be the main room of the facility. All the vents lead there. If she's not there, we'll have to see if we can check Myron's records."

"Lead on, then." And hopefully the princess would be in this main room. Vola wouldn't be in any shape to swing her sword if she had to do much more crawling.

About a hundred feet more and Lillie stopped beside another grate. She waved Vola forward. Behind them, Talon and Sorrel crowded around another grate.

A wide room opened below. This grate was all the way up the wall, near the ceiling, so they had a bird's-eye view of the center of the facility.

Myron stood in the middle of a large open room, fiddling with some brass valves that led into a tank glowing green and eerie in the darkness of the facility. One central tube shot out of the tank straight up into the ceiling above.

"What is he doing?" Vola said.

Lillie pointed along the walls. The floor at the edges of the room was raised, creating small platforms. Directly below their grate, a dead body was tied to a bed of goo on the nearest platform. Tubes ran from the body all the way back to Myron's tank.

"Is he trying to reanimate them?" Vola said. Lillie had mentioned he was experimenting with different ways to animate the dead.

"No, look," Lillie whispered. "It's already moving."

True. The corpse writhed under its bindings, splashing little bits of goo onto the raised platform.

Vola grimaced. "What is this, then?"

Lillie's brow furrowed, the green light below reflecting a mixture of horror and fascination on her face. "Are they the spell casters?" she said. "The dead spell casters?"

She bit her lip while squinting at the tank in the center of the room. "Oh my gods. I think he's trying to collect their magic. He's stealing magic from dead people."

"You can do that?"

"No!"

"Shhh," Vola said and covered Lillie's enraged shriek with her hand.

Below them, Myron stirred and looked up, eyes scrunched behind his spectacles.

The group froze, barely breathing until Myron finally shook his head and went back to his work.

Vola pulled her hand away. "Do you see Rilla anywhere?" she whispered.

Lillie shook her head.

"Talon? Sorrel? Do you see her?" Vola called softly back down the tunnel.

"Just Myron and a bunch of dead guys," Sorrel said. "She's not here, boss."

That was Vola's assessment, as well. It wasn't just the corpses in the beds either. Undead minions lined the walls but none of them matched Rilla's description.

"You wanted to check his records, right?" Vola said. "We'll need them to find Rilla if she's not just hanging around out in the open. Maybe you can figure out what he's doing from those, too."

Lillie's mouth pinched as if she was about to argue, then she scooted away from the grate and continued down the vent. Vola and the others followed.

Finally, Lillie stopped beside another grate and tested it for mobility. "It's like the others. Opens from the other side," she whispered.

"Is anyone in there?" Vola asked.

Lillie peered through the bars. "One zombie. But if we make a lot of noise, who knows what else will show up."

Vola ducked her head to check the room. One entrance. And there was a desk against the wall, right under the vent.

"We can risk it," Vola said. "Just be ready if anything comes through the door."

She shimmied one of the axes from her belt and wedged it

between the bars of the grate. Then she threw her weight against it.

The grate screeched, then popped off the wall. Vola wormed her way through the opening and dropped hands first onto the desk.

She turned the fall into a roll just as the sole occupant of the room lurched around to face her. Vola brought her heels down on the zombie's head and it dropped with a soft thud before it could even utter a moan.

She scrambled to the door to check the hallway while the others clambered out of the vent behind her. "We're clear for now. But let's be quick."

"What exactly are we looking for?" Sorrel said, opening a desk drawer and sifting through the contents.

"Anything that might point us to Rilla," Lillie said. "Prisoner manifests, staffing schedules. Anything."

"Dear diary, today I caught a princess snooping around my lair. I shut her up in cell block A with the rest of my unfortunate prisoners, mwahaha." Sorrel said, handing a stack of papers to Vola.

"That would be handy, yes," Lillie said without looking up from the stack she'd appropriated. "I'm going to see if I can find out what Myron is doing with the dead spell casters."

Vola tried to help. She went through the stack Sorrel had given her and squinted at the squiggly words until she forced them to make sense. But anything that looked remotely helpful she handed to Sorrel and Talon. Anything that looked personal she handed to Lillie.

"You know, he's actually pretty organized," Sorrel said, as she neared the end of her stack of papers.

"You have to be as a researcher," Lillie said absently. "You waste your time and funding if you retrace your steps by accident.

Most of the time you want to discover new things, not new ways to do the old."

"Who do you suppose is funding Myron?" Sorrel said.

"Whoever wants the power of dead spell casters." Lillie held up her papers. "He's definitely siphoning magical power from them into tanks, like those in the main room. It should be impossible. Once you're dead, you're dead, and your magic is dead, too."

"But dead is a relative term to a necromancer," Sorrel said.

"If he can make bodies walk, maybe he can make bodies give up their magic, too," Talon said.

Vola's brow furrowed. "But then what does he do with it? What does he want all that power for?"

"I don't know that he does," Lillie said, smoothing out a document on her knee. "He's shipping the tanks somewhere. I don't think he's keeping any of the power. These are the manifests."

"Who's it going to?" Sorrel said. "His boss?"

Lillie froze, eyes on the page in front of her. "Huh."

"What?" Vola said.

"Well, that's…odd. This shipping address. It's the same drop-off spot as the slaver we tracked from Water's Edge."

They all blinked at her.

"That dock where shady people rented shady storage for shady dealings?" Sorrel said.

"Not just the same dock." Lillie held up the page. "This is the same number. It's the same man who was going to collect those slaves from Lord Arthorel."

"So, not only does he want living people," Talon said. "He wants magic from the dead, too."

Vola crumpled the edge of the paper in her hands as she thought. "Is the princess a spellcaster?" she asked quietly.

Lillie froze, and then her hands crept to her cheeks. "Oh. Oh no. Maybe? There's nothing official about it. But very little about the Dagger Throne is made official."

"Stop freaking out before you have to," Sorrel said. She held up a page. "As I said, he's super organized. Here's his list of live prisoners. Not very many. Just those boys he caught snooping around. Good news is, he didn't kill them. Bad news is, Rilla's not on the list." She held up another piece of paper. This one was folded with several others. "Here's his list of test subjects. Every dead body he's used in his lab with a detailed description. He didn't bother with names. Good news is according to the description James gave us, she's not on this list either. Bad news is—"

"Bad news is she's not on any of the lists," Vola finished for her. "She's not here."

Lillie met her eyes. "She's not here."

Vola's heart sank to her stomach and knotted there. They'd been so sure they were following the right lead. Myron had been the last one to see Rilla alive. Myron had flipped out about her stealing his research. But if she wasn't here in Myron's lab, then where else could she be?

Cleavah herself hadn't been able to find her. Something had kept the goddess from seeing the princess.

Vola sifted through the racing thoughts and pulled out the ones that needed addressing right now. Before any other undead minions came to investigate the noise in Myron's office.

"All right," she said. "So, Rilla's not here. We've been tracking down the wrong lead. Not a big deal, we'll just backtrack. But the thing is, is it worth it to go after Myron now if the princess isn't here to be rescued?"

"He is a necromancer," Lillie said. "He should be arrested, anyway."

"By us?" Vola said. "When he's got hordes of dead bodies just waiting to be raised against us?"

"We should leave," Talon said. "Come back with the city guard. They can't ignore this on their doorstep. And with more numbers, we have a better chance."

"But he's got Maxim's Warhammer," Sorrel said. "We can't leave it with him."

"We'll come back," Vola started, but Sorrel stood, tiny fists clenching and unclenching.

"By then the monks will have gotten here. They'll get to it first."

"Wouldn't that be better than Myron running off with it again?" Lillie asked, head tilted. "Then it would at least be with your order."

"No!" Sorrel cried.

Talon glanced at the door and stood to listen at the crack.

Vola stood, too. "Then we can get it back from them," she said. "Sorrel, we're not abandoning this, all right? We're just retreating. We walked in here thinking we'd knock out a few zombies, kill a necromancer, and save a princess, but it won't be that easy. We'll come back. I promise."

"You don't understand," Sorrel said.

"You're right, we don't." Lillie stood as well. "Please, explain it to us so we do. Why is it so bad if your order gets the staff? They're not very nice, I agree. And I would like nothing more than to rub their faces in their defeat. But why is it worth risking your life?"

Sorrel's gaze flicked from Vola's face to Lillie's to Talon's and back again. Finally, she rubbed her eyes with her palms and paced to the wall with the vent and back again.

"The staff is just part of Maxim's Warhammer. The haft. Tallah already has the other part."

Vola nodded. "So, if she gets the haft, she'll have a complete divine weapon."

"Yes. And she shouldn't. I know no one believes me, but..."

"There's nothing to believe or disbelieve, yet," Lillie said. "We don't know anything."

Sorrel's mouth fell open, and she snapped it shut. Then she

gave them a weak grin. "I didn't mean you. Look, the old abbot, Father Naemon, he knew he was dying. He set a task for us. He said whoever could retrieve the head of Maxim's Warhammer from the catacombs below the monastery would become the next abbot or abbess. The next leader of the monastery.

"It was hidden there by Jodin Battlecalled. The founder of our order. It was all a big game at first. A way to test our skills. But we swore to honor his wishes. So there wouldn't be any infighting. I think he knew something was coming. Something we'd need good leadership and a divine weapon to fight."

"What happened?"

"We went down into the catacombs and when we came out, Tallah was the new abbess," Sorrel said in a flat voice.

"That's it?" Vola said.

"What else is there to say?"

"I don't know. Your god values strength and loyalty. I don't think you'd abandon your monastery or your family without a really good reason."

"You're right, he values loyalty. Something happened down there that made me think Tallah shouldn't be the one to wield any power. Let alone Maxim's. I tried to tell the others, and it made me an oathbreaker."

Sorrel stared at Vola, her gaze daring her to say anything. Vola kept silent. She'd known this. It didn't change anything.

"Why won't you tell us what happened?" Lillie said gently.

"Because it shouldn't matter," Vola said, holding Sorrel's gaze. "Maxim values loyalty. If Sorrel thought it was important enough to break that oath, then it was important enough to break that oath. And that's all we need to know."

Sorrel went red, and her mouth dropped open. But when she glanced at Lillie, Lillie just bit her lip and nodded to Vola. Talon hadn't moved from the door, but her hood ducked in a nod as well.

"We get it, Sorrel," Vola said. "We trust you. We trust this is important. Now trust us. We can't do this, yet. What good is breaking your oath to do the right thing if you die trying to get the rest of the Warhammer? We'll come back. I promise. And if Tallah has it by then, we'll get it back from her. No matter the cost."

Finally, finally, Sorrel let her gaze drop. "All right," she said, the words coming out on a sigh. "All right. Let's go get some help then."

TWENTY-TWO

VOLA KNEW where they were going now, and she took point back through the vents toward the front door where they'd come in. Lillie predicted they'd even be able to go around the initial storeroom with all the awakened undead and avoid a confrontation altogether.

Sorrel crawled behind them all, head down and silent. She'd agreed to retreat, but she grumbled under her breath at every intersection that took them further from Myron.

They came to an intersection Vola hadn't been expecting, and she glanced over her shoulder at Lillie. "Which way?"

"Right?"

"Are you sure? You don't sound sure."

"Look, half of this map is guesswork. The other half is smudged. It's dark and I'm tired and—"

Vola went right. The hallway that she could see through the grate seemed familiar, but all the hallways looked the same, so that was hardly helpful.

They crawled on for thirty more yards, and Vola ducked to glance out another grate and get their bearings.

This couldn't be right. They should be on top of the front door by now. Instead, they faced a long blank hall that ended in a wall and another grate.

Vola squinted. The grate opposite them moved. It swung open silently, and a dark, lithe figure slipped out into the corridor.

"Oh my goddess," Vola breathed as the figure stepped to the head of their hallway and knelt, touching the floor.

"What?" Lillie said behind her. There were murmurs from Talon and Sorrel even further back.

"That's why we haven't found her yet," Vola thought, kicking herself mentally. "She wasn't caught. She was hiding. Just like us."

"Who?" Lillie asked with an edge that said she was done waiting.

"What was Rilla's description again? Dark with curly black hair, last wearing a green and gold jacket?"

"That was it."

The figure stood and turned enough that the light lit up her features. She had a mass of black curls rising around her head and her skin was as dark as an ebony blade. She wore a dark green, leather jacket with dull gold highlights that was more armor than clothing. Just like her description. Although James had failed to mention the rows of knives gleaming along her belt.

Lillie craned around Vola's bulk to see through the grate. "It's her. That's the princess of the Dagger Throne."

"Guys," Sorrel called softly from behind them. "If that's our princess, we've got trouble."

Sorrel and Talon peered out another grate that let out on a nearby hallway. The sound of shuffling footsteps carried even to Vola in the lead.

"Oh, poop," Vola said, unwilling to chance a lightning strike in the vents again.

The princess knelt at the intersection of the hall, directly in the path of the zombies.

A wet snuffle made Vola jump and a dark shape came between them and the view.

"No, Gruff," Vola said desperately. "No, not now. Not here."

He threw back his head and howled.

Talon cursed.

Through Gruff's legs, Vola could see the princess spin, eyes darting between the distraught wolf and the hallway where the hordes advanced.

"He's gonna give her away," Sorrel said.

"Welp, this is happening," Vola said and then kicked the grate out.

She tumbled out into the hall in a clatter of armor and weaponry, making Gruff dance out of the way. Lillie shimmied out behind her, slightly more graceful this time.

Vola rushed for the princess, trusting the others to be right behind her. "Rilla," she called. "Rilla, look out."

The princess whirled. "Who—"

"The undead. They're coming; you have to—"

Vola stepped across the edge of a hazy circle where Rilla had knelt earlier. Green light sprang up around her, catching her in midstride. Her boots went out from under her and an invisible hand yanked her into the air by her feet. She swung there, her head three feet from the ground as her sword and shield crashed around her.

Lillie yelped and Sorrel darted around the green light, rolling toward the opening of the next hallway. Another trap sprang up around her, green lines flipping her upside down and fastening her to the ceiling.

"Oh for the love of all that's holy, who the hell are you?" Rilla said, throwing her hands in the air.

Vola twisted around, trying to keep the princess in sight while keeping an eye on the hallways. "We're rescuing you. There's a horde of undead on their way…"

Vola trailed off as she took in the setup. The long unbroken hallways leading to this intersection. The carefully placed traps. The horde shuffling down the corridor straight toward them. The princess standing there with her hands on her hips and a storm in her eyes.

"We walked into your ambush, didn't we?" Vola said. The blood rushed to her head, making it pound. "Oh, fuck."

Lightning cracked to the ground and the first line of zombies coming down the hall fell.

"My thoughts exactly," Rilla said and stepped to the wall. She lifted the grate and stuck one foot inside.

"Wait, Your Highness," Lillie called. She had her hands in the air, gesturing frantically as her eyes moved between Vola and Sorrel. "I can't dispel this."

The undead ambled forward, slow but inexorable. They'd reach Sorrel first, hanging from the ceiling, but the hallway behind Vola rang with the sound of shuffling feet and she'd dropped her weapons.

Talon darted between Sorrel and the horde, raising her bow and sending a stream of arrows into the masses, but unless she had a way of multiplying herself, she'd be overrun in seconds. Gruff darted into their mass and one or two fell with wordless cries as he took their legs out from under them.

Sorrel still held her staff, swinging it through the air upside down, muttering, "Come to me. Come on. Come on. Come on."

The princess froze, half in and half out of the vent. "How do you know who I—" She shook her head. Then she glanced between Vola and Sorrel and the zombies bearing down on them. She sighed. "Fuck my life."

Then she stepped back into the corridor.

The first wave of undead reached Talon and Sorrel, and Talon threw away her bow in favor of her knives. Sorrel laid about her with her staff, having much easier access to bash heads than she normally did. She couldn't move her feet, which were stuck to the ceiling, but she seemed to be having great fun poking at zombies' eyes.

"Lillie, get behind me," Vola called, trying to twist around to see the enemy coming down her hallway.

Lillie didn't budge. "Don't be ridiculous. You can't protect me while you're hanging upside down without your sword," she snapped.

"I'm damn sure gonna try."

"Oh, don't be so dramatic," Rilla said, stepping up next to Vola. She made a complicated gesture, and Vola fell to the ground with a crash.

She scrambled to her feet, rubbing the back of her head. "Great, now can you do that again, only to them?" Vola pointed to the first ranks of zombies.

Rilla scoffed. "I only have the two I can do at once. I waited for the perfect moment to lure them in."

Vola winced. "Of course. Lillie, did you see what she did? Can you get Sorrel—"

Lillie was already on her way, her hands twisting in an exact copy of Rilla's gesture.

"There's no way she learned to break my spell just by watching—"

Sorrel's feet broke free, and she fell on her enemies with a triumphant cry.

Rilla blinked. "Oh."

"Can you use those, Your Highness?" Vola pointed at the knives lining her belt.

Rilla bristled and suddenly there were three in each hand. "I castrated the last man to ask me that."

"Just making sure. Cause this is happening now."

Vola swept up her sword and shield and met the first rank of zombies head-on.

The undead stalked inexorably forward, but Vola sidestepped and used their confusion to take off three heads before they even knew what was happening. But that wouldn't stop many for very long.

"Lady," Vola whispered. "Do you have anything that could help?"

Vola's sword burst into a clear bright flame just like it had in the graveyard against the wraith. The light made the zombies stagger backward, giving Vola and Rilla a chance to slip in under their guard and hack away at the hordes of bodies.

"What's wrong with them?" Rilla said. "Afraid of a little fire?"

"They don't want to mess with the mother of sharp implements."

The ranks at the back of the hall rippled and surged and a niggling doubt worked its way through Vola's calm.

"What the —"

The zombies parted, falling back to make way for a huge figure that blocked the lantern light.

Vola's eyes widened as she looked up and up. "Uh oh."

"Will the mother of sharp implements impress that thing?" Rilla said, staring up at the giant made up of mounds of flesh. Like a zombie sewn together from the contents of a mass grave.

Vola glanced down at her sword, which seemed to splutter in the face of such undeath.

"Nope," she said.

The flesh monster stepped forward, lumps of different colored skin rippling as it swung a club that was little more than a broken column.

Vola dove to the side and rolled, coming up with her shield raised.

"Lillie," she called. "Any ideas?"

"What?" Lillie, busy with their horde of undead, spun to check on them and blanched. "Oh my."

"What is it?" Vola said.

"Flesh golem—"

The rest of Lillie's answer was cut off as the giant slammed a hand into Vola's shield and pressed down. Vola tried to match it strength for strength until her legs buckled and she cried out.

Rilla darted in and sliced across the monster's wrist, before dancing away again. It bellowed and shook its hand. Vola took the chance to roll out of the way.

Lillie skidded to a stop beside Vola and flung out her hands. Bolts of fire sped toward the thing, but they splashed against its flesh as if it was made of stone and it didn't even notice.

"Go for its eyes," Rilla said.

"Vola," Sorrel called from over her shoulder. "Toss me."

Vola fell to one knee, shield raised as Sorrel launched herself. The halfling landed feet first on the flat of Vola's shield and with a heave, Vola tossed her into the air.

The monk flew in a perfect arc, staff poised, and she fell with pinpoint accuracy between the flesh golem's eyes. She danced across the creature's shoulders, poking at it with her staff.

A twang and a zing made Vola duck and suddenly an arrow sprouted from one of the golem's eyes. It shrieked and clawed at its face. Sorrel lost her balance and rolled down the creature's back.

"Sorrel!" Vola called.

"Oh gods, its butt is even uglier than its front," her voice called.

Vola darted forward, dove between the thing's legs, and came up on the other side between Sorrel and the flesh golem that staggered in a circle.

It stopped, rumbled deep in its throat, and then made a grab for Sorrel. Vola lunged, and it caught her right around the middle.

Her stomach dropped as it hoisted her into the air, and Vola had a split second to be impressed with anything that managed to pick up a half-orc in one hand. It raised her, poised to smash her into the ground head first.

"Halt!" a voice called.

The flesh golem froze as Myron strode through the ranks of zombies. He bore a staff in one hand, decorated with intricate knots up and down the surface. His free hand he waved at the flesh golem.

It slowly lowered Vola to the ground.

"We could have taken it," Sorrel said from near the thing's ankle.

Myron squinted around at them behind his smudged glasses. "You?" he said. "Can't you four just leave me alone?" He peered at Rilla. "Five. I didn't realize they were with you."

"They're not," Rilla said mildly.

"This is unacceptable. Do you know how much of my work you've interrupted? I'm a necromancer, not a murderer, but I think I'll make an exception for you."

"Think again," Sorrel said and stuck her quarterstaff between his legs.

He went down in a tangle of limbs, his staff rolling away and his glasses falling to the stone floor. Sorrel threw her own weapon aside and tackled Myron before he could go for his staff again.

The flesh golem roared and hoisted Vola in the air again. She kicked and stabbed at its hand, trying to get it to drop her.

"Stop! Stop!" Lillie said, throwing herself at the golem. "We surrender all right. There's no need to kill us."

Myron threw Sorrel off himself, and Lillie grabbed her to keep the halfling back.

The necromancer hauled himself to his feet and touched his face. His glasses had fallen off and he took a few moments to search the floor for them before he gave up and squinted at Vola and the others where they stood or hung from the flesh golem's hands.

"Take them to the labs," Myron snapped at the golem. "Lock them in. I don't have time to deal with them right now."

TWENTY-THREE

THE FLESH GOLEM locked them in one of the abandoned laboratories. It didn't bother taking their weapons away before tossing them into the mostly empty room, which seemed like a huge oversight until it touched the wall and a crackling black and purple barrier sprang up, covering the door and windows. Vola stepped forward and reached a tentative finger out to test it. The snapping colors zapped her fingertip, and she jerked back with a yelp as the flesh golem grinned in a mockery of a human smile.

So, they wouldn't be able to use their weapons anyway unless it was on each other.

Vola sighed and turned to survey the room. It was very similar to the one where they'd found Cleavah. Bare walls, tile floor, a couple of lab benches, and a stool. No containers. No exits except the door and the windows that led back out to the hall where the flesh golem was disappearing. There weren't even any grates leading back into the vent system, either by accident or because Myron had guessed their trick.

Talon prowled the edges of the room, hood swinging back and forth. She was probably coming to the same conclusions as Vola.

Gruff sniffed along the opposite edge, snorting now and then. Sorrel crouched on the floor in the corner, her staff in front of her. She frowned at it, then touched it, then frowned at it again like it had personally offended her. Lillie kept wringing her hands, casting glances at the princess.

Rilla leaned back with her butt propped on one of the tables and crossed her arms. Her light brown eyes narrowed as she surveyed Vola and her team.

Vola's feet snapped together, and she straightened her spine, almost involuntarily falling to attention.

"Well, my mission's truly fucked now," she said. She had a throaty voice and clipped syllables that didn't give a damn what anyone else thought. "What are you doing here? And how did you know who I am? I specifically told my steward to keep any adventurers away from my investigation. Adventurers always screw things up."

Vola winced, then cast a glance at Lillie and Talon. Sorrel rubbed her forehead. "Um," Vola said. "Is your steward named James?"

"Squirrely fellow," Sorrel added. "Kind of nervous."

"Yes," Rilla said.

"He was the one who hired us to find you," Vola said. "He was convinced you were missing or dead."

She rolled her eyes hard enough to make her head rock. "I wasn't missing. Obviously. I was undercover. Protocol gives me two weeks without contact before he's supposed to panic. He must have gotten nervous and abandoned the script. He's fired. As soon as I get out of here."

Her gaze flashed across the bare room.

"I have a few spells that might help," Lillie offered. "If we could just get you through the barrier, then you could escape."

Rilla shook her head. "Forget that. I'm not leaving without

taking Myron with me. That's what I came here for. And it's only gotten more desperate since then."

"Because of the energy he's stealing," Vola said, hoping to impress her. She'd rather the princess stopped looking at them like a problem she wanted to delegate to someone else.

Rilla's gaze sharpened on her. "Yes. He's stealing magic from dead spell casters. He's been amassing enough to send to his buyer for weeks, and I'd rather it didn't actually get that far."

Lillie straightened. "Is there a way to reverse the process?"

"I don't know yet. I figured once I got my hands around his neck, he'd tell me fast enough. I was trying to lure him out of the facility. Outside, he's limited to raising only a few undead at a time. In here, he's nearly unlimited. He gets shipments of dead bodies he can turn into his horde nearly every day. I'm good, but I'm not that good. Unfortunately, now he knows I'm here, there's no way I'll be able to pry him out."

Vola and her party stared at their shoes.

She should at least pretend to be surprised that they'd screwed up yet another mission, but unfortunately, it was becoming a pattern.

If only she could think of a way out, they could make it up to the princess somehow. They could stop Myron and actually do what they'd set out to do.

Sorrel opened her mouth to say something.

Talon hissed from beside the barrier. "Heads up," she said.

Vola stepped across the space to stand beside Talon. Rilla stayed where she was, watching with narrowed eyes.

Vola didn't see anything through the shifting black and purple barrier, but she could hear something. A shuffle and a whisper. Someone who didn't want to be heard.

A figure came into view, hooded in gray.

"Oh, great," Vola muttered just as the figure caught sight of the barrier.

Tallah pulled the hood back and smirked at them. "Look at this," she said as two more monks came into view. "It's Sorrel. In a cage. And she even brought her friends. How cute."

Hazel came into view and bit her lip as she surveyed the trapped party. The last monk went to the end of the hall, keeping watch.

"It was quite clever, having Fang deter us." Tallah folded her arms across her chest. "But luckily I had Hazel following you from the beginning. She understands loyalty, even if that old hag doesn't. Even if you don't."

Sorrel's fists clenched at her sides. "You wouldn't know loyalty even when it punched you in the face, Tallah. One day, everyone who follows you will see the truth of you. And they'll see the truth of me."

Tallah shook her head and clicked her tongue. "And that's your problem, Sorrel. Monks are supposed to be humble. But you have no humility. Only pride. You desperately want to be recognized. You want fame and glory. But we already proved you aren't good enough for those. You're not a leader. All you're good for is to follow."

"Tallah," Hazel said quietly. "That's not what Maxim teaches."

"You're right," Tallah said, leaning back. "Sorrel can't even follow. She's an oathbreaker."

Sorrel's fist lashed out, striking the barrier right over Tallah's face.

The abbess lurched back even as Sorrel hissed in pain and shook her fist.

Tallah collected herself and then chuckled. "That's why you'll never be allowed back in the monastery, Sorrel. You'll never make a good monk until you learn that Maxim doesn't value pride. He values loyalty. Above all, loyalty. Good followers know that and don't seek recognition above the others." Tallah gestured to the other monks before her gaze settled on Vola. "I wonder how long she'll follow you before her pride makes her break another oath."

"*I* wonder just how strong this barrier is," Vola said, voice calm and calculating. She threw a punch at Tallah's face, just as Sorrel had done.

The barrier crackled and spluttered but held strong. Vola clenched her teeth tight on the pain and didn't let any of it show as Tallah glanced worriedly at the barrier.

Finally, the abbess scoffed. "You think it's an insult, but it's the truth. Sorrel swore an oath to follow me, but when it came time to fulfill that oath, she chose to lie. She undermined my authority and left. She'll eventually do the same thing to you."

Tallah raised her hand to call Hazel and the other monk to her side. "We're not letting you come back," she told Sorrel. "Maybe if you'd gotten to the Warhammer first. But that's what we're doing."

They flowed down the hall in perfect unison, leaving Sorrel, Vola, Lillie, and Talon behind the barrier.

As soon as they were out of sight, Vola bent over her hand, grimacing in pain.

"That was stupid," Rilla said, behind her.

Vola took a few deep breaths and straightened. "No. It was necessary." It had been necessary to rattle Tallah. And it had been necessary to stand with Sorrel, show her they weren't going to be moved by words.

But Sorrel stalked back over to the wall and flung herself on the floor without meeting Vola's eyes.

Lillie gave a fake little laugh. "Well, it's not like you wanted to return to the monastery, anyway. So really, they haven't taken anything away from you."

A muscle jumped in Sorrel's jaw and she hung her head, her hands clenched on her knees. "Actually..."

Lillie's shoulders drooped. "Oh."

Vola rubbed the back of her neck. She'd rather be doing anything else right now, but it wasn't like they had a way out of this place.

She leaned back against the wall next to Sorrel.

"I kept…imagining it in my head," Sorrel said. "I'd have the Warhammer, and I'd bring it back and everyone would all be lined up. Everyone who ever believed Tallah. They'd all look at me and know. They'd know she was wrong and it would be so… so good."

Sorrel looked up at them, blinking rapidly. "That makes her right? Doesn't it? I wanted the Warhammer to prove myself. To get them to admit they'd made a mistake. And that's just pride. Another way of betraying my people."

"Bullshit," Vola said and a little crack of lightning struck the tile in front of them. Vola glared at the ceiling. "Can you think of a better word for it?"

The ceiling stayed silent, and Vola assumed she'd proved her point. She turned her scowl on Sorrel, who was staring up at her. "No, a good teammate doesn't need to constantly be proving their worth," she said. "But that's because recognition is given freely."

Lillie dragged the stool over to them with a screech and perched atop it. Talon's hood swung like she was weighing her options, then she crouched on the floor just far enough away to feel comfortable but close enough to be one of them.

"You shouldn't have to prove yourself to your family," Vola said, deliberately using that word. "Because your family should already recognize your skill. And we do." She added the last part quietly. "A team that refuses to recognize the contributions of its members isn't worth defending."

Vola bent her neck, looking down at Sorrel. The halfling chewed her lip, tracing the edge of a tile with her fingertip.

"You said it yourself," Vola said. "Back in the graveyard when all this was starting."

Sorrel glanced up. "I said what?"

Vola pointed to Talon. "Talon's our tracker. Sh-They find ways to come at our enemies sideways. They're the unexpected arrow in the dark. I don't have to check that they're there, because I trust—no, I *know* that they will be."

Talon ducked, her hood hiding her face.

"Lillie's our brains. She figures out our enemies' weaknesses. She thinks and writes and plans, and when those things fail, she makes sure everything explodes."

Lillie went a bright, painful red, but she gave Vola a beatific smile. "And Vola is the one who keeps us together with her wisdom," Lillie said. "She says she'd prefer to swing a sword, and she's very good at it. But it's her words that hold us to one another. Her words, her strength, her dedication. She is a bulwark. A shield. And a sanctuary."

Vola shrugged as if to let the praise roll off of her, but she buried the words deep down where she could remember them later.

"Sorrel, you're our heart," Vola said.

Sorrel pulled a face.

"You're our passion." Vola ignored her reaction. "You're our muscle. You walk ahead of us and clear a path so we have a place to stand. So Talon has a place to appear, so Lillie has a place to think, so I have a place to defend."

Vola lowered her chin and didn't continue until Sorrel met her eyes. "We want you to be proud of what you do for us. We want you to be proud of who you are. Because that's where your strength is. And we'll keep telling you as long as you need to hear it."

The princess watched them from her place propped against one of the tables.

Sorrel let her knees drop, so she sat cross-legged on the tile. She scrubbed her hands over her face, holding them there for a second as if composing herself. When she finally looked up at them, her familiar grin wreathed her features.

"I suppose that means we'd better get out of here, then."

Vola nodded and stood. She walked to the door and examined the barrier without touching it. Unfortunately, Myron had sealed them in with magic so there wasn't even a lock to pick.

"You say that like it's as easy as walking out of here," Rilla said with a snort. "You've taken a look around, right?"

Vola raised an eyebrow at her. "Yes, but would you rather just sit there?"

Lillie stepped up to the barrier and held her hands out palms up as if testing it. "We're going to get out of here," she said. "And we're going to find a way to get Sorrel back into her monastery. With or without Maxim's Warhammer."

Sorrel chuckled under her breath. "It would be better with; otherwise, why did I snatch it?" She stood and used her toe to flip her quarterstaff into her hand.

The rest of them stared as the halfling spun the staff fast enough to make it blur, then struck the floor with one end. As they watched, the smooth wood under her hands writhed, forming intricately carved knots that glowed from the inside.

Maxim's Warhammer.

TWENTY-FOUR

Vola's mouth fell open. "You swiped the staff?" she said, her voice rising until it hit an octave that made her flush. She couldn't help the grin that stretched her cheeks. "You freaking stole Myron's staff?"

Sorrel pouted. "You didn't think I'd just jump on him in order to beat him to death with my fists, did you?"

Vola blinked and exchanged a look with Lillie and Talon. "Well…yes."

Sorrel opened her mouth to respond and then shut it with a click. "Okay, fair point. But I can multitask."

Rilla gave the halfling a little bow. "I'll admit to being a little jealous. Sleight of hand and theft are sort of my thing."

Sorrel shrugged. "I jumped him so he'd drop it. In the confusion, I made sure he grabbed the wrong one. And I knocked his glasses off so he wouldn't immediately be able to tell the difference."

"But the glow," Lillie said. "It wasn't glowing before."

Sorrel eyed it sideways. "Yeah, I'm not sure why it's doing

that. Unless…” She shook her head. “Doesn’t matter. I can make it stop.” And the staff stopped glowing. “Oh, and check this out.”

The monk tossed the Warhammer to Talon, who caught it deftly. In the ranger’s hand, the staff warped and flowed into an elegant longbow. Talon weighed it in her hand and drew it to test the action.

“That is the nicest thing anyone has ever given me,” Talon said. Then she handed the bow to Lillie.

The weapon instantly morphed into a staff, much more ornate than the quarterstaff Sorrel had wielded. Lillie nodded, running her hands up and down the carved surface. “Now it looks like what I remember Myron carrying. I was wondering if I needed spectacles, too.”

“Do Vola,” Sorrel said. “I want to know what it does in a paladin’s hands.”

Lillie held it out and Vola took it carefully. The staff twisted and stretched, and Vola almost dropped it, but it seemed anchored in her hand, like the most well-balanced weapon she’d ever held, and when it was done, she carried a warhammer almost as tall as she was. The haft was simple and smooth from someone else’s use, and the steel head was carved with sun rays, one point extending to a wicked spike that would pierce the toughest plate armor.

Sorrel’s eyes were wide. “That’s the head of Maxim’s Warhammer. This is what it looks like with both pieces together.”

“How do you know?” Lillie asked. She’d pulled her notebook out to sketch a picture.

“I’ve seen it. The head of his Warhammer lived under the monastery for a thousand years. It’s what we were sent to retrieve when Father Naemon died. I held it for a whole minute.” Sorrel shook her head. “Not important.”

“Why did you wait till now to tell us you took it?” Vola said.

“I didn’t know how to use it. It morphed when I grabbed it, and I didn’t want to draw Myron’s attention to it. I like a good fight, but I promise I think ahead at least some of the time. Then Tallah showed up, and I really didn't want her to know we had it. It's our best chance to get out of here."

"It does seem quite versatile," Lillie said.

Sorrel turned to Rilla. "Would you like a turn?" she said politely.

Rilla's lips quirked in a grin. "It'll just be knives. I've always liked them best, and they seem to like me. But I'd rather use it to get out of here, wouldn't you?"

Vola held out the hammer to Sorrel.

Sorrel looked up, eyes wide. "Are you sure?"

Vola gave her an incredulous look. "What do you mean am I sure? It's yours, of course. You're the one who's been looking for it, you're Maxim's follower, and you were the one who swiped it. Now take it and let's see what you can do."

Sorrel held out her hands, and as Vola dropped the weapon into her palms, it morphed back into a quarterstaff the perfect size and shape for the halfling. The haft remained smooth and simple, but a complex leather wrapping decorated the grip now.

Sorrel's fingers tightened on the grip, and she bowed her head for a moment. Then she sighed and stepped up to the barrier.

"I still think a wizard's staff is more suited for the occasion," Sorrel said under her breath.

"I had my turn," Lillie said. "I wouldn't dream of taking it from you, now."

Sorrel leveled the staff at the barrier over the door and poked at it gingerly.

"Really?" Talon said. "You're holding the weapon of a god and you're going to use it to poke?"

"Try again," Vola said. "With feeling."

"I can do it without all the commentary, thanks," Sorrel said with a glare.

She spun and with a feral yell, brought the end of the staff down on the barrier with a wicked slash.

Sparks flashed where the two connected and a gash as wide as Vola's fist appeared in the black and purple curtain. The barrier flickered once, twice, and then sputtered out completely.

Sorrel whirled the staff, planted the end, and then leaned on it with a grin. "Easy as slicing a cake. Vola?" Sorrel gestured to the closed door beyond. "Will you do the honors?"

Vola grinned and kicked the door down.

"There are some perks to being an orc," she said as the door clattered against the tile floor.

"Half-orc," Lillie said.

Sorrel clapped her hands and rubbed them together. "What now? We've got our princess. We've got the Warhammer, but Myron is still up there collecting dead people's magic for some nefarious purpose. Do we go after him?"

"Of course we do," Lillie said.

"Or we take our princess and run," Talon said. "We did the job. We get paid."

Lillie opened her mouth, golden brows furrowed.

Vola held up her hands to forestall an argument. "Let's make this easy. Rilla, are you still going after Myron?"

Vola turned to check on Rilla, but the princess was already out the door in the hallway. She was counting each knife in her belt.

"Of course I'm going after Myron," she said. "My plan was to lure him out of his hideout, but that was when I was working alone. Now I have four more players and a god's weapon on the field, I can take a more direct approach."

Vola gestured to the princess. "There," she told the others. "We can't leave until the princess does. So let's go get Myron."

TWENTY-FIVE

VOLA, Sorrel, and Lillie waited in the hallway while Talon scouted for the main room where Myron had been collecting magical energy.

The princess crouched behind them, her eyes moving between them and the door and the two ends of the hallway.

Vola glanced at her while they waited. "Do you want to take point, princess?"

Rilla grinned with her teeth. "I'm more of the creep around back and stab them sort of royalty. You lead. I'll follow and fill in where I'm needed." Her gaze was more speculative than accusing now, and Vola took that at face value.

Talon motioned them forward, and Vola crept to stand beside the ranger at the door. "What does it look like?"

"Like it did from the vents," Talon said. "But this time there's a lot of screaming."

"Screaming? I thought zombies were more into moaning," Vola said.

"Not the zombies," Talon said and her hood was back far enough she could catch Vola's gaze and hold it. "The monks. They must have walked right in there and gotten captured. He's got them hooked up to those tanks of his."

Vola pursed her lips. "Right. We're going in then." She gestured the others forward. "This has just turned into another rescue."

"Aw, yeah," Sorrel said, unhooking her staff. "I like getting to be the hero."

"Sorrel, take point. Talon's flanking. Lillie, focus on Myron. We need you to neutralize him if you can. Rilla, fill in the gaps."

The princess saluted with a wickedly curved blade.

"Charge?" Lillie said.

Vola rolled her eyes. "You can stop saying it like that."

"But it's tradition."

Vola kicked the door in and Sorrel zipped past.

In the center of the room, Myron stood fiddling with some brass knobs attached to the large tank. Green mist swirled behind the glass and made Vola's stomach roil.

Myron glanced up, brow furrowed. "More test subjects? No, no, I don't need more yet—"

Lillie launched a fireball at Myron's feet which exploded in a cascade of sparks and smoke. Myron choked and coughed as Sorrel sped past him.

The screams came from the edges of the room where the tables stood, hooked up to the central tank with tubes and wires.

Sorrel vaulted the pedestal on the far side of the room and landed on the edge of the slab. Her eyes went wide. "Hazel," she mouthed.

Vola launched herself at the nearest pedestal. A railing around the edge gave her trouble for about three seconds before she just stepped over it.

Tallah thrashed against her bindings, splashing bits of goo over the raised edges of the table as she screamed. Little rubber suction cups connected her to the tubes in the table, puckering the skin at her temples, wrists, and ankles. Her eyes went wide as she caught sight of Vola. Her screams grew louder as if she couldn't even form the words to ask for help.

Vola took it all in with one glance, then raised her blade.

Tallah's screams cut off with a moan.

Vola brought her blade down and severed the leather straps holding the abbess down on the right.

"Hey, leave them alone," Myron said as the surrounding smoke cleared. "Ugh, you're messing everything up. My results will all be skewed now."

He raised his hand and pulled down like he did when he was summoning his staff, but Lillie stepped up to him and planted her fist in his nose.

Myron cried out and stumbled back, aborting his attempt to get his staff. Instead he waved his hands and green lightning crackled through his fingers. He pointed at Lillie.

Lillie spat a word and threw her arms wide.

Myron's lightning snapped, and he cried out as it dissipated.

Cool, Lillie had learned a new trick. Vola cut the other straps and yanked the suction cups off Tallah. Across the room, Sorrel was doing the same for Hazel. Talon was at the third table, cutting the last monk free.

"I thought he was supposed to kill his victims first," Tallah said, voice shaking as she pushed herself to her elbows and rolled straight off the table. She landed on her hands and knees.

"Are you complaining that you're still alive?" Vola reached to help Tallah to her feet, but the monk cried out and clutched her head.

It didn't look like Hazel and the other monk were in any better shape.

Vola took stock of her party. Sorrel and Talon were just fine. And Lillie was holding her own against Myron.

The only ones who needed her help right now were the

monks. Across the way, Sorrel supported the slightly taller dwarf with her shoulder. She gazed up at Hazel with concern. Like whatever argument they'd had never happened.

"You had better appreciate this," Vola grumbled. She reached deep for that well she had inside, the one filled with white fire and cool water. And flung it across the room, trying to remember exactly what it had felt like the first time in the hospital. "Your power through me, so be it."

The power flowed out of her, pouring into the three monks at once, making them gasp and stagger. Pain pounded in Vola's temples, leeching the strength from her limbs, and she doubled over.

"What did you…" Tallah said beside her ear.

"I healed you. Now help us take Myron down."

Vola shoved away the pain—it would fade soon as Cleavah healed her from the inside—and vaulted over the railing to sprint for the necromancer.

His eyes widened as he heard her footsteps and spun. Then he reached behind him for his staff. He pulled out Sorrel's plain old quarterstaff and pointed it at Vola.

With a vicious grin, Vola brought her blade down and split it in two.

Myron stared at the two halves of his useless stick and choked. "My staff. What happened to my staff?" Then he glared at Vola. "You really don't want me to finish my work, do you?"

"Not if it involves stealing other people's magic, no," Vola said conversationally.

"Well, then," he huffed. "I guess that makes my choice easier." He reached over to the tank and turned a nozzle. Green mist poured from a tube, and the contents shifted and roiled.

Vola stumbled back from the swirling mist pooling against the tiles. But before it could reach her, tendrils wound up Myron's legs, and he began absorbing it.

"Lillie?" Vola called.

Lillie stood with her hands covering her mouth. "He's using it. He's using the stolen magic. Oh, shit."

Vola's stomach dropped. Never a good sign when the wizard started cursing.

A flicker of movement behind Myron made Vola pause. While he was focused on her, directly in front of him, he missed Rilla creeping up behind.

The princess flowed up and spun to strike from behind.

Her blade struck his back, but Myron's whole surface flickered and a shaft of light flung Rilla back. The princess landed, cracking her head against the nearest pedestal.

"Oh, fudge buckets," Vola said, staggering back a step.

"You might have taken my staff, but I have power beyond mortal magic now," Myron said.

Vola glanced around the room. Tallah and the other monk had disappeared, leaving Hazel standing pale behind Sorrel.

Myron advanced on Vola.

"Well, crap," Vola said and retreated a step. If Rilla's example was anything to go by, her weapons wouldn't do anything against him now.

"Vola, catch," Sorrel called.

The halfling threw the staff like a javelin, and Vola flung aside her sword to catch it one-handed. In her palm, the weapon shifted and morphed into the hammer she'd held in the laboratory.

Myron's eyes went wide.

"That's better," Vola said. And she swung the hammer in a perfect arc.

Myron's shield crackled again, but this time he was the one to stumble back, clutching his chest.

Vola pressed the advantage and struck again. A warhammer like this was built to be handled with two hands, but Vola was bigger than most warriors, and she swung it like a club, using its weight and momentum as her advantage.

Another solid blow and then Myron flung up a hand and shot another spell at her. Black, foul-smelling energy wrapped her chest, making her stagger. She fell to one knee as the spell burned into her skin, sapping her energy.

"Lillie," Vola whispered. And she threw the hammer.

Lillie squeaked and dodged for the weapon. It morphed the instant it touched her hands, and she cradled it to her chest.

Beside Vola, the princess pushed herself to her hands and knees, her head bleeding from the temple.

Lillie used the staff, powering her spells so they crawled up the intricately carved wood as wreaths of fire before she shot them toward Myron.

Vola took the chance to crawl to Rilla. She placed one hand on the princess's head and the other on her own chest. "Lady bless," she whispered, praying Cleavah's power was greater than Myron's.

A flash of light made Rilla gasp, and Vola's breath came easier as the sapping spell ceased and energy poured back into her. Even the mirrored wound on her head wasn't so bad. She must be getting better at the whole healing thing.

Myron yelled as white flames cascaded around him, eating away at the shield. But as he threw out his hands to retaliate, Lillie dodged. She landed on the floor with a thump as the spell sailed over her head. She rolled the staff away from herself.

Talon stopped it with a booted foot and flipped it into her hand. By the time it rested in her palm, it was a bow. Gruff snarled and threw himself at Myron, making the necromancer lunge to escape. Talon anticipated his movement and shot just as Myron turned to face the wolf.

Her arrow pierced his hand, skimming through his magical shield like butter.

"Now, Sorrel," Talon called and threw the bow.

Sorrel leaped to the edge of the table and caught the staff out of the air with a flourish. She hopped to the railing, and with a feral cry, leaped through the empty air over the top of Vola and Rilla.

Sorrel landed on Myron, the staff cracking against his shield. It flickered and died as Sorrel rained blow after blow on the necromancer, the staff a blur of color.

The halfling fell to one knee and swept Myron's feet out from under him. As he fell, she flung her hand out and her open palm struck him in the chest with a bang Vola felt in her ears.

The necromancer fell against the tile floor and lay still.

Sorrel straightened and planted one end of the staff against the floor to lean on it. "Ta-da," she said with a grin.

TWENTY-SIX

"Not bad," the princess said. "I can take him in—"

The whole facility shuddered, and the party staggered. Rilla used the railing at the edge of the pedestal to climb to her feet.

"What was that?" Vola said.

Lillie was staring up at the ceiling, eyes wide. "I don't know. Something changed."

"Well, duh," Sorrel said. "The earth moved. That's a pretty big change."

"No, I mean something in the spells around the facility changed. Myron's not conscious to keep them active."

There was a low shuffling moan that reached through Vola's skin and sent a shiver down her spine. "Shouldn't that mean they deactivate? Everything's shut down now, right?"

"Not necessarily," Lillie spoke quickly as Vola made a hand gesture and Talon slunk over to the door. "Anything tied to him should have gone down, but he had reanimation spells built into the facility itself. Those are still active, but without him to control them…"

Talon hissed from the door, the portal open a crack. "We've got hordes."

"There's no one to command them," Lillie finished.

"They're coming for me," Myron whispered. He pushed himself up to shaky elbows and raised his head. He blinked wide eyes. "The dead are angry."

"Probably has something to do with the fact that you zapped them back to life and stole their magic." Rilla strode forward and hauled Myron roughly to his feet.

"I don't care about their magic," Myron said. "It was only for funding. Research is expensive, you know."

"Tell you what," Vola said, "We'll stand behind you while you explain it to them. I'm sure they'll understand."

"You think so?" Myron said, hopefully.

"No, you twit," Lillie said.

"Can you regain control?" Rilla asked.

"Not now. You've ruined everything."

"We could let them have him," Sorrel said.

"I'd rather keep him alive." Rilla pulled Myron over to his tank. "He has an employer I'd like to pin down."

And it seemed like a cruel sort of execution to leave the necromancer here for his undead to tear into little pieces. They'd just have to mop up the horde anyway before it made it to the city.

"Where are the monks?" Vola said.

"Gone." Hazel climbed down from the pedestal. Red rings around her temples stood out from her pale skin but she didn't waver as she met Vola's eyes. "They retreated while they could."

Sorrel snorted. "So much for strength and loyalty. Vola saved your lives, you know?"

"So did you," Hazel said. "If you hadn't taken the Warhammer, we would all be dead by now."

Sorrel shrugged but also ducked her head so Vola only caught the flash of a smile.

"Here they come," Talon called. She wedged a piece of tubing under the door and retreated to stand beside Vola.

Vola glanced at Hazel and up at the grate on the wall. "If I give you a boost, you can probably reach the vents. Go now, while you can."

Hazel's lips thinned. "I'm not going anywhere."

The undead thudded against the door, making it buckle inward.

"Suit yourself," Vola said, drawing her sword.

Sorrel spun her staff, Lillie planted her feet, and Talon drew her bow.

Rilla finished tying Myron to the tank in the middle of the room. "So you don't even think about slipping out the back."

Myron whimpered.

Something big slammed against the door, and Vola's grip tightened.

"My lady," she said to the air. "We might need something a little stronger this time. I'd prefer to keep serving you, and I can't do that if I'm a puddle of red paste."

"Ew," Lillie said.

"Do orcs bleed red?" Sorrel asked curiously.

A warm breeze whispered past Vola's ear and her sword hummed in her palm. It started to glow.

Sorrel and Talon jumped as their weapons let off a soft white light as well. Even Rilla's daggers and Hazel's plain quarterstaff glowed between their fingers.

"Make the most of it," Vola said. "I don't think this will last forever."

One last blow hit the door.

It didn't just open. The door disintegrated in a cloud of splinters and the plaster of the wall crumbled as a swarm of animated bodies rushed in, tumbling over each other in their haste, forming an inexorable surging tide of undead.

Lumbering behind them came the flesh golem, huge enough its head nearly brushed the ceiling. Pieces of mismatched skin jiggled over twisted joints and lumpy muscles.

Lillie sent a fireball into the front ranks, and Sorrel used the cover of flames and smoke to rush the enemy.

"For Maxim!"

Hazel was only a second behind, wielding her own staff with deadly accuracy. Rilla followed, ducking and weaving around the undead.

Vola raised her shield and divided her attention between guarding Lillie and keeping an eye on Talon. The ranger sprinted around the edge of the room, keeping ahead of the undead with sheer speed, stopping only to launch a volley of arrows into their ranks. Gruff wove between rotting legs, snapping out to trip and rend and snap bones.

The zombies fell, one by one.

But the flesh golem came on, oblivious to the corpses it crushed under its feet.

"I'll draw its attention," Vola called to Lillie and Talon. "You go for its eyes."

Vola dove between its legs and slashed at the tendons behind the knees. A normal enemy would have fallen from that one stroke, but this thing just staggered around in a circle, its legs wobbling at funny angles until it could lunge for Vola.

Lightning wreathed the creature's head, zapping and crackling across its stolen flesh. It shook its head and then batted at the annoyance, striking its own ear with a meaty thud.

Vola took advantage of its distraction and swept her shining blade up, leaving a large slice in its abdomen.

Black sludge spurted from the wound, and Vola danced back with a grimace to avoid the mess. Hazel darted in beside Vola, weapon brandished, but the monk slipped in the sludge and landed on her back hard enough to knock the wind from her lungs.

Vola grabbed the monk and yanked her out of the way as the golem staggered forward a step, intent on crushing them. Vola chopped at the thing's foot, but it was too thick to sever.

"Does this thing even feel pain?" Vola cried.

Hazel scrambled back while Vola resettled her grip on her sword and double-checked Lillie. The wizard stood in a circle of fire that kept the zombie horde at bay while she concentrated her fire on the golem's head and shoulders. Talon kept moving, well ahead of any zombies chasing her. Sorrel stood amid a pile of bodies, creating mayhem while she laughed.

They seemed fine. But Talon would run out of room to stay ahead soon. Lillie's fires would go out before the entire horde was dead. And Sorrel…well, Sorrel had to run out of energy at some point. Though Vola had never seen it.

They had to end this.

Vola ducked her head and rammed the flesh golem in the knee. It bellowed and then swiped her off her feet, slamming her head into the ground. But she could take the hit. As long as it was focused on her, it wasn't chasing her party.

It grabbed her ankle, nearly crushing it, and lifted her into the air.

"Now!" Lillie called. "To Vola, now!"

Vines sprouted from the ground, shattering the tile floor and snapping up the flesh golem's limbs. Talon's carefully reserved magic.

The golem tried to swing Vola around but found its feet lashed to the floor. Then the vines grew thorns, and it thrashed, trying to tear itself free.

Rilla ducked and rolled between the vines and flung a knife with one hand. The blade lodged itself in the creature's left eye.

The flesh golem moaned and dropped Vola. Hazel darted

forward to drag Vola out of the fray as Lillie raised a wall of fire between them and the creature.

With a feral cry, Sorrel leaped through the flames and clambered up the flesh golem's arm, avoiding the thorns. It tried to swat at her, but a vine snaked out and lashed its wrist. The golem blinked at its trapped hand and flexed the shifting muscles under its mismatched skin. The vine snapped, and it swiped at Sorrel.

Sorrel dodged but lost her grip and slipped, dropping the Warhammer while she scrabbled for purchase. She recovered and scrambled the rest of the way.

Vola rolled, already planning to snatch the staff and toss it to the halfling, but before she could reach it, Sorrel threw out her hand. The Warhammer rose into the air and snapped into her palm as if she'd called it there.

Sorrel stood on the creature's shoulder, a tiny figure atop the giant made of flesh, and she brandished her weapon. A tracery of blue lines crawled through the wood, reminiscent of Cleavah's glow.

"For strength," Sorrel said. "And loyalty."

She launched herself into the air, flipped over, and came down with all the weight of a god's wrath.

A rift of flesh speared down the golem from its head to its groin, and with a groan, it split in two. The halves fell away from each other as Sorrel leaped free of the severed body.

It fell with a thud that shook the floor and shattered the glass in Myron's tank. He cowered beneath a shower of shards.

Sorrel landed neatly on one knee. As she straightened, she met Hazel's eyes.

The other monk stood beside Vola, gaping.

Sorrel gave her a small, distinct nod, and Vola had the feeling she was missing something. Something important only the two of them understood.

Vola put a hand to her head, which throbbed, and pushed herself up to survey the room.

Dead bodies lay everywhere, most in too many pieces to reanimate again. There were a couple that twitched weakly as if they were thinking about it, but they'd be able to mop those up without a second thought.

Vola's head and ankle ached, and she had black sludge caked in the gaps of her chain mail, but she seemed to be the only one hurt. Sorrel's cheeks were flushed, but she grinned. Talon still had her hood up, and Lillie didn't even have a hair out of place. Rilla and Hazel weren't complaining either.

"All that work," Myron moaned, shaking his head. "Wasted. I'll have to start all over now."

Rilla snorted. "Right. Well, that's our cue. Come on, Myron."

"Where are we going?" Myron said as she pulled him to his feet and slashed the cord binding him to the tank.

"Your new home. In prison."

Outside there was no sign of the man and the boy they'd left tied up in the bushes.

There was no sign of the swamp beast, either. Vola hoped the two instances weren't related.

When they stepped into the bright light of midmorning, Myron blinked up at the sky. Then he glanced around at his heavily armed captors.

Before Vola could yell a warning, he'd thrown a spell at Rilla's feet and ripped himself free from her grasp. Amid the smoke, he made a break for the tree line.

Rilla swore and started after him. But she hadn't gone two steps before he screamed and reappeared through the tree trunks, trailing his ripped robe behind him. He clutched the edges and stumbled back to them, gibbering.

The swamp monster paced placidly from the trees, chewing a long tear of cloth.

Rilla drew her knives. "What the fuck is that?"

"Good boy, Millford," Lillie said, approaching the swamp beast.

"It belongs to you?" Rilla said.

"'Belongs' is a strong word," Sorrel said with a sigh.

The swamp monster snapped at Lillie's outstretched hand, and she stumbled back with a glare. "You could at least try to be pleasant. We feed you."

"Sometimes," Vola muttered.

Hazel stood off to the side, giving the swamp beast a sidelong look.

Rilla fixed Myron with a glare. "You try to run again, and I'll let them feed you to that thing."

Myron wrapped his arms around his torso, much of which was bared now through his ripped tunic. "You don't understand. I just want to finish my work."

Rilla rolled her eyes. "One day, you might realize that stealing magic from dead people is evil."

Myron waved a hand. "I don't care about that part. That's just my side business. It pays the bills and funds my real research."

"And that is?"

"I'm trying to halt the aging process entirely. I'm close to stopping death itself."

Rilla's elegant brows drew down. "So, you owe no loyalty to the man who was paying you."

"I don't care who pays me, as long as it funds my lab."

Rilla tapped her chin. "So, this lab you want…would it be all right if it had unlimited meals, functional amenities, sturdy walls, no windows, and bars on the door?"

"To keep out research thieves? That sounds wonderful. I would need my equipment."

"Of course. It wouldn't be a lab without it. But you wouldn't be able to continue stealing magic from dead people. You'd have to focus entirely on the halting death thing."

Myron's mouth opened and closed once, twice. "You say this as if it's a punishment. I don't understand what the catch is."

"You'd have to earn this setup," Rilla said. "I will happily give you a lab in prison to continue your research on anti-aging, but you have to give me information about your previous employer. Everything you know."

"In exchange for funding from the crown?" Myron said, eyes wide. "Gladly. I'll tell you everything. I kept notes. Would you like them now? Can we go see this lab? When can we leave?"

Rilla's mouth quirked in a satisfied smile. "Just a moment, Myron. You're a valuable asset. I want to be sure you're taken care of."

The princess stepped away from her new necromancer and Vola rubbed the back of her neck.

"He knows he's never going to be able to leave this lab, right?" she asked.

Rilla shrugged. "I don't think that'll be a problem. And it's prison either way for him. This way I get his cooperation and the information I want. I don't even have to fight to get it." She frowned. "Actually, that last part is a little disappointing."

"It's very clever," Lillie said, diplomatically.

"I didn't get to be the princess of the Dagger Throne without learning to take opportunities when I see them." She eyed them up and down. "Speaking of. I think James owes you your commission. Stop by Cliffside Palace tomorrow morning, and I'll see that he pays you."

She gave them a little salute and turned back to Myron. "Come on then, let's go find you your new lab."

Hazel shuffled her feet and cocked her thumb over her shoulder. "I should…I should go, too."

"I'm sure Tallah is waiting for you," Sorrel said, and for once, when she spoke of the abbess, her voice wasn't filled with rancor.

"I'm not so sure. She seemed very eager to leave," Hazel said, gazing into the trees. She turned back to them. "Thank you for the rescue."

"Have a good life." Vola wasn't quite able to say it without the sarcasm. Sorrel might not hold a grudge, but Vola could do it for her.

Hazel shook her head. "This isn't over. And I have a lot to decide before the end."

She stalked off through the trees toward the city.

"Well, that sounds ominous," Lillie said.

Talon snorted. "At least she's thinking, now."

TWENTY-SEVEN

This time Vola walked up the front steps to Cliffside Palace by herself. The two guards standing outside the big double doors didn't even flinch when a heavily armed and armored orc tapped on the door. The city sprawled down the hill behind her, like a dirty patchwork quilt over a couple of knobbly knees. She couldn't even smell it from here.

The stone walls soared into the sky, more fortress than palace like the name suggested, but they'd made some efforts with the flying buttresses in the back and one spindly tower.

The door opened and a liveried servant ushered Vola into the palace proper, down long halls filled with mirrors and plush carpets, to a columned portico. Three figures and a wolf waited for her on the patio, staring down at the city. Archways let out onto a hundred and fifty-foot drop with only a railing between them and the view.

Lillie turned at her step and smiled. "How is Cleavah?"

Vola shrugged. "Not sure," she said. "She wasn't there." She'd stopped at the temple while they'd gone on ahead.

Sorrel hopped up to the railing and swung her legs as if

waiting for a story. She'd propped Maxim's Warhammer, now shaped like the hammer haft it was, on the stone beside her.

"Her temple was still there with the graffiti, but the devotee was different. This one was light-skinned and fair-haired and had no clue who I was."

Lillie clasped her hands together. "Oh no."

"It's all right. She was polite, gave me a generic sort of blessing for my trouble, but I got the impression that Cleavah's work was done in this particular city, so she left."

"Without saying goodbye?"

Vola gave a lopsided grin. "It's hard to say goodbye to someone who's always hanging over your shoulder. She'll stick her nose in my business when she wants to. Until then, I just need to be patient and behave myself."

Sorrel frowned and picked up the Warhammer. She stretched it out to poke at the air over Vola's shoulder. "Are you sure she's there?"

Talon reached out to push the end of the staff down.

"You'd think a monk would know better than to poke the gods," she said. "Especially with another god's weapon."

"Eh," Sorrel said with a shrug, leaning the haft beside her again. "We can handle it. We can handle everything so long as we're together."

Talon flinched. She'd worn her hood down today. Her hair was growing out of its short, jagged cut, and she'd pinned a piece back out of her eyes. It gave her the slightest hint of feminine flair, offset by the patchy beard growing in on her chin.

They hadn't spoken privately since Talon had said she was leaving. The ranger stood slightly apart now as if distancing herself already. Had she told the others she was thinking about leaving? Had she made her decision? Gruff sat at her feet and Talon buried her fingers in his thick fur.

"Talon—" Vola started.

A door at the very end of the portico opened, and Vola had to drop her arguments as James stepped in. The steward didn't rush, but his step was hurried as he came toward them.

Vola crossed her arms as he stopped in front of them and hesitated a moment before bowing his head.

"Hey, James," Vola said. "Where's Rilla?"

James shot a glare at her. "Her Highness, the Princess of the Dagger Throne, is quite busy. Many things piled up in her absence. And she...wasn't in the best of moods when she returned."

She'd been fine when she left them. Gleeful even. "She told you off, didn't she?" Vola said. "For sending us after her when she wasn't really missing?"

James's shoulders stiffened. "I am allowed to worry about my princess. It's my job to worry about her."

"Probably not your job to question her competence, though," Talon said.

James's lips thinned, and he paused like he was trying to backtrack. "Regardless, she would like to express her gratitude for your assistance. Even if she doesn't think she needed it." He pulled out a large leather purse which clinked invitingly and Vola's heart lifted. "Your pay, as agreed upon in our contract. Three hundred gold for the safe return of—"

"Your girlfriend," Sorrel said, jumping down from the railing.

"Her Highness," he said with a scowl. "And she was impressed with your skill and fortitude and has asked that I open the armory to you. You may each choose an item from the royal collection."

Vola's eyebrows hit her hairline. "You're kidding."

"I'm not," James said, lifting his chin. Then he sagged a little, relenting. "Consider it a bonus. I...I may have underestimated my princess, but I'm still glad I sent you. Thank you for returning her safely."

Vola clapped him on the shoulder, making him stagger. "You're welcome."

The sound of voices bounced from the wall behind them and Vola turned, eyes narrowed.

Tallah and four other gray-clad monks, including Hazel, came through the door onto the portico, chattering amongst themselves.

Sorrel stiffened right before Tallah saw them and stopped, feet planted on the elegantly patterned tiles. Behind the abbess, Hazel's eyes darted between the party and the monks.

"What are you doing here?" Vola asked.

Tallah sniffed and folded her arms. "The princess invited us."

Vola cast a glare at James, but the steward wasn't looking at her. He was smirking at Tallah.

"Ah, yes," he said. "My lady would like to offer you the hospitality of the palace."

Tallah beamed. "At least someone recognizes our contributions."

James's smile went sharp. "She thinks you'd be more comfortable here since you obviously find the real world a scary place."

Sorrel smothered a loud snort in her elbow as Tallah's smile soured and pulled into a scowl.

Vola didn't bother hiding her grin. "That seems fair. We get the Warhammer, and you get to spend some time in the pampered luxury you deserve."

"You can't keep Maxim's Warhammer," Tallah snapped. "It belongs with us. It belongs with its other half. We have the head."

"I think it belongs with me," Sorrel said, patting the staff. "It likes me."

"It won't obey you," Tallah said, planting her hands on her hips. "It will only obey the owner of the head."

Sorrel's gaze sharpened. "Is that so?"

Tallah rolled her eyes. "And it's not like you can keep it to blackmail us. We won't let you back into the monastery now, even if you bring Maxim's Warhammer."

"That's good," Talon said. "We'd rather keep her."

Tallah glared at the ranger. "It speaks."

Vola growled as Hazel cried, "Tallah!"

"Leave them out of this, Tallah," Sorrel said.

Tallah shook her head. "I don't know why I'm surprised you couldn't even be normal for two seconds. You had to pick the party of freaks."

Sorrel screamed and jumped Tallah.

The abbess lost her footing and went down. She raised her hands to guard herself against Sorrel's blows, but Sorrel had the upper hand.

"You can't fight on palace grounds," James shouted, but no one paid him any attention.

Gruff lurched to his feet, hackles raised.

"Oh, come on," Vola said, stepping forward. "Sorrel, are you really going to make me break this up when you know I'd like nothing more than to beat the crap out of her myself?"

Lillie rushed forward as Vola grasped the back of Sorrel's tunic and yanked her free while the other monks leaped to grab Tallah's arms.

All except Hazel, who didn't dive for the fray. She dove for the Warhammer.

"Hands off," Talon said, taking a menacing step forward.

"Good job, Hazel," Tallah said, ripping herself from the other monks' grasp. "Now, give it here."

Hazel's eyes narrowed, and her gaze shifted from Tallah, who held out her hand, to Sorrel, who dangled from Vola's grip.

The dwarf raised her chin, took a deep breath, and spun, flinging the Warhammer through one of the archways, out into open air.

"No!" Tallah screamed. "What are you doing?"

Vola dropped Sorrel, who landed on her feet. The halfling straightened and met Hazel's eyes. Hazel raised her chin.

A smirk quirked the side of Sorrel's mouth, and she held out her hand.

In the open air over the city, the Warhammer stopped short in its mad flight and hung there poised. It spun and shot back toward them.

Vola ducked, but she needn't have bothered. The haft of the Warhammer snapped into Sorrel's palm like it had been tied there.

Sorrel's fingers curled around it, and she raised her gaze to Tallah and the other monks.

They all stared at Sorrel, Tallah with her mouth hanging open.

"I can see your tonsils," Vola said.

Tallah snapped her mouth shut. "How—"

"It answered her call," one of the other monks said.

"The haft of Maxim's Warhammer only answers the call of the one who owns the head," Hazel said, enunciating her words very carefully. She kept her gaze locked on Tallah now.

The abbess flushed. "But I own the head."

"Do you?" Sorrel said very quietly.

"The hammer obeys Sorrel," Hazel said. "And yesterday in the necromancer's lab, I saw it obey her friends. It changed shape for them, matching their fighting styles and personalities." She looked at her hands. "It didn't change for me just now."

"It…it should obey me," Tallah said, but her eyes flickered back and forth between Sorrel and the rest of the monks. "It should obey us."

"A year ago," Hazel said, "four of us went down to find the head of Maxim's Warhammer. To determine who would lead the monastery after Father Naemon died. Brother Ferell was hurt in the trials, and I helped him back to the surface. Leaving you and Sorrel behind. When you came back, you had the head. We thought that was it. We thought your strength had won out over Sorrel's skill. But when Sorrel came back, she said she'd been the one to retrieve the head. She'd been the one to solve the trials. You only held it for her. We called her a liar." Hazel's mouth pulled down in a grim frown, and she lowered her chin as she gazed at Tallah. "What really happened down there? Who is the real liar?"

"I retrieved the head," Tallah cried. "I own it. You've all seen it. It's at the monastery in the abbot's rooms."

Sorrel shrugged. "That's easy to test. I'll just toss it again and you can grab it this time."

Sorrel cocked back her arm and took two lunging steps to gain speed.

"No!" Tallah flung out her hand. "Maxim curse you, you know I can't do it."

Sorrel planted the end of the staff on the colorful tiles. "I know."

"You stole it," Hazel said, horror lacing her tone as the rest of the monks grimaced and pulled away from Tallah. "You stole the head from Sorrel and claimed her rights instead."

"No," Sorrel said. "At least, not exactly. I needed her help. The last trial required two people. One to press the switch that raised the gate and one to grab the head. I climbed in while Tallah stood on the switch. Then I grabbed it and gave it to Tallah to hold while I climbed back. I trusted her."

"I was the one who returned the head," Tallah said, lips pulled back in a sneer. "I was the one named abbess."

"Clearly Maxim disagrees," Hazel said. "Strength and loyalty, Tallah. The only one here who's shown any loyalty is Sorrel."

Sorrel flushed.

Tallah's face darkened. "She left—"

"She left after we betrayed her. Loyalty requires faith in the people you're loyal to. And she couldn't trust us anymore."

Hazel gestured to the other monks, who all glared at Tallah. "I think we can all agree and act as representatives for Maxim. Tallah Forsmyth, you're stripped of your title and exiled from all of Maxim's monasteries. Don't bother coming back."

"You can't—" Tallah said as the other monks dragged her to the door. "Just because she says—"

"Maxim says," Vola said, tilting her head. "He doesn't say much, but he is your god. You'd think you'd learn to listen when he does speak."

The monks threw Tallah out the door as Hazel finally turned to Sorrel.

"I'm sorry," she said without hesitation. Too little too late, but it still needed to be said. "You're our abbess now."

Sorrel rolled her eyes. "You know I'd make a terrible abbess."

"What?" Hazel said, jerking back a step. "Then why did you —what was all this—Why'd you go after the head in the first place?"

Sorrel held the Warhammer out, balanced on both palms and her brow scrunched in concentration. The haft warped and morphed into a plain quarterstaff like the one Hazel already carried.

Sorrel handed it to Hazel. "I was always going to give it to you."

Hazel's fingers closed around the changed Warhammer even as her eyes went wide and stricken because she'd broken Sorrel's friendship and loyalty, and all the "I'm sorries" in the world couldn't make all that hurt go away.

"But I can't make it work," Hazel said. "It doesn't belong to me. It won't obey us."

"You don't have to. It's really just a symbol."

Sorrel glanced at the other monks, who stood a few steps behind Hazel. "You'll follow her because she's my representative, right? You'll give her your strength and loyalty because she's worthy of it."

The monks nodded even as Hazel protested. "I'm not—"

"No, maybe not," Sorrel said. "But neither am I, and I think maybe that's the point of leadership. Always striving to be worthy of the honor is a lot better than believing you're entitled to it. Right?" Sorrel asked Vola.

"That's what I'm learning," Vola said.

Sorrel let go of the Warhammer and stepped back.

Hazel's brow furrowed. "You're not coming? But you know we'd welcome you…"

Sorrel shook her head and cocked her thumb over her shoulder at Vola, Lillie, and Talon. "I've got things to do here."

"Why?"

Sorrel glanced back at them and smiled. "They're my family. They didn't need proof to trust me."

Sorrel probably hadn't meant it as a blow—it wasn't like her to kick a defeated enemy—but it struck like one, anyway.

Hazel winced. She cast Sorrel one last glance before she gathered her monks and left the palace.

TWENTY-EIGHT

VOLA STEPPED up to the open-air bar in the Underground, and three rowdy patrons turned to protest. They took one look at her with her sword and shield on her back and her new breastplate shining on her chest and backed off, leaving four stools empty right in the middle.

"Wonderful," Lillie said and sat delicately on the far right.

Sorrel scrambled up to sit beside her, her plain quarterstaff slung across her back so it hung down past the edge of the barstool.

Lillie leaned around Sorrel to grin at Vola. "I like your new armor, Vola," she said. "Very stylish."

Vola couldn't help glancing down at the shiny surface and tapping a fingernail against the metal. It gave a melodic "ting" and didn't even scratch under her nail. She'd only had the thing for a few hours, but she was already quite attached to its design: simple, functional, and elegant. Not to mention its blade-stopping effect. Always a plus.

"And I like your…er…headband?" Sorrel said, pointing one

knobbly finger at Lillie's forehead. She'd already signaled the bartender for a pint.

Lillie blushed and touched a fingertip to the silver band that circled her head and ended in a point between her eyebrows. A small blue-green jewel centered on her forehead matched her eyes.

"Thank you," she said. "It's a circlet."

Vola was going to go with tiara but whatever. "It's pretty," Vola mumbled trying to be diplomatic.

Lillie's lips twisted. "That's sweet of you. I know it's a bit gaudy, but it allows me to see magic without having to cast a spell, and it provides some protection against mental and psionic invasion."

Vola raised her eyebrows and nodded as if she knew what the hell that meant.

"What did you pick from the armory, Sorrel?" Lillie asked.

Sorrel stuck out her foot while slurping her beer and wiggled her toes, which stuck out from a pair of fine leather sandals. "Monks don't really go in much for worldly goods, but we do also walk a lot," she said once she'd swallowed. "They're super comfy and the grip is amazing. I'll bet I could walk up a wall with these."

Vola half expected her to leap off the stool to demonstrate, but she buried her face in her tankard for another swig while Lillie glanced around the crowded bar, blinking.

"Where's Talon?" she said. "I assumed they'd be right behind us."

Vola flinched, her shoulders jerking in response. Talon had been with them at the palace. She'd been with them in the armory, but Vola hadn't seen her on the way back to the Underground and now she wondered if the ranger had slipped away while no one was paying attention. She'd hoped Talon would choose to stay with them, but she hadn't had a chance to talk her into it. Not with all the running around after necromancers. And Vola had said it was Talon's decision. She had to respect that.

She rubbed her forehead, trying to find the right words to explain. "I'm not sure Talon is—"

"Here," a gravelly voice said behind Vola. "I'm right here."

Vola spun on her stool and her shoulders sagged. "Oh, thank Cleavah," she murmured.

Talon stood in the middle of the busy alley wearing a brand-new leather cuirass. This one tapered around her waist, giving her a slightly curvier silhouette.

"Does this mean you're staying with us?" Vola asked quietly.

Sorrel's face snapped up from her beer. "What?"

"Why wouldn't you be staying with us?" Lillie asked, turning wide, hurt-filled eyes on Talon and Gruff.

Talon stalked forward to stop a foot away from where they sat. "I thought I'd made my choice," she said, hood jerking toward Vola. "But I realized I couldn't make it without all of you knowing the truth. I've already told Vola, but you two have a right to know as well."

"Know what?" Sorrel slid her tankard back onto the bar and turned, giving Talon her undivided attention. Rare when there was beer nearby.

Talon heaved a gusty sigh, audible even in the hubbub, and raised a hand to pull down her hood. Her face was pale and splotchy. She'd obviously tried shaving again, leaving nicks and raw skin along her chin, but her eyes remained sharp and wide on Lillie and Sorrel. Vola tensed, waiting for it.

"I'm a girl," Talon said in a rush.

Lillie raised a hand to her mouth. Sorrel's brow furrowed.

"And?" Sorrel said.

Talon blinked. "No 'and.' I'm a girl."

"Oh, all right." Sorrel tilted her head, expression still quizzical as if she didn't see what the point was.

Talon looked at her out of the corner of her eye. "I haven't always been a girl."

"Okay."

"When I was little, people thought I was a boy." Talon's voice trailed off, hesitant, still waiting for the blow. "Even after I told them I wasn't."

"That was silly of them," Sorrel said.

Talon glanced at Vola, looking for help, but Vola didn't have any ideas.

"I want to be who I am, now," Talon said. "I want to live as a girl. And I don't want to keep who I am a secret from you or anyone." She stared at Sorrel.

"Would you like some help? Is that what the problem is?" Sorrel asked. "We can teach you how to be a girl. It'll be fun. We're all girls so it should be easy." Sorrel glanced at Vola. "Right?"

Vola shrugged. "Right, unless we're as incompetent at it as everything else."

Lillie squeaked behind her hands. Her eyes shone. "We can do all the traditional things girls do as they grow up. Buying new clothes and staying up late talking and having pillow fights."

Vola rolled her eyes. "Lillie's been trying to rope us into a slumber party since the swamp."

"You needn't act like I'm trying to torture you," Lillie said with a huff. "As Sorrel said, it will be fun." She reached out to touch Talon's hand, and wonder of wonders, Talon let her. "We can try all the things you've wanted to do and never felt safe or comfortable enough to try."

Talon swallowed so hard Vola watched it travel down her throat.

"Thank you for telling us," Lillie said softly as Sorrel turned back to her beer, crisis averted. Lillie smiled at Talon and raised a hand to gesture to her hood. "You should wear your hood down more often. I like seeing your face."

Talon blinked several times before her lips stretched as if creaky and unused, and that was the first time Vola had ever seen Talon smile.

"So, why did you want to leave?" Sorrel asked absently, staring down into her empty tankard with one eye.

"No reason," Talon said, voice rough even for her. "No reason that makes sense now."

Vola suppressed her own grin, worried it would scare Talon off, and offered her the seat on Vola's other side. Sorrel waved at the bartender for another drink. He slid a full tankard to her.

"You know, he's a lot quicker today," she remarked. "Do we just look tougher? Or has word spread that we can actually pay now—"

"You didn't bring that swamp monster back with you, did you?" a voice said behind them.

Sorrel jumped, sending a cascade of lager over the bar.

Vola turned to eye Fang. The ancient halfling stood in the middle of the alley, hands planted on her hips. Her sleek body-guard stood over her shoulder, eying the people on the street.

"No, Fang," Vola said. "We left it outside chewing on a cobblestone."

"Good, I've written new rules for the Underground. No swamp beasts of indeterminate breeding allowed."

"Wow," Sorrel said, swiping at the spilled beer. "Can you really spell all that?"

Fang's eyes narrowed, and Vola spoke up before she could kick them out. "Thank you for your help with the monks," she said. "You kept them off of us for a good long while."

Fang rolled her lips between her gums. "Not as long as I would have liked."

"Tell you what," Sorrel said. "You can teach me that little air walk, sneak up behind them, and punch them thing to make it up to us."

"I suppose I could," Fang said, eying Sorrel up and down. "Tallah wanted me to teach her as well, but she was too dumb to know how to ask. The only thing that covered up how dumb was all the lies."

"Hear, hear!" Sorrel raised her tankard for a swig.

"They're out of everyone's hair, now," Vola said.

Fang examined her fingernails. "Did they get what they came for, then?"

"Yes," Vola said.

"And no," Sorrel added.

Vola's gaze sharpened on her. Sorrel stared into her tankard, a smirk playing on her lips.

"What does that mean?" Fang asked.

Sorrel shrugged. "Let's just say they got what they deserved and nothing else."

Fang's eyes narrowed. "Hmm. So not much then. I approve. Just keep me out of it, next time. I'm not in the market for any more swamp beasts or monks." She paused. "Unless I'm feeding the monks to the swamp beast."

She wandered off toward the pit and her scaffolding, mumbling to herself. Her bodyguard followed.

Vola turned on Sorrel. "Spill," she hissed. "You look like a cat that fell in a vat of cream."

Lillie and Talon leaned in as Sorrel grinned, openly this time. Sorrel reached behind her for her weapon and pulled it forward. The quarterstaff shimmered and morphed, turning into the haft of a Warhammer they'd become intimately familiar with over the last few days.

"You switched them again?" Lillie said, voice rising.

Talon hid a laugh behind her hand, making Vola wonder briefly how many smiles had been hidden under her hood.

"Yup," Sorrel said. The Warhammer morphed back into the simple quarterstaff, and she slung it over her shoulder. "The head is safe with Hazel for the moment, but the haft is more useful out in the world. It's staying with me."

"Won't Hazel need it? Or notice the difference?" Vola said.

"She knows," Sorrel said with a shrug. "As I told her, the staff was just a symbol to get the monks to recognize her as their leader. She wouldn't have been able to use it, anyway. It belongs out in the world, kicking bad-guy butt and doing good."

Vola just shook her head.

"Of course it belongs with you," Lillie said. "But, Sorrel, why didn't you tell us what happened under the monastery?"

Sorrel ducked her head. "The last time I tried to tell someone the truth they called me a liar and an oathbreaker. Can you blame me for being scared?"

Lillie bit her lip. "I guess not."

"No," Talon said. "I don't blame you for being scared."

Sorrel's lips twisted in a self-deprecating grin. "Seems silly now to be scared of you guys, doesn't it?"

A figure slid onto the next stool over, and Vola did a double-take.

"Um, Princess, what are you doing here?"

Rilla sat there, dressed in her dark green leathers, curly hair long and teased out into a cloud around her head. She raised a finger, and the bartender hopped like a rabbit on fire to find a clean glass and something clear and golden to pour into it.

Vola glanced around to see if anyone noticed a princess sitting in their midst. But the alley bustled as it always did.

"I wanted to thank you, personally," Rilla said, as Vola turned back to her. "But palaces give me a rash."

"Erm, don't you live in a palace?" Sorrel asked.

"Only when I can't help it."

"Have you gotten anything out of Myron, yet?" Vola asked.

Rilla dipped her chin. "I have." She spun on her stool to face them. "He had some very interesting things to say about his boss and a certain noble or two in the capitol. I'm on my way to investigate." She glanced at Vola's breastplate and then her gaze settled on the full purse hanging on Vola's belt.

"How do you like the perks of employment?" she said with an elegantly raised eyebrow.

Vola's gaze narrowed. "It's nice to be paid for your work," she responded.

"Would you like that to be a regular thing?"

Sorrel spit out her beer. Vola glared her into silence.

"What are you suggesting?"

Rilla spread her hands. "I'm offering you a job. Employment on my payroll. I need a personal strike team. Someone I can trust to send into investigations. Similar to the Myron Vidal one." Her lips thinned, and she glanced away. "I hate to admit it, but I really shouldn't be traipsing through necromancer lairs myself. Not with the Dagger Throne at stake. It's just not smart. And I'm supposed to be smart."

Vola carefully kept her mouth shut on any kind of response.

"Would you like to be my team?" Rilla said.

Vola and her party exchanged a long glance.

"Why us?" Vola said.

Rilla's lip twitched. "I've seen you in action. And I've been asking around. You seem to be plagued with accident and mistake," she said.

Vola's eyes narrowed.

"But somehow you always spin it just right to come out on top. You take mishap and turn it into victory."

"I suppose that's a compliment," Vola said.

Rilla chuckled. "If accident were a person, you would be their champion," she said. "And that's something I can use. You're almost god-touched."

"Not almost," Talon said.

Rilla's gaze sharpened. "Yes?"

Vola met her eyes without hesitation. "I am chosen by Cleavah, goddess of vengeful housewives."

Rilla's eyebrows went up. "Really?"

"Yes, really." She waited for Rilla's full reaction. There was always a reaction.

Rilla shrugged. "All right. I'm not exactly a housewife. I'm a spy and an assassin. But I keep Southglen safe. It's my home. I know when I need people who can take the bad and spin it to good. I'd like to have Mishap's Heroes on my side."

Vola winced. She wasn't the only one.

"Aw, can't we be something cooler?" Sorrel said. "Like Agents of Justice? Or Southglen's Champions?"

"This is probably more accurate," Lillie said.

"Will you take the job?" Rilla said.

Vola opened her mouth, but Sorrel spoke over top of her.

"First," the halfling said. "Are you the bad guy?"

Vola groaned.

"She's not the bad guy, Sorrel," Lillie said. "She sits on one of the Thrones of Southglen."

Sorrel shrugged, unrepentant. "Just making sure. You can't be too careful."

Rilla rubbed the smile from her lips. "What's second?"

"Oh, I don't know," Sorrel said. "I haven't thought that far."

"I have," Vola said. "Any objections?" She met each of their eyes in turn. Lillie beamed at her. Sorrel raised her tankard. And Talon gave her a solemn nod.

Vola stuck her hand out. "We'll take the offer, Your Highness."

"Just Rilla, please," Rilla said, shaking her hand. "Unless

we're with company who'll be offended by practicality. Where we're going, it's more likely than you'd think."

"Yay, we have a job." Sorrel stood on her stool to wave to the bartender again. "Drinks all around."

Rilla grinned. "I'm game."

"A glass of red, please," Lillie told the bartender. "And please replenish whatever the lady on the end is having."

"Scotch, neat," Rilla said, raising her glass. "With a little umbrella, please."

Vola raised an eyebrow. "Really?"

"I think they're cute."

"I'll have the same," Talon said.

The bartender gave Vola a look. "And you, ma'am?"

Vola opened her mouth, but Sorrel beat her to it.

"Not tea," the halfling said. "This is a victory drink. You can't have tea."

"If it's a victory drink, I should be allowed to get whatever I want," Vola said with a scowl.

"Yes, as long as you want something that's actually exciting." Sorrel rolled her eyes. "Come on, Vola. Cleavah can't possibly disapprove. I've met her, and I'm pretty sure you've been making that up."

"All right, fine. Cleavah doesn't care. I just don't like it."

"Then find something you do like," Lillie said.

"You're down two already," Sorrel said, finishing her beer.

"Fine. I'll have, er, something sweet."

The bartender slid a drink in front of her. Green with little salt flakes around the rim. Vola scowled at it. "Do you think he's being cute?"

"Just because it looks like you…"

"It does not look like me."

"Try it," Lillie said. "You asked for sweet."

Vola sipped cautiously and smacked her lips. "Okay, yeah.

That's pretty sweet." Then she grimaced. "Oh, but the aftertaste. What is that?"

"Liquor prob —"

The world went black.

When Vola woke, her head pounded, and the earth moved under her, heaving like the deck of a ship.

She groaned and immediately a cool hand touched her forehead. "Easy now," Lillie's voice said. "Don't worry. We're all here. The only one who had a rough night was you."

Vola groaned again and rolled over. She cracked her eyes and found rough planking inches from her nose. When she turned her head, she saw the deck of a ship stretching away only to end in a sharp plunge into a brilliant blue-green sea. It heaved, too.

"Oh my goddess, I thought it was a metaphor," she mumbled.

"What was a metaphor?" Talon's boots came into view.

"Never mind." Vola pushed herself up to her elbows, testing her head and her strength. Her head still hurt, but at least her arms held her.

"I'm sorry. The captain didn't want us to put you down below for fear you'd vomit," Lillie said.

"He's justified," Talon said. "Considering how much vomiting Sorrel's been doing."

Vola squinted against the sunlight and found Sorrel's figure hanging over the railing of the ship, heaving into the sea.

"Where are we?"

"On the way to the capitol of Southglen," Lillie said, biting her lip and looking out at the horizon. "Rilla did say she wanted to get going as soon as possible."

"Right," Vola said. "Er, what happened before that?"

"At the bar?" Talon said. "You sipped your drink and passed

out." She paused. Her hood was back in place, protecting her fair skin from the sun. "So, when you said you don't like alcohol, you meant you don't like what happens when you drink alcohol."

"Sorrel must have had fun with that," Vola said.

"She did."

"She made lots of jokes and was very sad you weren't awake to hear them," Lillie added. "That is until we got on the ship and she started vomiting."

"If it makes you feel better, she's regretting a lot of what she drank last night."

"But," Lillie said. "We are on our way. Our quarry is ahead of us. We have an employer who is not a bad guy. And we are together. Southglen awaits."

"Hooray." Vola thrust her fist in the air, and then slumped back to the deck to close her eyes until they reached the capitol.

Thank you so much for reading!

The misadventures continue in *Trust and Treason*! Who is this man who's hunting Lillie? What did she ever do to him? And is working for a princess going to pay off or will politics get Vola and the others killed in new and interesting ways?

Ever wondered what happened to Vola, Talon, Lillie, and Sorrel before they met? Sign up here to get the Mishap's Heroes prequel, Creation and Calamity, and read their origin stories!

And finally, if you loved spending time with Vola, Lillie, Sorrel and Talon, consider leaving a review so other readers can find more stories about heroes who don't look like heroes but save the day anyway.

THANK YOU FOR READING

Keep reading for a preview of the next book, *Trust and Treason!*

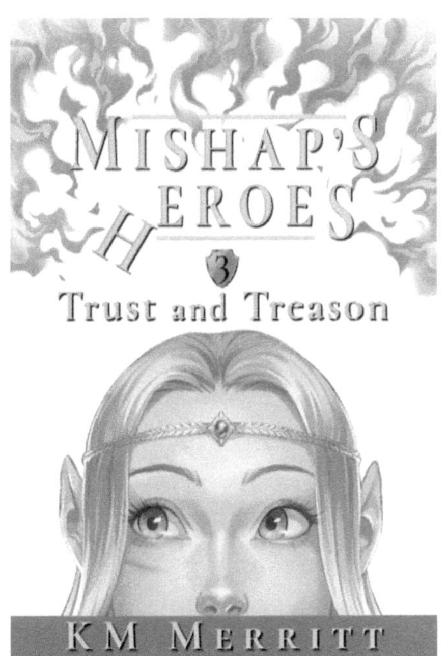

ONE

Vola eyed the murky water passing under the edge of their flat-bottomed barge, one dark eyebrow arched in distrust.

"You don't have to glare at it like it's going to leap up and eat you. It's just water," a voice to her left said.

Vola glanced at the speaker, a tall slim woman with dark skin, light brown eyes, and a wide halo of black curls around her head. Rilla. Princess Allellarilla to be exact. Guardian of the Dagger Throne.

And their new employer. She'd named them Mishap's Heroes—though Vola secretly hoped the name wouldn't stick—before she'd loaded them onto a ship headed for the capitol. It only took them three days to sail up the coastline this time, and then they'd traded the sleek ocean-faring vessel for this poor excuse for a boat in order to crawl up the meandering river. With wide logs rough-cut into a flat-ish surface and lashed together with some dubiously frayed rope, the barge looked a little like a child's school project.

"Believe me," Vola told the princess, stepping back from the edge. "We've been in some places where the water tries to kill you any way it can."

Rilla raised her eyebrows. "Sounds like a good story."

"Be fair, Vola," another voice said, this one more melodious, like it was born to accompany a lute. "There were plenty of other things that wanted to kill us as well. Each more dangerous than the water. I don't see any carnivorous flora, here."

A blonde half-elf, built short and round, and strikingly beautiful, gestured around at the broad plain where, true enough, there were no giant pink flowers waiting to eat them. Only waves and waves of green and gold grasses that marched all the way to the water's edge.

"And look," Lillie said with an indulgent smile. "Talon is enjoying it well enough."

Vola turned to find their ranger lounging on the edge of the barge, trousers rolled up to her knees so she could paddle her feet in the river. The rest of her was swathed in a dark cloak, her hood pulled low over her face.

The party as a whole had only seen Talon's face a couple of times. But even with her hood up, this was the most relaxed the ranger had seemed since they'd left the wilds for more civilized lands, and Vola wasn't about to ruin it by complaining about the murky water. Even Gruff, the big black wolf lazed beside her, panting like a lap dog.

"Sorry I didn't pick a more scenic route," Rilla said, but not like she was actually sorry. "I didn't want to announce our entry into the city."

Vola cocked her head. "Is this level of secrecy necessary? Or does it just come with being the spymaster for an entire kingdom?"

Rilla blinked. "I don't understand the question."

Lillie stood on tiptoe to whisper to Vola. "I think it's normal for the Guardian of the Dagger Throne."

Rilla turned back toward the front of the barge. "We'll be there soon. You can almost see the tiers."

"Good," a voice groaned at their feet. "I'm done with boats. No more boats. I beg you."

Vola bit her lip to hide her smile and tried to appear sympathetic as she peered down at Sorrel, a slim halfling who lay on the rough boards of the barge. Green tinged her normally nut-brown skin and errant curls of her red brown hair stuck to her sweaty forehead.

Lillie gasped. "I see it. Sorrel, if you stand up, you can see the city. We're almost there."

"No thank you," Sorrel groaned. "I trust you not to give me false hope. And down here I'm closer to the edge in case I barf again."

Ahead of them, the mid-afternoon air shimmered, glints and flashes of light obscuring anything beyond.

"It's the city's defenses," Rilla said. "Half the Shield Throne's time and energy is spent just keeping the wards up and running. It's a good precaution, but it does interfere something awful with the air currents sometimes."

A yelp sounded followed by a large splash behind the barge.

Vola turned to catch the poleman gaping at the frothing water inches from his pole. She sighed.

A scaly green head, topped with a filmy crest, surfaced about half a barge-length back and snorted. Water plumed from its nostrils and its yellow eyes narrowed before the head turned and started industriously down the river the way they'd come.

Vola sighed again, gustily, and glanced at her party members.

"Don't look at me," Lillie said. "I did it last time. I had to use a complicated spell for it, too."

Vola cocked her head at Talon.

"I'm only half-dressed," the ranger said. Gruff didn't even raise his head.

"Wouldn't it be better to jump in a river half dressed?" Vola said. "Then your boots wouldn't get wet."

"Nice try," Talon said, and Vola could almost hear the smirk in her voice. "But it's your turn."

"Sorrel?" Vola asked desperately.

"Nnnuueergh."

"Fine." Vola pulled the scabbard and the round, scarred shield from her back. "Hold these," she told Rilla.

The princess took them with a frown as Vola bent for her boots. "I'm not sure why you keep going after it. No one likes it, it's ill-tempered as hell, and it clearly doesn't want to stick around."

"Believe me, I'd let it go if I wasn't worried it would destroy the local ecology." She tossed her boots aside.

"If we let it go, it'll just turn into some river monster we have to fight later on when it starts eating the locals," Talon said as Vola grimaced and slid off the back of the barge. The water only came up to her chest.

"I suppose as one of the leaders of those locals, I should insist you retrieve it," Rilla said. "I'm not sure I want to, but I should."

"Aren't you some kind of animal handler?" Vola called to Talon as she waded after the swamp beast. It wasn't really trying to get away. Just trying to piss her off.

If Talon responded, it was lost in all the splashing as Vola chased the swamp beast down. She reached for the muddy lead rope still hanging from its neck but it waited until her fingers closed around it, then pulled the slippery line out of her hand. She scowled and tried again before the foul beast could swim away. The thing looked like a cross between a donkey and a crocodile with the personality of a serial killer thrown in.

The swamp beast's eyes narrowed and suddenly it yanked, diving underwater and dragging Vola with it. Its webbed claws pulled in strong strokes, hauling Vola through the water.

She planted her feet in the muck at the bottom of the river and pushed up so her head broke the surface. She sucked in a noisy breath and surged back against its pull. Luckily, she outweighed the thing—just barely—and she managed to yank it off balance. By the time it had floundered upright in the water, she'd hauled it back to the barge.

Vola climbed up beside the pole-man, who eyed her warily.

When they'd boarded back at the harbor, he hadn't been particularly happy to have a half-orc on board. But then he'd seen the swamp monster and decided Vola was the least of his problems.

Vola tugged on the swamp monster's lead, trying to get it to jump back onto the barge. It tugged back, treading water easily. It hissed at her.

"Fine," she snapped at it. "If you won't come up, you can just swim behind us the rest of the way." It wasn't like that would be a hardship. The thing was born for murky water ways.

She tied the lead off and left the swamp monster swimming behind. There was a chance it might try towing them backwards but she didn't think it was *that* strong.

By the time she straightened, her party lined the front edge of the barge. Even Sorrel had finally stood and stared with wide eyes.

Vola raised her gaze and caught her first glimpse of Glenhaven, capitol of Southglen. A solid wall of cliffs rose out of the plains ahead of them; tier upon tier of the city had been carved out of the white rock. A waterfall cascaded down over the terraces, which were wreathed in colorful strips of greenery and flowers. It was all white marble and glistening water, with little sparks and flashes of magic framing the image.

"Holy Cleavah," Vola said, coming up behind Lillie and Talon. They didn't even mention that she still dripped all over. They just kept staring. "That has to be at least five times the size of Brisbene."

"Six, if you count the farms around the base," Lillie said, then she flushed and shuffled her feet. "I mean, I think. I must have read that somewhere."

"I don't think this place even has an Underground. It's too clean," Sorrel said. "The whole thing is an Aboveground if you ask me."

That only seemed to hold truer as they approached. As the waterfall reached the lower levels of the city, it branched into five different streams meeting the rivers that meandered across the plains. Even their murky waterway cleared into a sparkling green by the time it wandered up to the dock set into the base of the cliff.

By the time they docked, the swamp beast seemed a little more cooperative and it climbed up onto dry land with only a half-hearted snort.

Vola had assumed the lower levels of the city would be slums, or lower income housing for those lesser races who had immigrated. Southglen's population was predominantly human, with elves coming in at a close second. But the area around the docks boasted large open-air markets surrounded by colonnades, marble banks, and restaurants with patio seating on the terraces. Humans and elves passed them in the streets, yes, but so did gnomes with their creased faces, dwarves in clusters with bristling beards, and a couple tall figures with bright scales and elongated snouts. They wore flowing trousers and skirts but looked tough enough to put Vola on her ass if they wanted to.

Rilla led them down streets paved in smooth flagstones to wide shallow stairs that marked the passages between each tier. And as far as Vola could tell, each tier was as prosperous as the next. She felt a little grubby in her travel-stained tunic and breeches, which were now soaked through with muddy water, and she wished she'd stopped to put on her shiny new breastplate instead of slinging the bag over the swamp beast's back.

Sorrel's face had regained its normal color, and she gazed

around with wide eyes. "Is it always this…shiny?" she asked Rilla.

Rilla surveyed the city, her lips pursed. "It is. I'm originally from Brisbene. You saw it there. Pretty normal. But Glenhaven is the home of the Fifteen Thrones. All the princesses live here, at least part of the time."

"Glenhaven profits from the direct oversight of its ruling body," Lillie said.

Rilla cocked her head. "Or meddling."

Vola craned her head back, but the lower tiers blocked the upper ones and only a sliver of the palace was visible far above them.

"Fifteen princesses seems like a lot," she said, well aware she was talking to one of them right now.

Rilla shrugged. "It's been that way for centuries now. The Thrones themselves choose the princesses. No one's really sure how it works; we've got wizards researching the process. But the magic seeks someone with the intelligence and skill to manage one small piece of Southglen's government. The Thrones imbue each princess with a specific type of magic dealing with their personal demesne."

Lillie nodded like this was old news. Vola tried to look like she knew what Rilla was talking about. Sorrel and Talon exchanged a glance, but it was Sorrel who finally said, "I have no idea what a demesne is."

Rilla blinked. "Think territory. Each Throne rules a certain territory of the government. There's war, justice, religion, health. Things like that."

Rilla, they knew, was the kingdom's spymaster. The Dagger Throne kept Southglen safe from treason and espionage and sabotage.

"How do you know who's in charge?" Talon said. "A wolf pack works in concert, but there is always an alpha."

Rilla shook her head. "We rule our territories equally. And if there is something that requires everyone's input, then we come together for a vote."

"You really don't have any kind of ranks?" Sorrel said. She wended her way down the street backwards so she could face them as she talked.

"No," Rilla said, then looked thoughtful. "Well, not officially. There are definitely princesses who are more popular with the public. The people love to throw parades for Justice and War." Rilla winced. "But the princesses of Public Works and Sewer Management don't get out much."

Vola hid a snort behind her hand.

Lillie did a double take as a tall, slender elf in a green dress sauntered by. Vola was close enough to notice the way she went stiff, and her limp grew more pronounced.

Vola's brow drew down, and she shifted closer to Lillie. The half-elf had admitted weeks ago that she'd originally fled from Southglen. And then, just in Brisbene, a man named Virvalim had sent a bounty hunter to collect her. He was nothing but a dark ashy smear on a wall now, but Vola still watched the crowd around them warily. She had no idea what to watch for except the name and that was only helpful if the creep walked around with a name tag, but no one would be snatching Lillie if Vola had anything to say about it.

Out of habit, she checked Sorrel and Talon, too. Sorrel was Sorrel, moving through the crowd with a grin and enthusiastic grace. The quarterstaff slung over her back didn't seem to weigh her down at all, even if it was half of a god's weapon.

Talon stalked beside the big black wolf named Gruff as usual. But while it was hard to tell her moods under the swathing hood and cloak, Vola thought the ranger moved with stronger stride and looser shoulders. While in Brisbene, she'd been wound tight and miserable. Either Talon was getting used to cities, or she was more relaxed after her decision to live as herself.

About halfway up the city, Rilla stopped outside a large inn. It hadn't been built with marble like a lot of the buildings so far, but the mahogany siding shone clean and smooth and the door didn't squeal when Rilla pushed it open.

The princess exchanged a nod with the proprietor who stood behind the bar on the ground floor. He jerked his chin in response and raised two fingers with a questioning look.

Rilla nodded and led them to the stairs. Vola was impressed. Every place they'd been to so far demanded your cash upfront.

"I don't want you to think I'm stiffing you," Rilla said, heading down the second-floor corridor. "Your fee includes room and board. But I don't want to lead you right up to the palace. I'd rather keep you a secret for a little while longer."

Vola nodded. "So, the whole city doesn't know you have us on retainer. Makes sense."

Rilla pushed a door open. "This is where I stay when I'm not at the palace. I've got a single next door. You can live here while you hunt down Myron Vidal's boss."

Sorrel bounded into the room. "Whoa, there's a bed for each of us. And look. We've got a second entrance. In case you want to skip out on the bill?" The halfling trotted over to a door that led out to some stairs. The inn had been built around a central courtyard, complete with decorative benches on one side and straw-stuffed practice dummies on the other. "This place is swank."

"Lots better than the Snuggly Bunny," Talon said, stepping into the room. Gruff slunk toward the fireplace and didn't hesitate to curl up on the hearth.

"The Snuggly Bunny?" Rilla said with a raised eyebrow.

Vola winced. "Long story."

There was a polite tap on the doorframe and Vola turned to

see a boy of about nine shifting from foot to foot on the threshold. He was clean and neat, and Vola guessed he was the innkeeper's son.

"I've been watching for your return, Mistress Rilla," he said breathlessly. "You have messages."

"Thanks, Pellor." She took the stack of envelopes from the boy. "Have my bag dumped in my room, and there's a…mount tied up outside the inn. See that it's stabled. Away from the horses. It bites."

The boy ran off as Rilla sorted through the messages quickly and efficiently, honing in on one toward the back. She broke the seal and read, her eyes scanning the text.

Vola hated to pry, but they were working for the princess now. "News?"

Rilla's lips twitched in an aborted grin. "Your first assignment, seems like."

Vola straightened, and the others perked up from their places around the room.

"I've been tracking the man who hired Myron." Rilla waved the paper at them. "The same person who was buying slaves from your Lord Arthorel. Even though slaving is against the law. One of my operatives has been trackng his correspondence. Seems Myron was right. He's up to something in Glenhaven."

Vola cracked her knuckles, remembering Henri's face behind bars. It made her growl. "What would you like us to do?"

"Find his messenger. Track down who he's contacting, what he wants, see if you can learn where he is. I'm going to work the problem from the other end."

"What do you mean?"

"Like finding the middle of the rope by following both ends. I'm going to pull on ropes and see which one yelps."

ACKNOWLEDGMENTS

I started out thinking I was writing something fun and light and hopefully hilarious. But it turns out I can't just write fluff. Meaning creeps in from the sides and makes its home between the lines. And then someone likes it, and I have to write more, and more meaning forces its way in, and suddenly it's a whole "thing." I blame these people:

First, the Kickstarter backers, for making all this possible. And for believing in the series before I'd ever sold a copy.

Mom and Dad, for reading every book ever. And always asking where the next one is.

Arielle, Betsy, and Alison, for being the first inspiration for a group of inept heroes who have no idea what they're doing and manage to save the day anyway.

Miranda and Lacey, for sisterhood which looks a lot like party dynamics sometimes.

Kevin and Andrew, for inviting me to play this little game called Dungeons & Dragons.

Kyle, Mary, Amy, Clark, Tim, Greg, Lauren, and Dave, and a host of other party members, for providing endless opportunities for inspiration. These books are all your fault.

Lucy Lin, for all the amazing cover art. I don't think anyone else could have brought Vola and the others to life the same way you did.

Fiona McLaren, for copy edits and flexibility. And for

enjoying my humorous fantasy as much as my slightly more serious stuff.

And Josh and Abby, for endless support. Especially when I decided to launch a series the same month I was supposed to have a baby.

ABOUT THE AUTHOR

Books have been Kendra's escape for as long as she can remember. She used to hide fantasy novels behind her government textbook in high school, and she wrote most of her first novel during a semester of college algebra.

Kendra writes familiar stories from unfamiliar points of view, highlighting heroes with disabilities. Her own experience with partial paraplegia has shown her you don't have to be able to swing a sword to save the day.

When she's not writing she's reading, and when she's not reading she's playing video games.

She lives in Denver with her very tall husband, their book loving progeny, and a lazy black monster masquerading as a service dog.

Visit Kendra at
www.kendramerritt.com

facebook.com/kendramerrittauthor

goodreads.com/kendramerritt

instagram.com/kendramerrittauthor

tiktok.com/@kendramerrittauthor